Exurbia

Also by Molly McGrann

360 Flip

Exurbia
Molly McGrann

PICADOR

First published 2007 by Picador
an imprint of Pan Macmillan Ltd
Pan Macmillan, 20 New Wharf Road, London N1 9RR
Basingstoke and Oxford
Associated companies throughout the world
www.panmacmillan.com

ISBN 978-0-330-41241-4

1 3 5 7 9 8 6 4 2

A CIP catalogue record for this book is available from
the British Library.

Typeset by SetSystems Ltd, SaffronWalden, Essex
Printed and bound in Great Britain by
Mackays of Chatham plc, Chatham, Kent

Visit **www.panmacmillan.com** to read more about all our books
and to buy them. You will also find features, author interviews and
news of any author events, and you can sign up for e-newsletters
so that you're always first to hear about our new releases.

For my parents

I cut the sentence
Out of a life
Out of the story
With my little knife

—Thom Gunn,
'Song of a Camera'

It's morning again in America. Today more men and women will go to work than ever before in our country's history. With interest rates at about half the record highs of 1980, nearly 2,000 families today will buy new homes, more than at any time in the past four years. This afternoon 6,500 young men and women will be married, and with inflation at less than half of what it was just four years ago, they can look forward with confidence to the future. It's morning again in America, and under the leadership of President Reagan, our country is prouder and stronger and better.

—TV advertisement, 1984

Exurbia

One

"You can follow a story as very small, an isolated event, or a sign that something sinister is taking place in the world at large." That was English class. They were reading about some lady getting stoned to death by her neighbors and friends—her own family, even—when she drew from a lottery box the marked slip making her the sacrifice that would help the corn grow tall. It wasn't so long ago, Lise thought. It wasn't Bible times. Maybe a hundred years ago a lady was getting stoned to death in America. Lise almost laughed out loud into the rickety quiet of the classroom. Stoned to death. She had to tell Trish about this. They would get stoned to death in the parking lot at Yum Yum Donuts. That would make Trish laugh. That would make Trish like her again. She checked the white-faced clock with its jumpy hands like a Hollywood lunatic, the relentless *tick* from one minute to the next: 2:59. Four minutes until 3:03, when she could get stoned to death with Trish and Jen, her best friends.

"What does this story show about mass psychology?"

Lise blatantly re-did her lips, then passed her new lipstick to Jen, across the aisle and one seat back. "Clinique," she mouthed, peeking over her shoulder. "Careful." She didn't want it to wear down too fast—Burgundy Bronze, bought yesterday at the mall.

Jen nodded, ducking behind her English textbook, which was propped on end on her desk; a mirror was taped inside the cover's hardback, alongside a list of every boy she had kissed in the last nine months, since school started: twenty-six names in Jen's bubble script, the i's dotted with little o's, tiny hearts, daisies, stars. Lise leaned forward and blotted her lips on the facing page of her own book—her and Jen's tag, repeated around school in all their class-rooms, on hall and bathroom walls and the library tables, and outside school, in the Galleria toilet stalls, on the mirrors at Phazes, stamped onto the vinyl booth of Hamburger Hamlet, right on the spot where they sat. Right on the seat, where the rips were mended with what looked like rubber cement, blobs to absently pick at while they waited to eat. The Booger Seat, the girls called it. "Eww," Trish had said, grimacing when they tagged it, a Menthol 100 cigarette poking out of her mouth like a lollipop stick. "Like, thousands of people have farted there and you guys *kissed* their asses." Lise and Jen giggled, tagging their plates, their napkins, their spoons, all over their water glasses, the napkin dispenser, and, finally, the check, sealed with a kiss.

"What rituals similar to this lottery do you participate in?" Mr. Feltman asked.

"Getting stoned to death," Lise muttered, and the pack of girls and boys around her cracked up. One boy pinched an imaginary joint to his lips, whistling as he exhaled ripe, Juicyfruit breath.

4

"I'm deaf after lunch duty," nervous Mr. Feltman said, demonstratively touching his ears, always careful of his New Romantic bouffant haircut, held together with Dippity-Do. He kept a jumbo tub of the hair gel in his bottom desk drawer, Lise knew, because Joey Havrilla had found it one day when Mr. Feltman was late to class. Dippity-Do, a bottle of mouthwash, breath mints, a toothbrush, a nail file, needle and thread, a dried red rose, and a pack of matches from Howard Johnson—each item held aloft and treated as a revelation. "Repeat your answer please, Elise," Mr. Feltman said, but the bell rang signaling the end of the day and Lise was already on her way out the door, her backpack fashionably slung over one shoulder, Jen on her heels click-clacking in wooden-soled sandals. They pushed through the crush in the hall, the girls' eyes the knife that flashes prettily before it gets you like a cramp in the side, slashing at the weak, the rotten, the diseased, crippled, and scarred. Their swinging, syncopated stride—trained and supervised by Trish—beat a tattoo that must be heeded: *here we come, move it, move it.*

Jen hacked into her fist as they hurried along. "Robo said he'd wait until 3:35."

"Nice smoker's cough," Lise replied.

"I like, smoked a whole pack last night. My mom was stressing me out *so* bad. I was starving and she wouldn't let me order a pizza, and then she finally did, but not until like, eleven o'clock. *And* she said I had to pay her back. That is like, such an un-motherly thing to do. She's supposed to *feed* me, and I hate the food she cooks."

"At least your mom cooks real food. Mine's too *oppressed* to cook. She *microwaves.*"

"That's cooking," Jen said.

The girls were approaching Millikan Middle School's social vortex: the Eighth-Grade Lawn. Here Lise knew Ray Savage, the Barr brothers, and Harley Pierce—collectively known as the Crew-Cut Crue, a bunch of FFF wannabes—would be lounging with caffeine-rich cans of Mountain Dew, idly flicking their skateboard wheels. Sometimes Lise saw them skating around the Yum Yum parking lot, scooting off at the last minute when they thought they were going to get caught watching everyone. They weren't FFF, but Lise thought they were cute.

"Julia Lopez is a *dog*. You're crazy," Harley was saying.

"I'm not crazy! Institutionalized!"

"Dude, I heard she's *suicidal*. That girl can skate. She's fucking Evel Knievel. She rides banks like waves. She's not afraid." The four members of the Crew-Cut Crue nodded their heads, impressed.

"Harley Pierce is the biggest babe," Lise whispered as she took Jen's arm. The girls adjusted their chins, lifting and tilting, drawing their eyes straight ahead, knowing they would be hawked as they passed, their pendulous hips like a hypnotist's watch. "Maybe we should go to Marina Skatepark this weekend and watch them skate."

"You look hot," Harley called to Lise and Jen. "Are you hot?" The girls didn't answer him—didn't even look.

"Those boys are only into skateboards and Donkey Kong. They're *young*. They're like, our age," Jen sniffed. "You can do much better than that. You need an *older* boyfriend. Someone like Robo."

"Oh, and what makes Robo so great?"

"He drives," Jen answered. "He drums. And he's got a big dick. The biggest I've ever seen. Bigger than *Playgirl* magazine."

"No way."

"*Way.*"

Lise slugged Jen playfully. "You bitch! You didn't tell me! When did you sleep with him?"

"I didn't. Not yet. I mean, I touched it. *You* know. Trish knows. You know what I did. My special trick. I'm turning into *such* a pro." The girls had reached the teachers' parking lot. "Ohmigod, like, I need a cigarette *now!*" Jen stamped her foot.

"Wait until we do this run," Lise said. Safely away from the gaze of their peers, the girls slipped both backpack straps over their shoulders and tightened them. Lise tried to relax, knowing it would be easier if she did: they had more than a mile to shift in twenty minutes. Every school day for the last two weeks they had done this run, and Lise had thought it would get easier; meanwhile the heat had intensified, rocketing from 74 degrees to 82, spring becoming summer. As they huffed along, she complained, "I hate this. I get totally sweaty."

"You should bring another shirt."

"I'm not changing in front of Robo!"

"He wants us to have a threesome," Jen said, her cheeks flushed, a purer pink than the peachy blush brushed high on her cheekbones. Her bosom—Jen had boobs, as she did broad hips and a round rear-end, unlike tiny Lise, flat and straight as a preteen—jigged in the polyester–cotton casing of her satiny top. Her clothes were always too tight, jeans

7

hugging the perfect slope of her butt, jersey tube skirts riding up. She advertised herself, Lise's mother said. That figure wouldn't last long, said Mrs. Blue, meaning Jen would go to fat soon, and even Trish said Jen dressed like a slut. Running, she coughed every few minutes, a startlingly violent, wet cough; Jen smoked Marlboro Reds all the way to the filter, cherishing each one. "A threesome. That's what he told me last night. You or Trish, he doesn't care."

"Jen, that's so gross!" Lise shrieked, her eyes popping in shock.

Jen punched her wheezing chest, as if to make it stop. Her naturally curly hair, straightened and weighed down with styling products, began to separate with sweat, looking greasy. "It's no biggie to do it, Lise. If you use a rubber it's like you're not even *touching*."

Lise didn't believe Jen. Lots of kids she knew fooled around and it was no big deal to do it, they always said. They had sex after school before their parents got home— just another thing to do. They shot hoops, watched soaps, had sex, and drank Cokes, or had sex, watched soaps, drank Cokes, and shot hoops. But Lise listened to her mom, whether she wanted to or not; she heard her mother's voice in her head, even though she tried to block it out: don't do it, an echo in the cavern of her skull, the words always there—sometimes Lise thought she heard her mother's voice in the middle of the night while she slept. Don't *do* it, her mother said, tackling Lise's subconscious. Don't even *think* about it, and now Lise was scared, oh was she scared of sex!

The girls skillfully navigated the grid of streets that connected the ocean to the city of Los Angeles, making

8

sudden detours to avoid cars they possibly recognized, cars that might contain classmates or, worse, their own parents, heading home from work early. Lise and Jen shifted through traffic and stoplights as if moved by a joystick, gobbling up the pavement, sucking down bugs for points. They weren't even talking now, but concentrated on their running, Lise with a stitch in her side that she longed to stop and pull at. Finally at Oxnard they slowed to walk and cool down some, combing through asymmetrically bobbed hair with their fingers and smoothing one lip against the other to even the color of their lipstick. They stayed on Oxnard to Ulysses S. Grant High School (where Lise would have liked to study the boys), which backed onto the small campus of Los Angeles Valley College. There, Robo waited for them in his Mustang convertible, banging his head to Van Halen.

"I go out with a totally hot guy," Jen said proudly. "Like, the oldest, most hottest guy any of us has ever gone with." Robo was twenty, and rich. He paid for everything they did. Jen was wearing a new wristwatch with gold hands on a black face and a black patent-leather band, reward for seven unsolicited blowjobs in as many days — her special trick.

Robo opened his car door and Jen bounced onto his lap, throwing her arms around his neck. "Ohmigod, like, hurt me, hurt me!" she cried. Robo's mouth swallowed hers, hard and active like he was eating, smeared to his chin with Lise's new lipstick. He suddenly pulled away. "You're fucking late. I was ready to leave."

"Mr. Feltman made us —"

"Who?"

"Our English teacher, Mr. Feltman. He had to talk to Lise." Jen looked at Lise. "Isn't that right? About your paper?"

"Yeah," Lise muttered. "We had to like, stay after class and talk to him about that."

"Mr. Feltman is a total butt-fucker," Jen declared.

"Get in," Robo said. "I don't want to hear about it. Maybe you guys forget I'm in college. I've already been through this shit."

Lise hurried around to the Mustang's other side and climbed into the backseat. Jen sighed and hopped from Robo's lap to the passenger seat. Immediately she reached for the radio's tuning knob.

"I had it exactly where I wanted," Robo said, slapping Jen's hand onto the zip of his shorts as the car started to roll. "Play with this instead."

Jen gurgled and happily groped, while Lise looked away. She didn't want to see Robo's big dick. She could look at Trish's mom's *Playgirl* magazines, but the real thing made her nervous. Instead, she concentrated on the front yards strung together like lights, red, yellow, and pink flowers pricked out in a screen of green, the terracotta roof tiles as continuous as the black macadam that lined the street. Robo, caressed, his voice mellowing, continued half-heartedly on the subject of Jen's musical taste. "Anyway, you listen to totally bad music. You like Top 40. Those drumbeats hurt my ears. Fucking fake drum machines, any ape can do it."

"I do not like Top 40," Jen said. Each word was distinct, crisp.

"Do so."

"No way," Jen sulked, snatching her hand away. "I like the Go-Go's like everyone else."

"You're still into Michael Jackson," Robo accused, grabbing for her hand, which was back on the tuning dial.

"He's sold more records than anyone, ever," Jen answered defensively—she couldn't help herself: Michael Jackson was a genius, according to Jen, although she wouldn't admit it in front of Robo. Instead, her hand in his lap wriggled like a puppy that couldn't find its legs to stand up. Lise knew Jen had taped a Michael Jackson poster to the back of her closet, behind her miniskirts, and that she did Jane Fonda to "Thriller," even though it was a totally old record.

"You want to sleep with him. You want to make Oreo babies with Michael Jackson."

"Do not!"

"You know you do."

"Do *not*. Do I, Lise?" Jen asked, turning around to the backseat.

"Um," Lise shrugged.

"We're going to listen to some *good* music now. I got some Aerosmith right here. The best band in the world," Robo announced, slotting in a tape.

"Cool. I love Aerosmith," Jen said, one hand on Robo's crotch, the other on the volume knob, ready to crank when the rewind popped so that music would leave a trail of wildly soloing guitars wailing behind them, like exhaust.

They pulled onto Coldwater Canyon, roughly following the Los Angeles River (itself a plausible road alternative, paved in concrete and drained of all but a trickle of running water) towards the hills that cradled Campbell Hall, Trish's private school. The closer they got, the more worry took over Lise, her stomach twisting in on itself, her hands clenched in fists. Was Trish still mad? Lise didn't think she could bear another day of Trish's short, sharp answers to her questions, nor the long silences in between while Lise tried to think of what to say next. At least Trish was speaking to her at all. In January she'd ignored Lise for a whole week after Lise's mom shrank her favorite Benetton sweater in the wash, plus Trish wouldn't let Lise borrow clothes for a further month—the ultimate sentence, Lise's vanity stripped back to the raw, green wood of life before Trish, before good clothes and parties, before everything about Lise had changed, except her name, of course, and where she lived, and her parents—things she couldn't change no matter how she wished on birthday candles blown out all at once and pennies found heads-up and butterflies or ladybugs or any pretty winged thing that happened to land on her person.

Robo pulled up to Campbell Hall and parked outside the main gate on Laurel Canyon; he would wait in the car while Lise and Jen went in, taking their backpacks with them so to look like students—despite that they didn't wear the private school uniform. Lise and Jen knew from experience to proceed confidently into the fourteen acres of athletic fields, science labs, playgrounds, gymnasiums, and art studios. Both girls knew it was a question of attitude, of showing they belonged: squatter's rights. Nostrils stiffened, chins high, they hurried toward the tennis courts where Trish waited for them every day in the pungent shade of a eucalyptus tree. Waving as soon as they saw her, pealing her name ("Ohmigod, she looks pissed *off*," Jen whispered. "Please, God, no. No more," Lise added in silent prayer), Trish only stared back, blank-faced. She wore her Campbell plaid kilt and a wilted, white-collared shirt, her thick white socks shoved down—bunched just so—to crowd Gucci 175s. Trish had *perfect* shins. She had pristine knees, unmarked by scars, and an abundance of long, slender, honey-colored limbs, waxed since she was eleven. Mrs. Blue wouldn't let Trish play sports, lest her calves and biceps overdevelop. The artful layers of clothing Trish added to herself, despite the day's heat, made her look even more petite—never like she was hiding something, some bulge or bone that stuck out. Today, it was an expensive lemon-yellow Ton Sur Ton sweatshirt with the sleeves cut off and the neck trimmed low, tens of multicolored rubber bangles up to her elbows, and purple Lycra biking shorts under her kilt. Her asymmetrical blonde bob was lilac- and fuchsia-streaked to match her outfit—or vice-versa. Trish was the knockout of the three girls, with prize features, a baby-doll complexion, the bluest eyes, and fingernails so long they curled, always color-coordinated with her lipstick.

Jen's single pearl-drop earring struck the padded shoulder of her Fiorucci graffiti shirt as she tossed back her bangs (orange-tinged with Sun-In as of last Saturday, after a day at the beach with Robo). Lise huddled, perfectly still. Both were waiting for Trish to say something first. Nothing came.

Lise picked at the clasp of her locket. "I like your new top, Trish. That's the one you told me about last night, right?" It had been a one-way conversation on the phone. She couldn't help her anxious tone: she wanted to make up their spat of last weekend when Lise, drunk, accidentally smoked the upside-down cigarette in Trish's pack. Her lucky cigarette. Trish had flipped out in front of *everyone*, her hands swimming toward Lise's neck as if she might strangle her, and Lise had fled into the bathroom of Phazes where she cried hard enough that her mother commented on her swollen eyes the following morning. If she wanted to be friends with girls like Trish then she needed to grow a thicker skin, Lise's mom had said.

Trish ignored Lise. "I need a fucking cigarette. I need a cigarette so bad." She put out her arms to Jen. "Help me up."

Jen pulled, saying, "Me and Robo are hungry. Let's go to Yum Yum."

"Yeah, and I want to get stoned to death." Lise hoped the joke would catch if she kept passing it, that the joke—a fragile, fulgent bubble—wouldn't smash like a light bulb at Trish's feet.

"We're not going to Yum Yum. We're going over to Melaina's house," Trish said, still ignoring Lise.

"We want to go to Yum Yum and then the park," Jen whined. "Me and Robo are hungry."

"Listen, you can eat maple logs and fuck your boyfriend in the bushes tomorrow, but today we're going to Melaina's house," Trish snapped.

"Melaina has a softball game in Tarzana. She's not home," Lise said.

"Come on, let's just go to Yum Yum," Jen said.

"Yeah, we want to get stoned to death at Yum Yum," Lise giggled—her sparkling fake laugh—and nudged Jen. "Like that story today."

"What? What story?" asked Jen, looking bewildered.

"I'm so sick of Yum Yum," Trish groaned. "Those guys are *nasty*. I don't know why everyone thinks they're so hot, because I don't."

Yum Yum Donuts was where FFF hung out, their customized VW Beetles filling the parking lot after school, the boys with their flattops spilling from the donut shop's doors. There was one FFFer Lise really liked, Mikey, the one everyone liked, a tall, dark, clean-looking boy. Lise had never met him. Mikey would only talk to the prettiest girls. Mini-featured Lise, with her bunny-slope nose and narrow face, wasn't pretty enough, but Trish was, and he had waved her over to his table one day. Trish just walked past him, saying, "I don't want to go out with some wannabe gangster." Mikey laughed, while Lise stood where Trish had been the minute before, hoping he would notice her next. He didn't. He was too busy watching Trish flounce across the parking lot. Lise scurried after her, copying Trish's walk—but when she turned around, another girl hung from Mikey's arm.

"Come on, let's just go to Yum Yum. I already told Robo," Jen said. "He wants donuts."

"We're not going to Yum Yum—all those stupid guys.

We're going to Melaina's house. We're doing something different today. Something new. Something fun," Trish said.

"She's not home."

"You already said that twice, Lise," Trish answered her finally, rolling her blue eyes. "I heard you, OK?"

Lise flushed. "Sorry," she mumbled.

Trish turned to Jen. "Tell Robo to take us to Melaina's and drop us off."

"Can't Robo come?"

"Doesn't he have his own friends?" Trish said, looking revolted.

"He likes me. We're going together," Jen said.

"Yeah, for two weeks. And you already gave it up to him. He's totally pussy-whipped. You should dump him, Jen."

Surprised, Lise turned to Jen. "You told me you didn't sleep with him!"

"So what? I did. Big deal."

Lise was horrified. Trish and Jen were keeping secrets! "When did you do it?"

"I don't know."

"She did it on the second date. At the movies. On the floor." Trish shuddered. "So gross. The *floor*."

"We had our clothes on. I mean, I wasn't *naked* or anything," Jen said.

Trish pressed her fingers against her temples and shook her head. Lise and Jen could tell she was stressed. They had stressed her out. They were always stressing her out. "I'm stressed," she sometimes said when Lise called her at night. "I was waiting for you to call and Alexis wanted to use the phone and you took *forever*. I never get to use the phone when I want to. I need my own line. I pushed Alexis and the David Hockney fell and my mother *screamed* at me because he like, *personally* gave her that painting and she doesn't have his number anymore and now I'm totally stressed *out*. All because of you." Alexis was Trish's older sister. She took classes at UCLA.

"The funniest thing happened in English today," Lise said, changing the subject. If she could just make Trish laugh—she *needed* Trish to be her friend again. Trish and Jen couldn't be better friends than Trish and Lise (or even Lise and Jen, although their friendship wasn't so important; both had wanted to be Trish's friend when she briefly attended fifth grade with them, enough to become friends with each other). Best friends like Trish, Lise, and Jen weren't supposed to keep secrets. Trish and Jen knew that Lise liked Mikey from FFF, and they all knew that Jen's dad had used his belt on her once and that's why Jen's mom left him, and that Trish's dad paid her mom $5,000 a month in child support. Trish and Jen knew that Lise had wet Trish's bed once when she was really drunk, which is why she slept on the floor now at Trish's house, but they hadn't told anyone. They *promised* her they wouldn't. These facts—these secrets—were what made them friends. *Best* friends, the kind that shared *everything*, including when they slept with someone. Lise should have known the details of that *immediately*. She tried again. "We totally laughed so hard in English. Remember that story, Jen? About the lady getting stoned to death? It was *so* funny."

But Jen was sulking and didn't answer Lise. She had her thumb in her mouth, a bad habit she couldn't break.

"Sounds it," Trish said, her jaw slack to make the words go flat.

"I want Robo to come!" Jen suddenly cried.

"He can't," Trish said. They'd almost reached his car and Trish had her cigarette pack out, ready to step through the Campbell Hall gate to freedom. The girls huddled together, making a wind block, while she and Jen lit up (Lise only smoked when she was drunk). Robo was banging his head to Dire Straits, that song "Money for Nothing" they always played on the radio. When Jen went to get into the car, Trish grabbed her arm and squeezed.

Jen said, "Robo, we need you to drive us to Sherman Oaks."

"The Galleria? No way. I'm totally sick of that place."

"We need to go to our friend's house. She's expecting us. And her mother," Jen added. "They're both like, expecting us."

"I'm not going over to some stupid friend's house to play Barbies," Robo sneered.

Jen looked at Trish, who glared back. "We need you to drive us," Jen said, still looking at Trish. "It's really important. Come on, Robo, just this once. We *need* you to drive us."

"Money for Nothing" was over. Robo reached for the tuner button until he found it again, or part of the song, at least. "Why don't you call your mommies?" He twisted the rearview mirror to groom his hair, yellow with Sun-In where Jen's was orange. "Or like, walk."

"We already walked *so* far today. I'm totally tired. My feet hurt." Jen limped to Robo's door and leaned against it, panting slightly. "They *hurt*."

Robo ignored her, polishing his Ray Bans with his T-shirt.

"Fine, we'll hitch a ride," Trish said, beginning to roll the waist of her Campbell plaid.

"What are you doing, Trish?" Lise said.

"Well, we have to get a ride, don't we? I'm doing what I have to do to get us a ride. Roll up your skirt," Trish ordered, pointing to Jen's ruffled white miniskirt.

"I'm wearing jeans. What should I do?" Lise asked.

"Get in the fucking car!" Robo yelled. "You'll like, get killed if you do that. Don't you read the paper? Three girls got raped in Van Nuys last week by some guy with a van."

"Of course we don't read the paper. It's totally boring," Trish snorted.

Lise shivered. "Did they die?"

No one answered her; they were busy fitting themselves into the Mustang, dumping their schoolbags on the floor. Lise climbed into the backseat next to Trish, who sprawled grandly, her shins flashing in the sunlight, the moisturized skin burnished as if flecked with gold. "Thanks, Robo," Trish said, patting him on the head like a good dog.

Jen was fiddling with the tuner button. "I want KISS," she said. "Give me KISS. I need to hear some hits."

Trish pulled a can of Evian spray from her bag, spritzed the hand that had touched Robo's hair, and wiped it. She moistened her face—it dried quickly in the wind that rushed to embrace them when the convertible roared away from

Campbell Hall. "Is my mascara running?" she asked, turning to Lise.

"No. You look awesome." Lise would have liked to cool her own face, but Trish had already put the spray away and turned her attention to the passing scenery. Lise looked, too, over Trish's shoulder, not wanting to miss what Trish saw. She began to count the elongated shadows of telephone poles, a compulsive habit when she was nervous (sixteen, eighteen, twenty-three, twenty-four ... would Trish ever talk to her, like, *really* talk to her again? No, Lise told herself, don't even *think* that thought ... forty-two, forty-three, fifty ...).

Ten minutes later, they were at Melaina's house, where no one was home, where Robo dropped them off and drove away, at Trish's insistence.

Two

When you're sixteen you start playing for real. That's what the cops told them. They said right back at the cops, "A kid who tells on another kid's a dead kid." Just like the movies.

Ed Valencia was almost eighteen and hadn't been nailed for anything yet, but the cops hassled him plenty, hassled all of the punks who stuck out like a Nazi uniform on the streets of casual, pastel Los Angeles. The cops stalked the shows, which were always oversold, and what looked like fighting to the bouncers and cops was only dancing to Ed Valencia and his friends. The cops broke up the crowd that gathered outside Poseur on Melrose, and crashed parties to carry off the keg or a cooler stocked with bottles and cans. Finally, the cops surprised Ed Valencia and the other Rats at their favorite skating spot, the carved-out banks of the Los Angeles River—the very river they had named themselves after, not really a river at all but a storm channel paved in concrete—threatening them with arrest for trespassing, vandalism, destruction of public property, and, if they struggled against the headlocks the cops caught them in, resisting arrest.

Ed Valencia only really got mad when the cops ripped

his clothes, like his D.O.A. T-shirt and his dad's old plaid flannel shirt, both treasured, worn thin—but more than that, Ed Valencia didn't have clothes to spare. His mom had just so much to go around, and Ed Valencia was considered unemployable by most Los Angeles businesses because he wore a six-inch jet-black Mohawk and tattoos and his clothes were blatantly secondhand (except his band T-shirts. Ed Valencia bought new T-shirts at shows when the band was good). One potential employer had even told him to go back to Hollywood Boulevard with the other punks, like Ed Valencia was some kind of rent-boy trying to make good at a hotdog stand. Tricking was for runaways, kids who didn't have three bucks to get into a show because they had a drug habit, who delivered babies in alleys and left them for dead, who got stabbed or overdosed or tied up in a stranger's bed, gang-banged until they bled. Kids who starred in snuff films and were never seen alive again. Kids who became hearsay on the street, the stories of what happened to them a useless warning to the same troubled kind bound for a violent end. Tricking wasn't for Ed Valencia, who lived at home with his mom and sister and went to school and stuck by his friends, the same loyal pack since grade school. He generally steered clear of petty crime and getting wasted—he was almost straight-edge. Almost. He jammed econo, life on the cheap and straight. Definitely not criminal.

The trouble was, the cops were everywhere, or at least everywhere there were punks. The cops thought all punks were the same: *asking* for it. Fuck the cops.

Ed Valencia, in his tiny bedroom, was getting ready.

Tonight he and Bones, another Rat, were going over the hill to see some new bands play at the Cathay de Grande, an early show, five dollars, all-ages. Ed Valencia stripped off his T-shirt—wet from that afternoon's skating—and selected a fresher one—Fear, "I Love Livin' in the City"—from the floor. Agent Orange played their hit, "Blood-stains," on his stereo, and Ed Valencia sang along as he swabbed the six holes in each ear with alcohol before inserting the various ornaments he always wore: an Iron Cross, a dangling skull, a sharpened chicken bone, his one and only ex-girlfriend's pearl stud, a black rubber scorpion, a crucifix, numerous safety pins and silver hoops. He rubbed Vaseline into the new tattoo on his forearm—a red-eyed black rat with dripping fangs. Then, with considerable care, he doused his hair with school glue and blow-dried his Mohawk upright.

In a cage on his bedside table, a rat slept in a hammock made from an old nylon stocking. Ed Valencia poked him. "Wake up, Darby." Darby Crash stretched, his tail flicker-ing. Ed Valencia opened the cage door and reached for the rat. Darby Crash would ride on his shoulder tonight. He, like Ed Valencia, liked to prowl L.A. after dark.

With Darby Crash roaming his neck and sniffing his ears, Ed Valencia checked the window for sight of Bones. Sure enough, there he was, dealing with a cop who had followed him into the apartment block's parking lot. Bones' car was illegal, an easy target: a fifteen-year-old Chevy Malibu held together with Duck tape and thickly layered gunmetal-gray primer paint. The brake lights had been kicked out, hood and roof dented by the steel-capped toes and nail-studded heels of combat boots (belonging to the Rats, dancing hard at an outdoor show), while the radio aerial—a wire coat hanger twisted out of shape—bore the anarchist's black flag. As the cop wrote out a citation, Bones leaned against the Malibu, his mouth a furious line. A large Iron Cross pendant reflected the intense late-afternoon sun, its black enamel molten-looking, melting into his chest like a wound, an unblinking eye. When the cop was gone, Bones balled the flimsy script and tossed it onto the backseat of his car, from where it would surely escape to become part of the litter cycle governed by traffic and sky.

Minutes later, he was banging on the door. "Get that, will you?" Ed Valencia called to his sister, who was listening to the *Rocky Horror Picture Show* soundtrack in the living room.

"Get it yourself."

"You're right there. I'm still finishing up in here." Darby Crash nibbled the scorpion that dangled from Ed Valencia's ear. Ed Valencia shook his head, playing tug-of-war, watching his Mohawk in the mirror to make sure it held.

Bones pounded, making the door chain and accompanying five bolts rattle. "Valencia! Valencia!"

"He'll kick the fucking door down in a minute and then Mom will really let you have it," Ed Valencia shouted to his sister.

Kelly replied, in sync with the mythical audience of her record, "The man you are about to see has no fucking neck. Where's your fucking neck?"

Ed Valencia stormed out of his bedroom, Darby Crash's nails digging in for the bumpy ride down the short hall, Ed

Valencia navigating the obstacle course of *stuff* for which there was no room, left over from when they lived in a house, not a rented two-bedroom apartment in crappy North Hollywood. "I'm going to crack that fucking record over your goddamn head," he growled.

"You would, would you?" Kelly replied. She had daubed her face with white pancake, then drawn on oversized red lips to match the little red bow tie cocked at her throat. Her mother's gold lamé evening jacket finished the outfit, draped on her scarecrow eleven-year-old frame like a bedspread. She was ready to do the Time Warp at the drop of a hat.

"Anybody home? Valencia? You there?" Bones treaded the Welcome mat, jangling the hardened steel shackles he wore as bracelets.

"I'm here," Ed Valencia said, fumbling with the locks.

"To take you," the record said.

"Where?" Kelly said.

"Turn it off, Kelly. I mean it. Bones doesn't want to hear this shit."

"Hear what?" Bones said, stepping inside.

"When Brad Majors," the record said.

"Asshole," said Kelly.

"Ignore her," Ed Valencia said. "She's not talking to you. She's talking to a fucking record."

Bones dribbled his limbs into the small, square, all-purpose living room, dominated by Kelly on the couch, an outdated turntable and receiver (their father's last family purchase), and a ten-inch black-and-white TV. Bones was called Bones because he was the most elastic, relaxed skater any Rat personally knew: boneless, made of rubber bands. "Man, I got hassled by this cop who tailed me with his fucking high beams on, grilling my fucking back. Told me I have a week to get my car fixed and that he was personally going to check up on me. He has my address."

"He can't do that. I know for a fact that he can't do it. It's an invasion of your privacy, the Fourth Amendment or something like that," Ed Valencia said. He was the smart one, the leader of the Rats.

"Oh yeah? It's bullshit, all that Amendment crap. It don't mean anything. Those guys do what they want. They fucking rape and pillage. Fuck," Bones said, shaking his head, "I'm having a bad day. Why does it have to be like this? Just one fuck-up after another. That fucking cop, he asked me where I went to school and then wanted to know if I *knew* anything, like who's dealing and shit like that. Told me he'd let me off if I could give him a name. They're a bunch of blackmailers, so fucking corrupt." Bones punched the air, then clutched his arm. "Dude, you got to see this. It's not right." He carefully rolled up his long shirt-sleeve to reveal a weeping rat tattoo, identical to Ed Valencia's. "Mine fucking kills. Is yours sick too?"

"You got to use Vaseline. It'll keep it all moist and protected. I already told you that."

"It hurts," Bones complained.

"Yeah, they always hurt for a while. But if it gets infected bad, you'll need a doctor, Bones."

"No way," Bones shook his head. "My mom can't find out. Then I'll really be fucked. Why do you think I'm wearing this shirt when it's two hundred degrees out?"

"Grab some Vaseline from my room," Ed Valencia said. "It's on my dresser."

"Is it true you're constipated?" Kelly said, still glued to her soundtrack.

"Shut up or I'll tape your fucking mouth shut," Ed Valencia warned her.

"There were dark storm clouds," the record intoned.

"Describe your balls," Kelly said.

"Knock it off, Kelly." Ed Valencia turned to Bones, who had returned and was slathering his arm with grease. "Dude, get me out of here. This place is too fucking small for me and *Rocky* fucking *Horror*."

"At least you have your own room," Kelly said. "At least you don't have to share with Mom."

"You ready, Valencia?"

"Why do you call him that?" asked Kelly. "It's not his name."

"Can you just shut up for one minute, Kelly?"

"On a night out they were going to remember," the record said.

"For how long?" asked Kelly.

"A very long time," the record answered.

In the car, Darby Crash patrolled the backseat, pausing to investigate tangles of sandwich cellophane, empty Coke cans, and a spare Converse All-Star (black canvas, always, its sole Duck-taped where it had worn through). Ed Valencia held the battered boom box that served as their sound system, its tape deck held in place with more Duck tape; he was ever-ready to haul the box to the window at red lights and blast the car to his right with the Buzzcocks or the

27

Germs or whatever. When he did, the targeted driver gulped like a goldfish, eyes bulging behind sealed window glass at the sight of the Malibu and the various River Rats who begged a ride in it from day to day. L.A. punks had a violent reputation. They were a force to fear, according to the media—and yet the boys' expressions below their Mohawks were indefatigably pleasant, benevolent even, convinced of their superior moral universe. Until the cops turned up, that is.

For now, no sign of cops, but Ed Valencia and Bones were keeping watch. "Dude, I heard about this show tomorrow night in South Pasadena. Some dude is going to shut down his street and Black Flag are playing," Bones shouted over the Circle Jerks.

"It'll get busted for sure. You remember last time, they started arresting people just for standing on some asshole's precious lawn," Ed Valencia yelled back.

"I don't care if they arrest me. Fuck the cops."

"Red light!" Bones braked sharply as Ed Valencia launched the boom box from his lap and turned up the volume. A fat, middle-aged, Mercedes-driving man turned to stare at him, nostrils flaring in white rings, his tiny pink nose, raw and snubbed as a newborn's, mismatched with the rest of his face. Nose job, Ed Valencia decided. Everyone was having nose jobs these days. His sister wanted a nose job, to plane a small bump, and she had threatened to have her boobs done if they didn't grow big enough. "You take what you're given," Ed Valencia told her, "and that's enough. You got to use what you got." He tried to explain the punk econo ethic—cheap, efficient, buying used instead of new all the time—but she waved him away.

"You smell like mothballs," Kelly said. "You wear dead people's clothes. That's totally gross." It was true that Ed Valencia wore clothes from the Goodwill Bargain Barn, where he could buy a pound of T-shirts and pants for twenty cents. All his friends did. They washed the stuff, didn't they?

The light turned green and the Mercedes shot off into the distance where street overtakes street to eternity—or so it seemed to Ed Valencia, who had only ever lived in Los Angeles. Satisfied that the Rats had given another obvious go-getter something to think about, the music was turned down to a more humane decibel level. "If you knew some-one died in the clothes you were wearing, would you still wear them?" Ed Valencia asked Bones.

"Yeah. Doesn't bother me. I wear the bathrobe my grandfather died in. It's totally rad, paisley flannel with satin lapels. You've seen it. I wore it to school last week."

"But don't you like, lose control of yourself when you die? I mean, don't you shit and piss yourself when you die?"

"They wouldn't give away those clothes, or they'd wash them first if they did. My grandfather's robe is fine. No stains. Hey, I heard dead guys can fart, too. You know whose dad is a mortician?"

"Who?"

"Karen Lightner. Lightner's Funeral Home in Burbank."

"Someone should go out with her," Ed Valencia said.

"You'd get to drive the hearse around. Maybe you'd be out one night and she'd get called to pick up a body."

"Not her, dude, her dad."

"Maybe her dad would be too busy."

"Check it out," Bones said, pulling up in front of the Cathay de Grande. "There must be fifty cops here already. This isn't even a big show. It's fucking *Tuesday*."

"Hurry up and park," Ed Valencia said, his pulse provoked. He wanted to be in the middle of the crowd, feeling what it was all about, ready and waiting if anything took off, if some kind of riot started. He found it exhilarating, like dogs did the weather, the hairs raising on the back of his neck. Ed Valencia twitched his long legs, gripping the door handle, Darby Crash likewise raking his shoulder in anticipation, while Bones parked up.

"Are you here to see a bunch of deadbeats? Can't you afford a fucking haircut? Do your parents know where you are tonight? Are you looking for a fight? Are you FFF? The LADS? Suicidal Tendencies?" the cops asked, naming the suburban punk gangs they knew to haunt the shows.

"What are you talking about?" the kids replied, winking and flashing hand signals to let their friends know everything was all right. "FFF? What's that?" Better yet, be political, declare, "I have nothing to say," like the professionals did, who were used to being picked up and interrogated. Even Bones was smiling now; it was easier to deal with cops in a crowd than one-on-one in a parking lot bearing the brunt of the full California sun.

Every night in L.A. a show was on: at clubs in Hollywood and Downtown, at the Polish Association's meeting hall in Venice, or an abandoned storefront on La Cienega so close to LAX that planes sometimes overtook the song. The scene was organized, prolific, effective in that it got up the snouts of the cops, despite that the original 70s punks had dropped out, telling everyone punk was dead. Those carriers of the bug—the old timers—were actually deceased, or dying, or working for family businesses, while journalists (with their buzz-buzz and their bite, the lumps they dealt) were only interested in what was happening in England. The kids now infected—many in the early stages of the disease, self-medicating on music the way horses did on herbs and grasses—were confrontational in every way: politically, socially, theologically, artistically, sexually, *physically*. Their music was crushing, a sound not just heard but encountered, boiled down to basic drums and guitars, revved-up in speed, symphonic to its disillusioned listeners. This was hardcore: anti-parent, anti-nice. People called them boneheads and muscleheads, just looking for a fight, but the kids knew it was something more.

The Cathay's marquee listed five bands for five dollars, none of whose music Ed Valencia knew yet, but whose names sounded familiar: Hematoma, Stand Up, Parental Attitude, Candyland, The Buried. It was an early show, squeezed in before the metal show at 9 P.M.—but a show was a show was a show.

One of the bands playing tonight, Candyland, was supposed to be a bunch of juniors from Grant High School, the same age as Ed Valencia and the Rats. Seeing their name on the flyer made Ed Valencia wish he had a band to play out with. *He* could drive a hundred adrenaline-loaded kids to slam until their clothes soaked through. He could do that. He knew he could, but stupid things were holding him back, money most of all, and something specific to shout about. He was pissed off, that's for sure, full of steam hell-bent on release. They all were. That's why they were there: everyone was against them. But he couldn't just write a song saying, "I'm pissed off." He had to say it another way.

Inside the Cathay, the shirtless boys who crammed the shows (plus a handful of girls with *Star Trek* makeup, or no makeup at all to mask their pimples) milled, casually bumping as the room filled. Getting things started. Warming up, swinging arms, shaking out legs, easing the cracks from their necks with a tick-tock nod or a roll, the shaved strips of their heads gleaming like oiled ball bearings. The crowd's T-shirts bore the names of the adored: Crass, the Exploited, Black Flag, the Subhumans, Misfits, Minor Threat, DRI, the Germs, Dead Kennedys, Fear. Bouncers stood by their posts, ready to pound any punks who might push their luck. There was to be no stage diving, it was announced. Everyone laughed. Then the first band charged from somewhere backstage, somewhere hidden and dark, bearing bottles of Colt 45 they smashed over the heads of the devoted frontline, kids who never turned their eyes from what was happening onstage, who bled and begged for more, who reached out cupped hands to catch the singer's gob and smear it all over each other. "Are you ready? Are you ready?" the singer screamed. Next to Ed Valencia, someone was pissing into a plastic cup, ready to shower the band with a water bomb. The crowd pushed from every direction, the first dancers clustering in the pit. The speed of the music was way above the normal rhythm, two or three hundred heartbeats per minute, and the kids responded the only way they knew: blown into each other, jerking and jigging, touched by electrodes.

"Listen, we got to be ourselves, live our own lives, and fuck social values," the singer shouted into the microphone, before someone jumped onstage and shoved the mic into his teeth, the noise like a chainsaw biting into a tree.

Darby Crash, who had been hovering on Ed Valencia's shoulder, dove down his shirtfront, surfacing from time to time to sniff the atmosphere, swiveling his sleek head, taking it all in before diving to safety again. Ed Valencia stood stock-still in the crowd with his arms crossed, a defiant position, his usual stance. Bones was in the pit at the front, dancing a hysterical hoedown. He lassoed a young kid around the neck with the crook of one elbow and swung him round, then threw him down. The kid—athletic, crew cut, good-looking—bounced up and threw a punch that landed in the middle of Bones' face. Bones, in turn, went down.

"Get up! Get up," the kid screamed, kicking him. Darby Crash, his nose poking out of Ed Valencia's collar, sensed trouble and disappeared just as Ed Valencia flew at the kid, a full-on body blow. But the kid wouldn't fall; he was some kind of football player, the way he planted himself. Fists up, he batted at Ed Valencia, arms moving like a conveyor belt. He wouldn't turn off—this kid was like he was plugged into a wall socket.

Never back down, Ed Valencia's head told him. To back down was scene suicide—and then he was tackled from behind, landing hard on the floor alongside Bones. More bodies dropped, everyone jabbing, grabbing ears and noses, knees in groins, leaning on femurs, fibulas, ulnas, pinning shoulders and throats. This is what happened when hard-core dancing went wrong. This was why the cops dogged them so: when violence, the moment before theatrical or comical, became suddenly real.

Within minutes, cops were streaming in from all doors. The first band was just three songs into their set and the show was already over, lights up, the club manager on the microphone telling them to get the hell out of there, threatening the end of punk bands at the Cathay de Grande. Ed Valencia was yanked to his feet, his young opponent likewise held, the kid's split lip showing juice and pulp. Ed Valencia's right cheek had swelled up like a blister in water and his nose leaked. He started to complain before a blow from a cop stopped him speaking. Both boys were cuffed and frisked, the cops haranguing them long after everyone else had left—including Bones.

"You think this is war? Think you punks are going to win? We got every resource available to us, and let me tell you, the LAPD is mobilized."

"Didn't do nothing," Ed Valencia muttered.

"Are you FFF? Do you have a knife on you?" The cop gripped Ed Valencia's calf, searching, twisting his jeans' leg to make the skin burn. "Come on, tell me something, give me an answer. Put your hands in the air. Get your hands

34

on your head or I'll blow your fucking head off. Give me a fucking answer, you fucking pussy."

Still Ed Valencia's head spoke clearly to him: don't back down. "Do I look like a cop?" He tried to sound tough, but his voice was higher than usual.

The cops squealed, mimicking him. "You sound like a girl," one said.

"You *look* like a fucking asshole," another one jeered, ratcheting Ed Valencia's handcuffs a couple notches, then leaning on them.

The metal cuffs bored into Ed Valencia's wrist bones. "Not resisting! Not resisting!" he cried. Beside him, the face of the kid was very red, but he was silent. He was taking it.

"You punks better start doing what you're supposed to be doing. We could book you, no problem. We'd come up with something. Try telling your folks what you were really up to tonight when they thought you were at the fucking library." The power of the uniform, Ed Valencia was thinking. The power of the uniform to destroy the outsider—it was a line from somewhere, a song maybe, a refrain that sang through his pain. Suddenly the cuffs came off and the cops were gone, Ed Valencia and the kid bolting from the club, the kid faster, by far, but Ed Valencia didn't care. He just wanted *out* of there.

Bones was waiting in the Malibu, nervously checking his mirrors. "Sorry, dude. I got kicked out like everyone else. They wouldn't let me back in. There was nothing I could do." He started the car. "You picked the wrong guy,

Valencia. That clown was definitely FFF. Let's get out of here before they come looking for us." Bones pulled out into the cruising traffic of Sunset and put his foot to the floor, the whole car vibrating as he accelerated but not moving very fast: he needed an uncluttered stretch on which to build momentum, before the Malibu could fly with the rest.

"You started it, Bones."

"I was only dancing. You're the one who threw a punch. The minute I knew that kid was FFF, I was done."

"How do you know that kid was FFF? He looked about twelve. He's too little for FFF."

"FFF is big, dude. Huge. They got kids all over the place now. They're fucking recruiting, like the army. They know *everything*, like they've got some weird kind of intelligence operation going on. They know who we are. We're dead, dude."

"No way," Ed Valencia said. "They don't know us. I've never seen that kid in my life."

"They know, dude. Believe me, they know. FFF is blood-thirsty, man. They fight anyone. They'll want the Rats now. They'll take us down," said Bones.

"I don't believe this. What you're saying is nuts."

"Don't believe me, then. But you're stupid if you don't."

"I'm not stupid. Back there was stupid. That kid was stupid. Even if he's FFF."

"He's FFF."

Ed Valencia shook his head. "He was a *little* kid."

"He knocked you over, didn't he?" Bones said.

Ed Valencia pounded the dashboard, making the glove

compartment rattle. "Stop the car! Where's my fucking rat? Where's Darby Crash?"

Bones transferred the rat from his jacket pocket to Ed Valencia's shoulder. "I found him on the floor of the Cathay. He was crawling around, totally fine. He's not hurt." Darby Crash promptly began to lick Ed Valencia's neck of sweat and blood, grooming him affectionately. When he was done, Ed Valencia fed him a Milkbone dog biscuit, cupping rat and biscuit in his palm.

"Got any more of those, Valencia? I'm fucking starving."

Ed Valencia just laughed.

"I'm serious, dude. There's nothing to eat at my house. My mom hasn't been to the store for weeks," Bones complained.

Ed Valencia pulled out another Milkbone. "Where are we going? We can't go home. It's not even dark out yet."

Three

Melaina's house was almost identical to Lise and Jen's houses, situated not quite in the middle of a flat street, the house a regular rectangular shape of 1,300 square feet in the popular Spanish Colonial style, its red-tiled roof and pink-stucco walls shaded by crape myrtle and eucalyptus trees. Upstairs were three bedrooms and a family bath cluttered with shampoo bottles smelling intensely of fruit—raspberry, strawberry, and apple in Technicolor, wholly unnatural—and downstairs, the living room and dining room, a kitchen with Formica countertops and stainless-steel double sink and garbage disposal, plus an attached garage. The girls paused at the front door, Lise ringing the bell while Trish and Jen inspected the windows. When no one answered, Trish led them around the side to the back door, somehow knowing its key was hidden in a palm's pot. She pointed. "There."

Lise bent obediently, grazing her right forearm on one of the plant's spear-edges as she groped the powdery, pebbly soil. A line raised in blood, stinging worse than a paper cut. "Shit!" she cried, used to being dramatic about these things.

Trish snatched the key from her. "Shut up. You want to get us caught?"

"What are we doing?" Lise whispered, gripping her sliced arm to stop the bleeding.

Trish unlocked the house. Then she wiped the key with her shirttail and dropped it back in the pot. "Come on," she said, and stepped inside the kitchen.

"Why are we here? What are we doing?" Lise asked again in a louder voice, sounding panicked now, her wide eyes clicking side to side. "Nobody's home."

"We're just going to look around. No biggie," Trish said. Jen was already snooping in the refrigerator, helping herself to a handful of green grapes—"Ohmigod, seeds!" she gagged, spitting down the garbage disposal. "*So* gross." A swig of orange juice from the container to rinse, and then she was rustling in a bag on the countertop, powdering her nose with a custard-filled donut.

"What are we looking for? We shouldn't be here if nobody's home." Lise heard her voice as if it were caught inside a helium balloon: tinny, distant. She wanted to grab hold of something to ground herself; her head was floating off its neck-pole, drifting toward the strip-light. It was chilly in Melaina's house, the air-conditioning left pumping all day to cool the family at night, and still Lise was sweating. She stared at her bleeding arm. Blood always made her feel queasy. She never licked a wound to put the juices back into her system, or nibbled an aging scab, gray in its wrinkles and cracks. She reached for a kitchen chair back—

"Don't touch," Trish snapped. "Only touch what you're going to take. You too, Jen. No fingerprints. That's the easiest way to get caught."

"I'm like, eating the evidence," Jen giggled, her mouth full.

"You'll get fat," Trish warned.

"Get caught at what?" Lise asked, her lips thick and dumb, getting in the way like too many hands, all thumbs. Black clouds crowded her pupils, leaving just a spark to light the way as she followed Trish and Jen into the living room. "What are we doing?"

"Like, take whatever you want," Trish said.

"Cool," Jen said, licking confectioner's dust from her fingers.

"From Melaina?" Lise asked.

"From anyone. Take little stuff you can carry." Trish was climbing the stairs, not touching the rail. "I need some makeup. And Melaina has a charm bracelet. I want that."

"I want it," Jen whined, following Trish.

But Lise's knees had locked. When she tried to breathe, ribs of girded steel groaned—she was all frozen up. Her ears buzzed, every noise of her body amplified, pulse a cannon, head full of static, mouth a cavern in which dried spit crackled like chaparral in the fire season. This was a whole new test, she thought. Trish was always testing Lise, who she suspected was weak: afraid of boys, afraid of dogs, afraid of the dark, sleeping with a night-light and her head under the covers.

"Lise, what are you doing down there?" Trish called. Her sharp voice cut to Lise's naked self: the girl who needed her friends more than anything in the world. Lise willed her soul to be strong and pushed one leg forward over the linoleum. Her Reeboks yelped, first left, then right—"Help!

Help!" they cried. She was on the stairs, feeling, as she climbed, like she was falling backwards. Trish met her at the top wearing Melaina's charm bracelet, jiggling her wrist so the trinkets tinkled. "Look what I got," she said.

Jen, just behind Trish, held Melaina's locked diary. "There's got to be a key here somewhere."

Trish shook her head and, simultaneously, the bracelet. "No way. Totally obvious. You'll tell everyone what she wrote and then she'll know it was us."

"But I want to *read* it."

"She probably writes about what she ate for dinner," Trish said scornfully. "And what boys she likes. No big deal. We all know she likes Kyle Goodman—she's always following him around at Phazes, trying to get him to dance with her. Melaina's *so* immature. I bet she's never *done* anything. Put it back where you found it. We should get out of here soon."

"What about the other rooms? Did you look in them already? Like, what about her brother's room?" Lise was trying to participate now, to show her allegiance to her friends. She would do it. She would always do it, and once she had done the bad thing the first time, it was easy—easy to taunt a fat waitress, to call the house of the poorest girl in her math class and pretend it was Woolworth's she wanted, asking how much their couch cost, their TV, their beds. Soon Lise would forget that she had ever been afraid. "Should we look in Greg's room?"

Trish wrinkled her nose. "*Gross.* He's a total masturbator."

Moving into the bathroom, Lise grabbed anything she

could reach: nail polish, lipstick tubes, cans of hairspray and mousse, a glass bottle of Listerine, body lotion, shampoo, all the products a family could need shoved into her backpack, dumped on top of her books, some of the tops only half-screwed, some entirely topless. She didn't care. It was more important to take something than worry about the mess.

They were in and out in ten minutes. Trish ordered them to muss the beds, kick over lamps, fling cushions to the floor, and open all drawers, being careful not to leave fingerprints. As they were about to walk out the door, Jen leaned toward a windowpane, her thickly glossed lips poised to kiss.

"No!" Trish smacked Jen on the side of her face.

Jen flushed, shocked by the blow. "That hurt!"

"What the hell do you think you're doing?" Trish demanded.

"I was just going to tag it like we always do."

"Are you kidding? They'll know it was us, stupid. That's like, evidence."

Trish pushed her through the door and Lise followed, Trish the last one out, using her shirttail on the doorknob. Then they were walking down the street, totally normal again, three friends, the best of friends, backpacks slung over one shoulder, although considerably heavier now— Lise was stooped with the weight of hers.

Jen said, "Now where? Who else's house?" She was excited. She dipped her pinkie into a pot of Melaina's lustrous, pearly lip-gloss and smeared her lips frantically, piling it on.

Trish's eyes gleamed. She wore Melaina's charm bracelet,

with a few more baubles tucked away inside the folds of her clothes. That was all she took, Trish, as always, sophisticated—she wasn't as *needy* as Lise and Jen. "Now we go to the Galleria and call my mom."

"How are we going to get there?" Lise asked.

"But I want to do another one!" Jen cried. "We should have had Robo wait for us. We could go to Jody Simpson's house—she lives around here. Her mom does window dressing at Robinson's and Jody gets like, free clothes, as much as she wants."

"We have all this stuff to carry," Lise said. "What's your mom going to think?"

"How's she going to know? It's all in our backpacks. Anyway, we just went shopping." Trish grabbed Lise's arm and squeezed. *Hard.* "You better not tell. You know what will happen if you tell."

Lise nodded, but Trish told her anyway, very close to her face. It got worse every time, what would happen if Lise or Jen didn't obey. "I'll tell everyone, including your parents, that you had sex with four guys in the parking lot at Phazes. Four *Black* guys."

Lise squirmed. She smelled Trish's lunch: potato something, mixed with other things, Diet Coke, Thousand Island salad dressing, and jelly beans, probably. "OK, OK. Like I'm going to tell. I didn't *say* that."

"Seriously, we should have told Robo to wait," Jen said. "I mean, at least we wouldn't have to walk to the mall. I swear, I'm only going out with guys who can drive from now on. My feet are *killing* me."

"No Robo. This is between the three of us. Don't *ever*

43

tell him, Jen," Trish warned. "We could get in a lot of trouble. My mom might not let me hang out with you guys if we get caught. She'll think you're a bad influence." Trish pulled out her pack of cigarettes and Jen's fingers twitched for one. Lighting up set off Melaina's charm bracelet, the silvery fringe of softball, Eiffel Tower, baby bootie, and shamrock effervescing, flashlit by the bright afternoon sun.

The front door of Lise's house opened right into the living room—no large front hall with a decorative wrought-iron staircase winding up and a broad banister for slithering one's hand down like at Trish's house, not even a small foyer in which to hang up a coat. Lise let herself in with her own key after Mrs. Blue dropped her off right out front; there was no point in Lise pretending that she didn't live where she lived, although she had tried at the beginning of her friendship with Trish, two years ago. Inside, the TV was on, tuned to *The Love Boat*. Lise's mother lay on the couch, a washcloth over her eyes, her heavy thighs pooled in the well of sagging cushions, knobbly yellow feet unshoed and stickered all over with corn pads.

"Hi."

"Hi," her mother replied grimly.

"Do you have a migraine?"

Lise's mother sighed. "Yes." Lise's mother always had a migraine, or the makings of one.

"I'm sorry," Lise said. Then, in a tiny voice, she asked, "Was your day OK?"

"They think their ideas are so great. They think I'm their

secretary. Excuse me, I don't *do* dictation." Mrs. Anderson worked on copy at an ad agency, although lately, because of her headaches, she had been leaving the office early at least one day a week. Lise, who was used to having the house to herself until six o'clock (even if she wasn't at home, she knew it was there, empty and waiting), resented the intrusion.

"I'm sorry," Lise said again.

"Where have you been?"

"At the mall. You know, with Trish and Jen. Trish's mom brought us home." Lise always made sure to cover the important details—who, what, where, and when—as quickly and succinctly as possible. She dropped her backpack to the floor with a reckless thud, freezing as she heard the jangle of loot and smelled the heady perfume of oozing lotions and shampoos.

Mrs. Anderson grimaced and held her head. "Elise, please. I've had noise all day."

"Sorry," Lise whispered. She wished her mother was younger and didn't complain so much. She wished she could talk to her about stuff, like being interested in boys and wanting sex. She wished that her mother would give her makeup tips, like Trish's mom did, or take her on shopping sprees at the mall, like Jen's, spending on Lise whatever was left after the bills were paid. Instead, Lise had to rely on borrowed bits and pieces from her friends (pretending their information wasn't new to her) and guilty $5 handouts from her dad.

"Why do you girls need to spend so much time at the mall? It only cultivates materialism."

"I don't buy that much stuff. I just like to look."

Her mother raised an eyebrow. "Like I believe that. You stink of perfume or something. Some kind of fruity perfume." She wrinkled her nose. Lise's mother didn't wear perfume; she smelled of toothpaste and Secret deodorant. On her bathroom shelf she kept a bar of ordinary bath soap, her toothbrush and deodorant, and a family-sized bottle of aspirin. She didn't even use face cream.

"Um." Lise shrugged. "Just some makeup. I left it at Trish's."

Mrs. Anderson sat up, the washcloth plopping into her lap. "I thought you said you went to the mall. You didn't say you went to Trish's house, too." It was missed details like this that she latched on to, evidence of secret fun. Trish and Jen always said you couldn't lie to Lise's mom. She pointed out their lack of eye contact, their fidgeting hands, doodling toes, and that they laughed too much but only half-smiled. She was suspicious by nature. She suspected, and expected, the worst.

"I mean I gave it to Trish to keep at her house. It's just to mess around with. Because I'm not supposed to wear makeup." Lise had scrubbed her face clean in the Galleria ladies' room while Trish and Jen touched up theirs. Every day Lise washed her face before she went home—especially now that she couldn't be sure if her mother would be there. Not until she was fifteen could she pierce her ears and mend the faults of her face with liquid foundation and blusher swept high up the cheekbone, and not until she was *sixteen* could she officially date.

"Why on earth did you buy makeup, then?" asked her mother, amazed.

"To practice, I guess." This was true. Lise was always playing with makeup in her room, and while Mrs. Anderson didn't approve, Lise didn't get into trouble. As long as she didn't leave the house wearing what her dad called war paint, looking—according to her mom—like she was asking for it.

"Why don't you act like a kid? You're in such a hurry to grow up. Next thing you'll be saying you're on a diet. You're thin enough. I don't want that kind of dumb behavior from you. Trying to look like a model in a magazine—it's just not healthy, Elise."

"I'm fine. I think I'm fine." Her mother *resented* her daughter, Lise sensed, but she didn't know why, or for what, just that this was the way it always was, for as long as Lise could remember. Her mother's dissatisfied mouth was a net to catch Lise doing something wrong. No other mothers she knew were like hers, with no-color hair parted down the middle and frayed at the ends, her oversized glasses magnifying her headache squint.

"You know I don't think Trish's mother is an appropriate role model."

"What are you talking about, Mom? You're just being mean. Trish's mom is fine. She's really nice to me."

"Of course she is," Mrs. Anderson answered in a strained voice.

"Leave me alone. You totally get on my nerves. I thought you had a headache," Lise said.

"What's that supposed to mean?"

"For someone with a headache you sure can talk."

"That woman." Mrs. Anderson paused. "I just hate to see you poisoned by peer pressure to look and act a certain way. When I was thirteen, I didn't care how I looked."

"So?"

"I think you care too much."

Lise hoisted her backpack to her shoulder. "Are you done? Because I have a lot of homework," she said, not waiting for an answer, heading upstairs.

Barricaded inside her small blue-paneled bedroom, the flimsy desk and chair pushed against the door, Lise set about unpacking that afternoon's spoils. She worked fast, hardly seeing what she handled. Her hands shook, making her fumble the slimy bottles as she bundled them into an empty pillowcase, then she set about wiping her school-books; next week was the end of school and she had to return them as good as when they had been signed out to her at the beginning of the year, or pay for them. No way was she spending money on books!

From under the single bed, simply covered in a quilt (stitched by her grandmother's own two hands, better than any pink ruffled bedspread with a matching canopy, Lise's mother always said), she pulled out the oversized dress box from I. Magnin that Mrs. Anderson's good work suit had come in. Here Lise kept the few love letters she had received ('I think you're the hottest girl in sixth grade. Will you go with me? Love, your friend, Steve'), plus the letters ending those courtships and beginning others, often dated within a week of each other ('Steve says he doesn't want to go with you anymore. Will you go with me? Love, your friend, Justin'), and letters she herself had written and never sent (every one of them addressed to Mikey from FFF), as well as a few sun-bleached swimming ribbons, spelling certificates, a detailed report on the fallen leaves of the San Fernando Valley (including crumbling specimens), and—most important—in well-handled boxes, her tampon and maxi-pad collection, for which she had no need yet. Into the dress box went the sticky, rainbow-stained pillowcase, the box slid back under the bed. Lise was free of her plunder, even if the air around her was saturated with its scent.

Now she set about her usual routine, what kept her busy until bedtime. Using a compact mirror (her mother didn't believe in bedroom wall mirrors, saying they only encouraged vanity), Lise ringed her eyes with gray pencil, coated her lashes in blue, then sent high beams of white eye shadow up to her brows. Next, a beauty mark dotted in coral on her left cheekbone. Finally she frosted her lips in purple grape-flavored gloss and teased her hair on one side—the long side—making a bird's nest. She wished she had highlights like Trish, candy-colored stripes, *so* cool, kind of punky, even if Trish said they weren't; they were *London*, which was even better. Lise stared into the mirror at herself for a long time. Her eyes were dark with feeling, with guilt. She didn't look innocent.

She heard the garage door begin to rumble, the red tongue withdrawing to the roof of its mouth. Her father was home early, too. What was their problem? They couldn't even stay at work like normal people. Within minutes, the muted strains of her parents' first fight of the night drifted upstairs. Theirs was a long-standing, malignant argument that neither could trace to its root: who did what that was so insensitive, so offensive, despicable, and cruel. Lise was beginning to understand that this had little to do with dirty socks stuffed under the couch or crumbs left to draw ants on the kitchen countertop, a lingering glance at another woman's breasts, the size of their respective paychecks and how money should be spent on what. This argument was more essential, more elemental, having to do with the people they really were, not the people they had pretended to be when they married, and now both had found out they'd been tricked.

Lise tried to think of other things, like if she was rich and could just go shopping all the time, or if Mikey from FFF liked her back and asked her to go with him. Or the day her parents might actually split up, when she would have adult dinners in a restaurant with her father on Wednesday nights and her mother would have a makeover and become her best friend.

The microwave beeped insistently; Lise could hear the kitchen discord just below, as if she was in there with her parents, sitting at the table. She picked through one of the *Cosmo* magazines she kept stashed under the mattress like porn—but she couldn't concentrate with all the noise. Her father banged the ice-cube tray to free the last stubborn plugs and Lise heard ice cubes clatter to the floor, triggering her mother to shout more. She crept into her parents' bedroom and dialed a number so familiar it was a song in her head. Trish answered on the fourth ring, as she always did. "Can I sleep over?" Lise asked.

"Sure," Trish said. "How are you going to get here?"

Four

After racing in the wheel all night, Darby Crash collapsed in the shoebox that was his bedroom, just as Ed Valencia woke in his own snug, carton-sized room. He could hear his mother and sister arguing next door in the bedroom they shared, then Kelly was crying, muffled sobs that meant she had buried her head in a pillow and was taking in cotton by the mouthful. Soon she would choke on it and throw up, triumphantly ending the dramatic ordeal. When Ed Valencia got home late last night, he had found his mother asleep on the couch; she only stirred to say that Kelly had wet the bed again—no doubt what they were fighting about.

On the kitchen table, the *L.A. Times* was spread open to "The Singles Scene" section, in which a number of items were circled. Ed Valencia's mother came into the kitchen and picked up the paper. " 'How to be Your Own Best Friend.' That's what I'm going to learn tonight," she announced, then added, "Since I don't have any friends. Since I don't have a *life.* "

"Sounds great, Mom," Ed Valencia mumbled as he poured a bowl of corn flakes. *Store-brand* corn flakes. They tasted the same, his mother swore, but Kelly wanted to do a taste-test with Kellogg's, like they did in the Pepsi commercials on TV. Kelly and Ed Valencia would wear blind-folds and their mother would monitor the contest—but so far she had refused. ("I don't need some fancy box to make food taste good to me," she said.)

"I need you to stay with Kelly."

Ed Valencia shook his head. "It's Friday night, Mom. I made plans."

"I never go out, Eddie, and you're out every night of the week. I need a life, too. I'm working so hard for you. This is the first time I've asked in a long time. Do me a favor just once."

Ed Valencia was silent, staring at his corn flakes, already bloated with milk, colorless, tasteless, inedible, exactly what his sister—a slow eater, easily distracted, chewing each mouthful forty times until nothing remained but the gristle of meat or a bay leaf tough as vinyl wallpaper—ranted about. He wished his mother would give him a chance to wake up before she started in on him like this. The sound of Kelly's crying had been withdrawn, and yet it seemed to him that an everlasting wail hung in the atmosphere of the apartment: the three of them feeling sorry for themselves.

"So you'll stay with Kelly?"

He wanted to help his mother, he really did. She worked full-time as a corporate secretary, staying late with her boss until after seven most nights, on call on the weekends, all for a pathetic salary. She had raised Ed Valencia and Kelly alone since their dad left, without child support. But the dark two-bedroom apartment they lived in, stacked high along every wall with packed cardboard boxes, made Ed Valencia feel claustrophobic, and he spent as little time at home as possible. He wanted to be with his friends—they were his real family, he felt, all-accepting, unconditionally loving. There was no emotional pain with his friends, no torment, no knife twisting in the back, not like this. "I told you I can't."

"Do me a favor just once," she pleaded.

"I have to do something really important."

"What? What's so important? You went out last night, didn't you?"

"We didn't really do anything last night," Ed Valencia said. "We just drove around. Tonight we're doing something."

"What?"

"I don't know." Last night's fight came to mind (Ed Valencia touched his tender cheekbone, puffy as if sleep-swollen, which is what he would let his mother believe if she asked—but she wasn't asking *that* question). He couldn't tell her that he needed to meet the Rats to come up with a plan to deal with FFF. She was always threatening to call the school counselor and have him brainwashed clean anyway. When she did, Ed Valencia would reply, "You want me to be a prep, but they're worse. All they want are designer clothes. They don't care about anybody but themselves. They're too cool to let anything matter."

"They go to college. They play it straight. *They* don't party in cemeteries. *They* don't get tattoos. They don't have pet rats and Mohawk hairdos."

"So I have tattoos. So what?"

"When did you get so nasty? It's those kids you hang around with. They're a bunch of bad kids. A *gang*," she insisted. But the Rats weren't a gang. They had no turf to defend. They harbored no grudges, unless against society in general, writing on their clothes with black indelible marker, "Who Cares?" and "Mass Production Killed the Self" and "Remember the Altamont" and "Elks Lodge Massacre 1979." The Rats weren't out beating up homeless people like the preps did, and while their T-shirts may have been objectionable, at least they didn't read "Trollbuster." They would never plant rat poison in garbage cans for those forced to eat there. Ed Valencia didn't shoplift or vandalize, and he prided himself in his open attitude, challenging his ideas about the world every day: what was normal, what was right. He was seventeen years old, going through a lot of shit, and life seemed very tricky to navigate. He was doing his best. He was doing OK.

Where he lived, the sun was deceptively warm, the inhabitants apparently calm. There was always the beach to liken life to, but there was an ominous feeling, too, something sinister under the surface of bouncy, sunny L.A. that could no longer be denied. Ed Valencia heard it in the shrill, insistent tone so many people used in stores and fast-food restaurants when the lines were long or the service was slow—and the way some people drove ("Too close, too close," his mother muttered under her breath in the car)—and nuclear war hanging over them all like a deep, percussive note, an endless tone.

The Rats gave vent to steam at shows. They skated hard, hurting themselves, always going back for more. If he had a car—or, for that matter, a driver's license—Ed Valencia could have driven around and tried to calm down that way, like so many people did. They were most themselves in their cars, was a theory. They drove somewhere to think, a special place they had found by chance one day, having gone the wrong way, or a place from the past, a view, a scent: smoking wood, cowpats, honeysuckle, a spoonful of the good old days to sweeten experience. Or maybe they just cruised to nowhere and back again, but *away* for a couple of hours, away from every sigh that rippled the pages of the *TV Guide*, the popping of his mother's joints as she creamed her hands at the end of a long day, the dripping kitchen faucet—Chinese torture to Ed Valencia when he was trying to sleep, headache-making, *physical* pain.

The Rats weren't really a gang, although that's what they were called sometimes, now that gangs dominated the news headlines, shooting with impunity and generally terrorizing the streets of South Central L.A. The Rats would never call themselves a gang, like FFF or the Lads did, and not "best friends" either, like girls or people who knew someone famous were likely to say. The Rats were just friends who stood by each other, better than family. Better than their dads.

Back at the breakfast table, Ed Valencia's mother grimaced as if with an interior pain. "Eddie, please."

"Please what?"

"Please tell me what you're doing tonight."

"Why do you care all of the sudden?"

"I have a right to know what's going on in my kid's life."

"Nothing," Ed Valencia replied. "There's nothing going

on. I'm not doing anything special tonight. I'm doing what I always do, which is nothing. There's nothing to do."

"Then you can stay home with Kelly."

"I told you, I'm going out."

"She can't stay home alone, Ed," his mother pleaded.

"Why not? I did when I was her age—with her. I've been babysitting Kelly my whole life. I'm sick of it."

"Well, there's no one else I can think of to do it."

"So? Like it's my problem." Ed Valencia stared at his corn flakes. He felt an impulse, long dormant, to overturn the bowl and take a bite from his orange juice glass instead, crunching the rim like it was fresh, crisp corn flakes he chewed.

"There are rapists out there, Eddie. *Rapists.* They dress up like the police. They come and knock at the door and that's how they get little girls."

"Like she'll be here anyway. It's Friday night. She—"

"Shut up, dickhead," Kelly said from the doorway. She, as ever, wore her Magenta costume: bow tie, fishnet stockings, hot pants, ankle socks, and a pair of cracked patent-leather tap shoes, too big for her feet, tied smartly with ribbons.

"What?" their mother said. "What did you just say? What did you call him?"

"He doesn't know what he's talking about," Kelly said. "He's dumb. Just look at his grades. He's like, failing school. He's even failing *parenting* class, the easiest class ever. Everyone gets an A in *parenting* class." Ed Valencia had dropped the egg he was supposed to care for like a baby, the very first day—but only because Bones' rat Dinky bit him (before Bones' mom killed Dinky because she thought that rats carried AIDS. Bones' mom thought that AIDS was in everything, including the produce at Albertsons, Oki Dogs, and beer on tap. Before AIDS, Bones' mother had suffered from Freeway Phobia, meaning she didn't work for three months and the family went on benefits. Not fun, Bones said. You can't eat what you want on benefits).

The phone rang. Ed Valencia answered. "Yeah?"

"Is this the Costello residence?"

"Who's this?"

The voice was pleasant, polite, a man's voice, melodic in a practiced way. I'm *reasonable*, the voice said. He probably sang in the choir at his church, Ed Valencia thought. A good provider, he went to every one of his son's baseball games, driving like a maniac from work to get there on time—but he made it, and that was the point. He made every game, home or away, chanting his son's name when he went up to bat, hassling the coach if his kid didn't play enough. Ed Valencia knew from experience how savage a man like this—a bill collector, a MasterCard representative, a repossessor of TVs and furniture, anything to do with credit—how savage this man could turn. "I'm looking for Mr. or Mrs. Costello, please. I have this as their current telephone number."

"Don't fucking call here again!" Ed Valencia shouted, hanging up. His mother stared at him, furious, then understanding: not in front of Kelly. No talk of money or bad credit or moving house in the middle of the night, like years ago when Mrs. Costello was still a cocktail waitress.

"What's going on?" Kelly said.

"Some pervert," Ed Valencia lied. "Just some jerk-off breathing heavy down the line."

"Yeah right. So don't tell me. See if I care." Kelly poured a bowl of corn flakes.

"You already had breakfast," their mother said.

"I threw up," Kelly replied, dashing a few splashes of milk into the bowl; she preferred her cereal paper-dry to sodden, lifeless mush.

"Corn flakes don't grow on trees, you know."

Kelly looked in her brother's bowl. "He didn't eat his," she accused.

Ed Valencia escaped when his mother wept, head in her hands, elbows on the table, while Kelly hammered corn flakes to dust with her molars, ignoring her mother's tears. He had seen his mother cry too many times. She was tired, that's why, she always explained after. "I never thought I'd be so tired. I'm not even forty. This isn't what I thought my life would be like, working my butt off, for *nothing*. Nothing for me. When is it my turn? When do I get to have a life?"

Kelly was too young to remember, just two when her parents divorced, and she only knew her mother as a troubled woman. Ed Valencia remembered the happy Costello family before everything bad happened, when there was enough money for a house in Burbank and two decent cars. But the Costellos couldn't stay together any better than curdled milk. Ed Valencia's dad left when he was seven. It was the same with every kid he knew. They were refugees from failed families, undernourished with junk food, out every night with no curfew. It was inevitable that these kids would find each other when they left home for the day—and days sometimes became weeks, months, even *years* before they returned. Sometimes forever. Leaving, kids learned, was easier the more it was done.

His mother's problems weren't his problem, Ed Valencia told himself. He had his own problems, and last night he had slept badly, dreaming about knives that made rashers of him, chains that scalped his Mohawk, the shorn 'hawk like a dripping mop head spattered around a room. If he had to choose his battles this morning, he was going to fight FFF, not his mother, and he needed to save his energy for the possibility of that.

Ed Valencia could skate to North Hollywood High School from their apartment, which meant he never broke down—not like Bones in his Malibu, who lived close enough to walk to school but drove out of pride. It was flaming June, a week before the end of the school year, and the heat haze was already intense at 7:30 in the morning: dense, yellow, unblinking, what would take hours to burn off, when the day became blatantly solar. Ed Valencia skated the shady side of the street, past small lawns of neon vibrancy radiating from cells revved up to near-combustion by the constant, remorseless Los Angeles sunshine. As he skated, the school glue holding together his Mohawk became more fluid and his scalp itched like a litter of just-hatched, ravenous cobras—but Ed Valencia didn't scratch.

He wouldn't risk wrecking his careful work, fifteen minutes at least with a hair dryer.

Since FFF had taken over Yum Yum Donuts, the Rats were forced across the street to Taco Bell where a dollar didn't buy much, just a single, soggy, skimpy Breakfast Burrito and a small Pepsi—not Coke, like Ed Valencia preferred, not even *New* Coke. Before, the Rats had feasted on day-old donuts, a dozen donuts for a dollar, and Ed Valencia missed the sugar rush of four donuts piled in one after the other, washed down with cool custard sucked through a straw from a donut hole, his sinuses clogged with confectioner's angel dust. The Rats snorted donuts. They shredded them into cottony tufts, stuffed the dough in their ears and up each other's noses. They cut neatly into donuts with plastic knives and removed their jelly hearts, replacing them with odd-end objects—pencil erasers, used Kleenex, chewed-out chewing gum—and passed those donuts on to unsuspecting classmates, siblings, mothers, teachers. With a dozen day-old donuts costing just one dollar, they could afford to be wasteful. Nothing had pleased the Rats better than a donut sitting heavy in their bellies and the knowledge that more were to come.

They were all at Taco Bell when Ed Valencia arrived: Jeff Air, who dared skate vert ramp while the rest of them stuck to the street; Steve Cashdollar, his real name; and Michael Pelletier, better known as Pellet Head. Bones was ordering his food while the other Rats lounged at a table near the front window, the same table where they always sat, listening to Cashdollar talk. Cashdollar was a motor-mouth.

Jeff Air looked up from his burrito, his foot-high

Mohawk grazing a piñata—empty of candy and toys, the Rats knew, having once slit one open with Cashdollar's pocket knife. "Valencia!" he called.

Ed Valencia lurked behind the condiments counter. "Shut up. I don't want them to see me."

"Who?"

"Who do you think?"

"I don't know. Hey, shut up, Cashdollar," Jeff Air said. "Valencia's here."

"Shut up yourself. I'm talking," Cashdollar said.

"I had to sneak in the back," said Ed Valencia.

"What are you talking about?" Jeff Air said.

"FFF put a price on my head last night," Ed Valencia announced.

Everyone stopped eating and looked at him. "What?" said Pellet Head.

Bones appeared, tray in hand. "I got you a Pepsi and a burrito," he said, retreating to a booth in the back. Ed Valencia followed. Looking at each other, shrugging, the other Rats shuffled over with their trays to join them, settling into the cool plastic contours that would soon stick to their bare legs.

"What the fuck is going on?" Cashdollar asked.

Ed Valencia paused before he spoke, looking seriously at each one. "I got into a fight with some FFF asshole and the cops shut down the whole fucking show. They wanted to cart me off to jail."

"I missed it. I can't believe I missed it. Dude, my mom wanted to come with me—she joined this group of moms called Parents Against Punks and they want to like, escort us everywhere we go," Pellet Head said, his mouth full of beans. "It's totally ridiculous. There's no way I'm going to a show with my mom."

"Parents Against Punks. PAP," Jeff Air said. "That's like, a smear test. Do they know that?"

"Of course they do. It's a bunch of moms," said Pellet Head.

"Smear Test is a good name for a band," Cashdollar said.

Ed Valencia rattled the ice in his Pepsi. Bones said, reminding them, "Valencia got jumped by FFF last night."

"Those guys are bad-asses," Pellet Head said.

Cashdollar snorted. "Fist-fucking faggots?"

"Friends fighting friends?" Jeff Air said, laughing with him.

Bones scowled at them. "Dude, those guys are hardcore. They *slayed* the guys from New Regime. They fucking trashed the Grant football team. They even wasted the Suicidals—it was sick, totally sick, with guys wounded, like a fucking war. How could you forget that?"

"Bullshit. Don't believe the hype," Jeff Air said. "They're not that bad. They just *think* they're bad. They tell everyone they are."

"Dude, they're bad. They're the baddest. They use weapons and shit. And there are about a million of them, all these fast little kids Ranger recruited. I do not want to fuck with those guys," Bones said.

"Ranger's gone, dude."

"How do you know that?" Bones asked.

"It's what everybody says. Have *you* seen him around?"

"I've never seen that guy in my life," said Bones. "I don't *want* to know him. He's brutal, dude."

"You've never seen him because he doesn't exist," Jeff Air said.

"Maybe he evaporated," Cashdollar suggested.

Ed Valencia didn't say anything, just finished off his burrito in three big bites, then drained his Pepsi down to the ice, his straw whining for more, scraping wax from the cup in curly slivers.

"Yeah, well, whoever's running FFF is calling the Rats out to fight," Bones said.

"Is that what they said?" asked Pellet Head.

"I can *feel* it. I was there. You were tucked up in bed with your mommy guarding the front door."

"Dude, my mom wanted to go to the show with me. I *told* you." Pellet Head rolled his eyes.

"Listen, we got to get a plan together," Ed Valencia said. "That's why we're here."

"Are we going to fight for real?"

"Like they even know who we are," Jeff Air said.

"Bullshit. They know who we are. We go to the same shows. We're all serving the same scene," said Ed Valencia.

"The same school," Bones added.

"Yeah, first thing: no school. We bail today," Ed Valencia said.

"Sounds good to me. We can go to my house," Cashdollar offered. "My mom's at work."

"So is everyone's," Jeff Air said.

"I got my own TV," said Cashdollar. "And cable."

"We know, we know. Like you let us forget."

"Hey, all over the Valley, nobody's home. Maybe we should take advantage of this, now that we're badasses, ready to take on FFF. I'd like an Apple computer and a new skateboard and a big fat steak, please, Mr. Santy Claus of Woodland Hills," Pellet Head said, rasping his palms.

"Let's go for it," Cashdollar said. Everyone laughed, except for Ed Valencia.

"That's exactly what the cops *think* we're doing," he said very seriously, so that no one laughed, just looked at each other around the table—looked *guilty*. "From now on, we got to watch our backs."

Five

Jen complained of cramps, stopping once to dry-retch into a storm channel big enough to fit a whole collie (and sometimes dogs got washed down the drain when the floods came, but you were supposed to keep them on a leash anyway, and clean up their waste with a Pooper Scooper and a plastic sandwich bag). She couldn't run, Jen said, because it hurt too much. The girls walked the rest of the way to Los Angeles Valley College, where Robo was unsympathetic to Jen's distress (gas-related, Lise thought, who remembered the half-pint of chocolate milk gulped at lunch, the two hotdogs and many briquettes of hash browns hosed down her gullet). Jen apologized repeatedly for being late, while nervous Lise ground the toe of her Reebok into the tarmac, but still Robo refused to unlock the car doors and let them in. It was only when Jen's sorry tears trickled across his thigh that they finally set off for Campbell Hall, Robo swerving and weaving, braking sharply, as if to test whether Jen was really sick or not.

It took a few minutes before she threw up over the side of the convertible, the colorful confetti of her vomit—a bag of Skittles during sixth-period study hall, Lise saw then— vandalizing the red car.

Robo went ballistic. Jen gagged like she might puke again, one hand clapped to her mouth. Flecks of vomit clung to her sunglasses. "It's not my fault. I can't help it," she wailed. Lise handed Jen some Kleenex, conveniently stowed in her pocket just in case her mother suddenly loomed, when Lise would pretend to sneeze and wipe her face clean of makeup, a ballet of practiced movements that ultimately appeared as if she was blowing her nose.

"Jesus, you reek. Bag your face or something," Robo said.

"Robo," Jen pleaded in a baby voice, reaching for his hand, used to being soothed, even honored when she was sick ("Who's my brave soldier?" Mrs. Lucarelli would coo, stirring the bubbles from a glass of ginger ale).

Robo pulled over the car and jumped out, running around to Jen's side to investigate the damage. Lise tried to help him. With a thick wad of Kleenex, she swiped at the vomit, before she, too, thought she would be sick, dropping the Kleenex in the gutter because she didn't know what else to do with it. Blood, puke, mucus, the sight of a pustule decorated with an oversized dandruff flake on the neck of the boy in front of her in the cafeteria line—all made the contents of her stomach eddy. Lise turned away.

"Stop being so mean, Robo," Jen cried.

"You're a total rookie. Barf is totally corrosive. My car is *fucked*. I don't have *time* for this. I don't have *time* for people like you."

"What?" Jen choked. "Robo? Are you breaking up with me?"

"Just get out so I can go to a car wash, OK? I really need to wash this shit off before it like, eats my paint job."

"But Robo—"

"Get out!"

Jen's car door opened slowly, heavily, a great weight for her to shoulder. "You can't break up with me just because I got sick," she blubbed. "That's totally mean." Lise scrambled after Jen. Robo, meanwhile, had leapt into the front seat, stuntman-style, not using the door. A moment later he pulled away, inevitably screeching the Mustang's tires.

"Ohmigod. Ohmigod," Jen hyperventilated. Lise spread wide her arms and she fell into them, her fevered, tear-slopped face like a hot-water bottle on Lise's breast, making her sweat. Lise looked around, hunting shade, but there were no proper shadows in the Valley at three o'clock, and so the two settled in a heap on the pebbled sidewalk, Lise fanning them with her math notebook.

"You'll be OK," Lise told her. "He probably didn't mean it."

"I've never been dumped before," Jen hiccupped. "Usually it's me who breaks up, that way they always want me back. Remember what Trish said?"

"Yeah." Trish, who was a conduit for her mother's proverbs, based on Mrs. Blue's long career as a merry, four-times-married divorcee, also said a girl should never get rid of her old car until she had a new one parked in the garage—but Jen didn't need reminding of that one just then. Besides, Lise only pretended to have experience with boys, reiterating what she heard from her friends about love and loss. Lise lacked courage when it came to fooling around; she was uncertain of what to do with the persistent tongues of the two boys she'd kissed, and the farthest she'd ever gone was a hand job—it went all over her face. Plus the guy *talked*. He told his friends and they started calling her Glazed Donut. For a whole week, they called her that—an eternity, weeks to teenagers what minutes were to babies.

"Ohmigod." Jen began to wail again. "Ohmigod, what did I *do*? I puked in front of Robo!"

"I'm sorry. I'm so, so sorry," Lise repeated, stroking Jen's head, careful to avoid the gelled half of her asymmetrical cut. Jen would kill Lise if she messed up her hair. Jen regularly wept over her hair, a curly auburn nest that she straightened with an iron, waking at six on school days no matter how late she had been out the night before.

"I barfed on his car. I *barfed* like, everywhere. All over. I just barfed," Jen sobbed.

"What about Trish?"

"What about her?" Jen sniffed.

"You know, she's like, waiting for us." They needed to get moving or Trish would be furious.

"Shit." Jen blew her nose. "Robo is such an asshole. He *knew* we had to pick her up."

"How are we going to get there? Is your mom home?"

"No, she's at work."

"Mine too."

"What are we going to do?"

Lise thought for a minute. "We really have to walk, I guess."

Jen shook her head. "It's too far, and too hot out. It's miles. It'll take forever to get there. And I'm sick—I can't *walk*," she gulped, looking like she might cry again.

"We'll hitch." Lise didn't know why she said it.

"We can't hitch. We're not allowed. It's dangerous."

But Lise was thinking fast now. They *had* to hitch; it was the only way to get to Trish. Jen was right: they couldn't *walk* that far—and they didn't know how to take the bus. "I bet some mom will give us a ride. A mom with a baby in the backseat and she'll let us play with it while she drives." The thought of a baby made Lise happy. She *loved* babies. The thought of a baby overrode her fear of hitchhiking, of what could happen to them. A baby represented joy, not horror. No one with a baby would hurt them, just like no one would hurt a baby.

"You think so?"

"Yeah. I totally think so," Lise said confidently. She remembered what Robo had told them about the three girls from Van Nuys who got raped when they climbed into a stranger's van. But Lise and Jen wouldn't get into a *van* with a *man*. They weren't *that* stupid. Besides, it was clear, bright daylight, the roads full of mothers in oversized, safe cars full of kids. "We're like, cute and clean-looking. Some mom will take us, for sure." Lise dislodged Jen and stood up. "You stay there. Look really sick, OK?"

"OK." Jen curled on her side, using Lise's backpack as a pillow.

Lise loitered at the curb, her right arm hooked, thumb jutting north, hip cocked. Sweat wandered from her armpits, soaking her top. With her free hand, she fixed her hair, showing a couple inches of bare, pale skin when she lifted her arm.

"Don't look so sexy. We want a mom to pick us up, remember?" Jen said.

Lise straightened her back and smoothed her skirt. She pushed the hair out of her eyes and tried to look hopeful and worried at once, directing one thumb toward the heavy traffic on Magnolia, the other in Jen's direction, who was heaped like baggage on the sidewalk, ready to be taken in hand and swept away home. They didn't have long to wait: a wood-paneled station wagon was reversing to reach them. "This car is just like *The Brady Bunch*. It's a mom—and she has some kids with her," Lise told Jen, her voice sharpening with excitement. She had been right! She could see *two* babies in the backseat!

The wagon's power window shot down, air-conditioning spilling out. Lise wanted to dive into the cold, let it seal over her head, a baby for each arm, like water wings. "Are you girls OK? Is there something wrong?"

Lise said, "Kind of. My friend's sick. We need a ride."

"How sick?"

"She threw up. She's really hot. She's getting worse, sitting in the sun."

"Hi," Jen said listlessly. She tried to wave, but her hand flopped back to her side.

"You shouldn't be hitchhiking," the driver scolded. "Even if your friend is sick. There are too many nuts around."

"We were going to ask a policeman for help, but we haven't seen any," Lise explained.

"There are fake police officers out there. There's a rapist on the loose right now who dresses up like a police officer. It's all over the papers."

"Oh," Lise said, looking at the ground. On cue, Jen moaned.

"But if you need a ride, better me than some lunatic rapist," the driver admitted. "I mean, that's why I pulled over."

"So you'll take us?" Lise asked. She glanced at the babies and—she couldn't help herself—waved at them. Lise loved babies. She would have been a babysitter, except that she had such a busy social life. No way was she staying in on a Friday or Saturday night. Not even a weeknight, because sometimes she went out, if she could sleep at Trish's house.

"Where are you going?"

"Campbell Hall?" It was a question, not an answer.

"Is that your school?"

"Kind of," Lise said. "We have to meet our friend. Her mother is picking us up." The lies rolled off her tongue like a tune that was easy to hum.

"OK," the woman said, finally releasing the door locks. Lise helped Jen up and the girls slid into the front seat, Lise first, giving Jen the window in case she got sick again. Behind them sat the babies, strapped into their plastic buckets, dumbfounded and silent, staring like clocks. Their mother reached across the girls' bare knees to the glove compartment, producing a neatly folded plastic bag—Fashion Bug, a discount store where the girls would never, ever shop. She handed the bag to Jen, saying, "Use this in case I can't get over fast enough. The traffic's bad today."

"The traffic's bad every day," Lise said, her tone knowing. It was the kind of thing her mother would say in the way of conversation, should she chance to meet other parents or when she was in a store, talking to the checkout clerk, and it embarrassed Lise, who wished her mother wouldn't say anything at all. Lise blushed, hearing herself.

Jen smiled gratefully. For once, she seemed happy to be in the presence of a mother. She looked better, brighter, color percolating in her cheeks, even if she still smelled of sick. "Do you mind if we listen to the radio?"

"Go right ahead."

Lise turned around to the backseat. "Wow, are they twins?"

"Yup." Their mother looked proud. "You don't see many of those, do you? It runs in my husband's family."

"Are they identical?"

"Uh-huh. Katie and Polly. They're eighteen months. They're just starting to talk. It's twin talk, their own special language that only they can understand." The twins looked nervous when Lise pulled a face at them; one wrinkled her brow as if she might cry, while the other made a square with her mouth. Lise quickly faced front again.

"You're so lucky. I'd love to have twins," Jen said.

"Not yet, I hope," the woman said, laughing. "How old are you girls? Fourteen? Fifteen?"

"We're—" Lise started.

"Fifteen," Jen finished. "Almost sixteen. We'll be driving

soon. My dad says he's going to buy me a Rabbit convertible for my sixteenth birthday. Then I won't have to hitch ever again," she added. Jen was lying, too. She hadn't seen her dad for three years, since he whipped her with his belt.

"When I was your age, it was safe to hitch. That was the Seventies. God, we were so naïve! California was one big, happy family. You can't trust anyone now. That jerk Reagan—he's made sure everyone's only looking out for number one. People just want to get rich. They don't want to help each other, they want to rob and kill and bomb each other and steal each other's land. And if he drops the big one—but don't get me started on nuclear war," she said, shaking her head.

"Um. We don't normally do this. We're really, really grateful," Lise said. She didn't know what else to say; she didn't know anything about politics. Her parents never talked politics at the dinner table. Lise remembered the one time they did, her dad accused her mom of sounding like a Democrat, as if it was something bad. Lise didn't know who was good or bad in politics, if it was the Republicans or the Democrats or some other party whose name she couldn't remember. "*Really* grateful."

"Will you buckle up?"

"What?" Jen said.

"Put on your seat belts. People drive like nuts. People drive like they think they're in the movies. But hey, it's L.A., right?"

"I don't get it," Jen said, like it was a joke. Jen never wore her seat belt, especially in front of boys. Lise, meanwhile, was struggling to fit the metal pieces together, finding her belt too tight, then too loose. She nudged Jen to do the same. Jen rolled her eyes, but did as she was told.

"I'm all for making seat belts mandatory. They did in New York. Usually it's California leading the way, you know. We're good like that. Seat belts and airbags, those are my things. That's what I write letters to the editor about. Did you see my letter in the *Times* last week? Michelle Davidson, that's me. If I'm going to be famous for anything in this town, I'll be famous for writing letters to the editor. My husband works in the coroner's office and last year they handled two hundred and seventy-four traffic fatalities. If all of them had been wearing seat belts, they'd be alive right now. Pretty soon they'll be fitting airbags in every new car," Michelle Davidson chattered. "Your dad should buy you a big car, like my station wagon, not one of those little Rabbits. Especially not a convertible. If you roll in a convertible, you're dead meat. It'll take your head off, believe me. My husband's seen it all. Haven't you read Ralph Nader? They should make it mandatory reading in high school—*Unsafe At Any Speed*. It shook up the automobile industry and changed everything. Just like Rachel Carson. Have you read *Silent Spring*?"

"I think we read part of it in school," Lise said uncertainly.

"You want a lot of metal between you and other drivers. My husband tells me what he sees. The worst accidents are those little cars. He drives a Wagoneer because he likes to sit up high and know what's coming at him."

Jen snapped the tuning knob between her middle finger and thumb, making it spin. Lise wondered how she ever knew if she had landed on something good to listen to.

Suddenly Michelle Davidson said, "You two aren't runaways, are you?"

"As if," Jen said, sounding offended. "Do we look it? Do we look all scummy and stuff?"

"Excuse me?"

"No," Lise said in her best polite voice, her voice for teachers. "No, we're not runaways."

"I just wanted to make sure. I always want to help," Michelle Davidson explained. "You're dressed nice, but you never can tell. There are so many throwaway children on the street these days. I read all about exploitation. It's hard enough being a kid—no vote, no lobby. I mean, you guys are really under-represented. And if your parents aren't safeguarding you, then you don't stand a chance. Not with all these villains hanging around. Now they're doing those milk cartons with pictures of missing kids. I bet you girls have seen one or two of those kids. You could tell me. I'd like to get someone home safe so they're not just another government statistic."

"Maybe at school," Lise said.

"At school? I never heard of a runaway who went to school. I think school is part of the problem. A pointless, weakened public-education system—that's what you kids are suffering from."

"Tell me about it," Jen said.

Michelle Davidson glanced at the backseat, where the

twins were sucking their thumbs, looking somber. "I just hope I do a good job with these guys. I'm not going to work a job outside of the home. People think I'm crazy when I say that, but no way am I going to turn myself into a pretzel trying to hold down two jobs. And motherhood is a full-time job, you know. Don't let anyone tell you it's not. It's your life's work, girls. I'm a feminist, but even I think motherhood is my life's work."

Jen had caught the end of a Duran Duran song. "Shit! I missed it!"

"Please don't swear in front of my babies. They're learning how to talk," Michelle Davidson said.

"Sorry," Jen said, reeling through the stations again.

"Wait!" Lise cried. "Go back, go back!"

"What? What did you hear? Did you hear 'Shout'?" Jen asked. "I totally want to hear that song right now."

Lise had heard rough guitar feedback, snotty vocals, and drums like mortars, hundreds of them lined up, firing one after the other, rat-a-tat-tat, like the shivers. "I think it was one of the college stations."

Jen snorted. "Figures. Why can't you listen to normal music like everyone else?"

Lise, against her friends' wishes, had a Clash tape that she listened to at home. Mikey liked punk. All the FFFers did. There were shows in Hollywood that she knew he went to, but Lise couldn't get Trish and Jen to go with her, and she was too scared to go by herself. "I don't like it that much. I like what you guys like," she reassured Jen.

"Here we are," Michelle Davidson said, pulling up in

front of Campbell Hall. "I personally believe in the public-school system, but I can see why your parents would want to send you here. Have you girls taken your PSATs?"

"Our what?" Lise said. She didn't know what PSATs were.

"Isn't it time you start thinking about the future? I have a friend who runs a great prep course, much better than the Princeton Review. If you hang on a sec, I'll write down her info. She has this amazing theory about how to take the test. You won't need any other book," Michelle Davidson said, scribbling on an envelope.

Lise turned to wave at the twins. "Bye-bye." The twins blinked. Their young moon faces were so changeable—a second later and they didn't look like themselves, as if a shadow had slid across, tarnishing what had been light, revealing an inheritance from an uncle, long dead, or a cousin once removed.

"I wrote down my number, in case your parents want to call me for a recommendation. Tell them I'm the lady from the newspaper. Michelle Davidson. They publish my letters at least every month."

"Thanks," Lise said, taking the envelope. Turning it over, she saw the grocery list in pencil, a sprawling cursive vine that ran right up to the edges and climbed the sides, each item crossed out and no doubt safely put away in Michelle Davidson's home, wherever that was. Trish could always guess where a person came from by the way they dressed or talked or what kind of car they drove.

Michelle Davidson turned to the twins. "Say bye-bye."

The twins began to cry and Lise and Jen scrambled out of the car like they had broken something.

"She was nice," Lise said.

"Don't tell anyone, OK?"

"Of course not. My mom would kill me if she knew I was hitching."

"I mean don't tell Trish I got sick in front of Robo," Jen pleaded. "We're so late. She's going to kill us. Ohmigod, I feel sick again. I might barf—"

"Swallow it," Lise ordered. She began to run.

"Slow down, Lise. I can't keep up," Jen complained. "You're the one wearing Reeboks—*I'm* wearing heels."

It didn't matter anyway. Here came Trish, whizzing at them like a golf drive. Before they knew what was happening, she had thrown her arms around her friends. "I met one of the Romeos!"

"Ohmigod, you're not *serious*?" said Jen. "We saw them at the mall, remember? They were *so* gorgeous."

"Oh yeah," Lise said, but she didn't remember—and she would have remembered a Romeo. When had they seen the Romeos? Was it that time Lise was sick and couldn't go out for like, four days? But Trish and Jen had called her every evening. They would have said if they saw the Romeos, unless they were keeping secrets. Were they? Were they leaving her out on purpose?

"Here he comes! He's going to take us home," Trish said.

His teeth were white as bleach, his dark pompadour gelled in plastic-looking waves, blue eyes flawless aquamarine, mined from somewhere far away, a color you couldn't buy in a contact lens. The Romeos were gods, the gilded ripples of their well-built bodies revealed by open shirts and tank tops, gliding as they walked, making the grass sing. Girls were known to prostate themselves before a Romeo at parties, suggesting the bushes, the dining-room table, the bathroom floor, anywhere, anywhere at all. Lise had heard, but she had not seen, and now here was her first Romeo, coming closer. He would reach them in a moment—he would be within touching distance. His smile was for them, or for Trish, at least.

"Ohmigod, he looks like a soap star," Jen muttered.

Trish arranged the wide shoulders of the white blazer she wore over her uniform, fluffed the white lace cravat at her throat. "Smile, girls, but not too much. Remember your braces."

Six

The River Rats packed inside Steve Cashdollar's black-painted garage-cum-bedroom, eating Cheez-Whiz sandwiches and drinking orange juice in preparation for that evening's mosh pit (when a band went fast, the Rats wanted to go fast with them). A black light made the white Wonder Bread glow, as well as Cashdollar's prized secondhand white Creepers, freshened weekly with shoe polish. The light picked out the flecks of laundry soap in their black jeans and T-shirts, showing up the dandruff on Pellet Head's bowler hat, the toothpaste caulking the corners of Jeff Air's mouth, and their teeth, in that light, looked as L.A. teeth were supposed to: so white they were blue.

The room was dark so that Cashdollar's nocturnal rat Mugger would stay awake and play with them instead of camping out under the bed like he usually did during the day. Cashdollar held a tub of strawberry Yoplait between his knees, periodically dipping his fingers and extending them to Mugger, who licked them clean. Between licks, Mugger nibbled at the processed cheese leaking from Bones' sandwich or sniffed the dog biscuits Ed Valencia kept in his jeans pocket for Darby Crash, scratching the denim with his teeth.

Many days this loyal core of boys had gathered in Cashdollar's room instead of going to class, hidden inside until three o'clock, when Operation Stay in School's representatives returned to their offices to process that day's log of truants. The Rats did nothing in particular on their days off: they listened to music, taping and labeling meticulously, or watched skateboarding videos, MTV, reruns of *Mork and Mindy*, *M*A*S*H*, and *Soap*. Inevitably, being teenage boys, they had to eat, and when they did they tried to eat sparingly so that Cashdollar's mom wouldn't freak. One might melt butter and sugar in a pan to caramelize, while another thinned an egg with milk before scrambling, or dribbled ketchup on leaves of Iceberg lettuce. Bones often ate a salted raw potato because he couldn't wait for it to cook and he didn't believe in microwaves. "I'm not putting radiation in my food," he said. "I got enough of that already with the bomb hanging over my head."

Other kids were cutting class as often as the River Rats, the richer kids hanging out in hot tubs and home cinemas and visiting their parents' racquet clubs to order lunch with Jack and Cokes or Screwdrivers or whatever was the cocktail of the moment. Some kids went on midday crime sprees armed with compressed-air guns to shoot out a lock—better yet, equipped with spare keys and alarm codes, prepared to rob each other's houses. Some left school and home altogether, moving into apartments their parents rented (and where parties were soon established, running uninterrupted, as long as the lease, or until eviction notice was eventually enforced), while the less fortunate took up residence in a Dumpster or Goodwill depository box, drinking their beers on the street.

"I heard she was going out with one of the guys from Dogpatch Winos," Jeff Air was saying as he fiddled with Cashdollar's turntable, trying to figure out whether the new Black Flag EP should be played at 33 RPMs or the usual 45. It was hard to tell.

"I heard she was going out with *all* of those guys."

"Dude, she's like, twelve. It's *sick*," Cashdollar said, shaking his head. "I don't care how hot she is. That's just wrong."

Ed Valencia thought of Kelly. She wore that Magenta outfit all the time, hot pants and fishnet stockings, a saucy bow tie at her throat—what might have been provocative on a developed figure, but not on scrawny, boobless, eleven-year-old Kelly. Her surfaces were all planes, her body more like an outdated theory of the world's shape: flat, not globular in any way, except her head. Other girls, though, were just the opposite. There were girls out there growing up so fast they looked like women before they officially entered their teen years. They were ready for experience, unafraid, willing to get into a car and be driven anywhere, to park late around the canyon's rim, vocal in their pleasure. They had practiced not on stuffed animals, but on the very real, animated parts of boys—and men, some of them—and their fingers crawling down the treasure trail were knowing, eager.

Not Kelly. Ed Valencia couldn't imagine his sister doing that, ever. "Can we talk about something else?" he said.

"It's almost tempting to go to Phazes. Those girls will do anything. It's like they have no morals," Pellet Head said.

"I heard about this one girl and a golf club—"

"Just shut up about it," Ed Valencia shouted. "No one's going to Phazes. It's the most stupid place on earth."

"How do you know? You've never been there," Pellet Head replied. "Seriously, it's not that bad. At least it's somewhere to hang out."

"Have *you* been there?" asked Jeff Air. Pellet Head ignored the question, scooping up Mugger instead. "*Have* you?" Jeff Air repeated, jabbing Pellet Head's side to get his attention. Pellet Head wouldn't answer, giggling as Mugger tiptoed up his shirt-sleeve to his armpit.

"If I hear any of you went there, I won't ever talk to you again," Ed Valencia said.

"You sound like someone's dad."

"You sound like a Republican."

"It's just a stupid fucking teenybopper nightclub, Valencia. It's not that bad. FFF hang out at Phazes and they're supposed to be the coolest guys in town," said Pellet Head.

"How do *you* know, Pellet Head?" Jeff Air asked.

"I seen them when I'm skating past. They're out in the parking lot and hanging around the door."

"Yeah right, skating past," Jeff Air sneered. "You're in there looking for some twelve-year-old ass."

"Fuck you," said Pellet Head.

"Dude, FFF are not the coolest guys in town. I can't believe you said that," said Ed Valencia.

84

"I said *supposed* to be the coolest guys in town," said Pellet Head. "I personally don't believe it. We're much cooler than FFF. That's why they want to kill us."

"Maybe we should just bomb Phazes. That would get FFF," Bones suggested. "I know what to do—I got a copy of the *Anarchists' Cookbook*."

"By the way, I do *not* go to Phazes," Pellet Head said.

"They got a drink there named after you. Mother's Ruin," cackled Jeff Air.

"That's gin," said Cashdollar.

"Why are we talking about stupid fucking Phazes?" shouted Ed Valencia. "I fucking hate that place! I won't hang out with the losers who hang out there. A bunch of social fucking climbers, that's what they are. Bunch of suckers." There was silence. Mugger slurped yogurt from Cashdollar's fingers. No one dared look at each other.

"We should talk about FFF," Bones finally said. "I mean, for real. About what we're going to do."

"I think we should wait. If we get jumped, then we'll fight, but I don't think we should call them out," Jeff Air said.

"We're definitely not going to Phazes. We're not finding them *there*," said Ed Valencia.

"Maybe they forgot already," Cashdollar said. "Maybe they don't really want to fight."

But the Rats knew otherwise: FFF didn't forget.

"What time is it? Let's get out of here. I'm sick of sitting around," Pellet Head complained, dumping Mugger on the floor. "This is totally boring."

"It's almost three. We should roll anyway. Sometimes my mom gets home early on Friday. The last thing I need is her shit," Cashdollar said.

"What are we going to do?"

"Go to Poseur?"

"I'm sick of that place. It's full of poseurs," Ed Valencia said.

"Isn't that the point?" Jeff Air asked.

"Isn't it supposed to be ironic or something?"

"You don't even know what ironic means, Pellet Head," Jeff Air said.

"Nobody knows what ironic means."

"That's ironic," Jeff Air said.

"There's that show in South Pasadena. Black Flag are supposed to play on some guy's street. You know, like a punk-rock block party. They're going to crack open a fire hydrant," said Bones.

"Dude, it's hot enough. Too fucking hot to be in school."

"School's air-conditioned," Jeff Air reminded them.

"Are you guys sure it's three o'clock? Because I can't get caught ditching again or they'll kick me out."

"The school year is over, Bones. They can't suspend you when there's only a week left," said Pellet Head.

"Those fuckers can do anything they want, dude. They can hold you back a year if they want. They can throw away your grades and keep your diploma. School sucks," Bones said.

Everyone agreed. What was the point of arguing? There was nothing any one of them could do.

Seven

"Maybe you're car sick," Lise suggested when Jen emerged from the bathroom.

"No way. I've never been car sick in my life. I love cars." Jen swallowed hard. "Where are they?"

They were at Trish's house, as they so often were—never at Lise's, only sometimes at Jen's, and usually just Lise spending the night then. Trish was funny about where she slept. She said her back hurt if she didn't sleep in her own bed, or she didn't like what was offered for breakfast. Plus she was used to her own bathroom; the family bathrooms in their houses were too cramped, too *used* by too many people. Like, once she saw one of Lise's dad's pubic hairs— it had to be his, it looked like a man's, Trish said—on the bath mat and that was it: Trish never stayed at Lise's house again.

"Upstairs." Lise was eating a bowl of Froot Loops and watching *The Love Boat* on the kitchen TV.

"Ohmigod, that smells *disgusting*." Jen turned on her heel and bolted for the bathroom.

A couple were strolling on deck on TV. On board the cruise ship, in love (at first sight, always, on cruise ships), the couple kissed passionately, the woman arching backwards over the ship's railing. She clung to the man. Her silky white gown fluttered in the wind: surrender. Lise shivered. Her own mouth parted as she tried to imagine herself one-half of *The Love Boat* kiss—but Jen returned, interrupting with a sour burp. Lise glanced at her and said, "I think you're really sick, Jen. I think you should go home. You're like, green and stuff."

Jen shook her head, her mouth willfully clamped shut.

"Trish's mom is out by the pool. We can ask her to drive you," Lise suggested.

"No way am I missing the mall with a Romeo. Everyone will see us with him. We'll be totally made. Those guys are so gorgeous. They're like, movie stars, or their dads are movie stars or something," Jen said.

"I heard they all live next door to each other in the Hollywood Hills."

Jen nodded. "His car is so cool. I love Wranglers. Don't you think he looks like he's in Duran Duran?"

Lise spooned cereal to her mouth, chewing openly, showing her food. "He's like, Simon le Bon."

The pong of ersatz Froot Loops proved too much for Jen. "Ohmigod," she muttered, fleeing the room again.

Thinking she should act fast while she had the chance, Lise stepped outside, making sure to shut the door behind her and keep the air-conditioning in. Sometimes the shock of going from cold to hot made Lise feel like she would wet her pants. "Hi, Mrs. Blue," she said.

Trish's mom lay in the shade of a Mexican fan palm, additionally screened by large dark glasses and a tennis visor, her nose white with sunblock. She didn't need to look up to recognize the voice: Lise and Jen were as familiar to her as her own daughters, the girls together constantly, wearing each other's clothes. "What is it, Lise?"

"Jen's sick, Mrs. Blue."

"Is she?" Mrs. Blue sounded uninterested.

"She barfed everywhere."

Mrs. Blue sat up and pushed her sunglasses on top of her head, dislodging her visor. Her eyes flashed with heat, concentrating on Lise. "In my house?"

"No, in somebody's car."

Mrs. Blue looked relieved. "Has she been drinking?"

The girls had no reason to lie to her. Trish's mom had done *everything*: nightclubbing in New York at Studio 54 and Max's Kansas City, orgies in Greece, the mile-high club, even a date with Sam from *Cheers*. She told the girls her stories, the four of them tucked up in her big bed, Mrs. Blue often with a wineglass in her hand, Trish prompting her with details: the sheer red blouse with flamenco ruffles that all but exposed her breasts and what David Bowie said when he saw her wearing it, or how she had been skinny-dipping with her friends in the middle of the night at Club Med when this guy turned up who was supposed to be English royalty, and he told Trish's mom he would make her a duchess, but she didn't want to move to England where it was so *cold* and *rainy*, even in June (she knew from when she was a model working in London in the Sixties). Listening, Lise pulled a pillow to her chest and breathed Mrs. Blue's perfume—Fracas—and something else that she thought might be the smell of sex.

"She's just sick, I think. She must have eaten something bad. You should see what she eats for lunch."

"Are you telling me this because Jen needs a ride home?" Mrs. Blue's gaze remained fixed on Lise, who scratched herself nervously, first her arm, then her neck, then she reached halfway down her back and dug deep between her shoulder blades, scraping one wing and then the other. "Don't scratch, Lise. That's not attractive."

Lise snatched back her hand. "Sorry," she mumbled.

"Why do I feel like I'm always driving you girls around? I suppose Jen's mother is at work. Yours, too."

Lise nodded. Mrs. Blue was the only mother she knew who didn't work, who treated divorce like a venture capitalist, breaking up families if need be (once, out shopping at Saks, she had been publicly slapped by an ex-wife who called her a home-wrecker in front of the entire shoe department). Divorce was their entitlement, she told the girls, especially if that cash cocktail a husband was meant to serve up just wasn't intoxicating. Get out while you're ahead, was her advice, and never shrink your fund. "She puked like, six times," Lise said.

Trish's mom sighed and settled her sunglasses on the Roman bridge of her sunblock-marbled nose. "Give me twenty minutes. Tell Jen to hang on. I only just sat down."

Lise retreated to the kitchen, where Jen was slumped in a chair, left ear suctioned to the tabletop. She, too, wore sunglasses, by now wiped clean of vomit. Her mouth was drawn like she was dehydrated, and when she saw Lise, she groaned.

90

"Trish's mom is going to take you home in a little while," Lise said.

Jen nodded sadly and sniffed—but even so, snot bubbled, leaking south. She scrubbed at it with her fist. She looked really bad, Lise thought. *Really* bad. Her makeup was a mess, faded in some places, clumped in others, streaked here to there, and her hair was stringy from riding in Romeo's open-top car.

"He likes Trish anyway. He's not interested in us," Lise said.

"His *friends* might like us. The other Romeos." Jen sniffed, and sniffed again, then again, until Lise had to turn up the TV to drown out her sniffing. Now Jen swallowed repeatedly, an anxious look on her pale face, glancing in the direction of the hall toilet. Once, she leaned forward, as if about to bolt, but ebbed back into her seat, breathing hard, swallowing her spit. What was taking Mrs. Blue so long? Forty-five minutes passed before Trish's mom came in, tying a robe over her bikini.

"Where's Trish?" she asked.

"Upstairs," Lise said. "She's with someone."

Mrs. Blue didn't look surprised. "Do I know him?"

"He's a Romeo," Jen gulped. "Totally hot. She's so lucky."

"She met him at school. He just like, walked up and started talking to her," Lise said.

"And?"

"He gave us a ride home. In his *Jeep*," Jen said. She hadn't thrown up in the car, although she had looked like she wanted to, taking in great breaths of air through her mouth (she looked like a dog with her tongue hanging out like that, Lise had thought), eyes closed against the world whizzing past. "His hair is so cool. Like Simon le Bon."

Mrs. Blue nodded her approval. She knew who Simon le Bon was, unlike Lise's mom, who didn't listen to music. Music made Lise's mom's head ache—the radio was just noise to her. "A Romeo. That sounds promising."

"Like, everyone wants to go out with them," Lise said.

Jen moaned, ever so softly.

Mrs. Blue sighed. "Not in the car, OK? I just had it cleaned. Are you coming with us, Lise?"

Lise shook her head. "I think I'll stay here. Trish said we might go to the mall."

"Will you call me tonight?" Jen asked tearfully.

Lise hugged her. "Of course I will."

When Trish and her Romeo finally emerged from upstairs, holding hands, Trish had changed into a Naf Naf floral jumpsuit and yellow Reeboks, a cute new outfit Lise had never seen before. "Did my mom go out?" Trish asked.

"She's taking Jen home."

Trish looked surprised. "What's wrong with Jen?"

"She barfed *everywhere*," Lise said, relishing the moment of revelation. "You missed it. All over Robo's car and then like, at least ten more times here."

"Ew." Trish and her Romeo were unimpressed. "Totally rookie."

"Jen and Robo broke up."

"Really?"

"Really. He was bumming about his car." Lise had to be careful about the way she was saying things: she had promised Jen not to tell Trish that Robo dumped her. But if Trish was more on Jen's side right now—as Lise feared she was—then Lise needed to pull her back.

"That guy was too Valley. Don't tell Jen, but I thought he was a total Val from the start. The way he dressed—and totally not cute, either. His *hair*." Trish wrinkled her nose. "I can't believe she went out with him for so long."

"I know what you mean," Lise agreed. She could never go out with a guy who dressed like Bruce Springsteen.

"Anyway, we're going to the mall," Trish announced. Of course they were. Docked on Ventura and Sepulveda boulevards in the southeast corner of Encino, the Galleria was a three-tiered promenade where kids could strut and flirt until their hearts and nether regions fluttered. Late afternoon on a Friday, any visible parent-types were too busy getting a head start on their weekend to-do lists to visit the congested food court, seemingly designed for the teenage appetite: potatoes, dough, grease, cotton candy, super-processed meat-n-cheese, all designed to oil their bones.

Strolling along the Galleria's crowded avenues with a Romeo, Trish and Lise were studiously examined. Teenagers always stared at other teenagers, checking out clothes, hair, gait, whether nails were manicured or badly kept (bitten to the quick with angst), what shoes were worn, what shade of lipstick. Their eyes screamed, "How do I look? How do I look! How do *you* look? Will I look like you someday?" and yet their eyes rarely met as they passed, so intent were they on the physical aspect. Since meeting Trish and Jen, Lise had believed more than ever that she would fit in—not only that, she would be popular, *desired*, the first love of newly hormonal boys, the serious choice of older guys with cars. Now here she blew on the strongest wind yet, a Romeo for her guide through the mall's multiple carpeted levels, her credibility soaring just for being associated with him. What a day it had been, with the night still to come, taking form even as they browsed a selection of tapes that were four for three, privy to the invitations tossed by passing peers whose parents had decided on a last-minute get-away weekend. The place to spread the word was here.

On their way upstairs to the food court, Romeo had them cross the esplanade to avoid a gang of strolling homeboys, stripped to the waist, their gold-plated chains and religious medals kindled by neon as they popped their muscles, heckling guiltless pedestrians, following too close on the heel. They were looking for attention, looking to start something for no reason. They were desperate, Lise sensed, and therefore dangerous—at the very least, their attention was embarrassing: vocal, focused on the weakest available fault in a person, punctuated with whistles and swearing. Boys like that didn't belong in the Valley, and yet increasingly they were there, driving around slowly, hauntingly, having appeared as if from nowhere like a ghost fleet. *Scaring* everybody.

Romeo bought Cokes and led the way to a conspicuous

table in the middle of the food court, its top picked clean by the wandering homeless. Like homeboys in the Valley, the homeless were to be ignored—and more easily were, despite their exhaust-stained skin in the land of the clean and tanned. Holding her breath like she did when passing a cemetery, Lise used speed to pass them. *Them*—but Lise didn't even think of them as people.

"Do you like New Coke?" Trish asked Romeo.

"Gross," he said. Trish wrinkled her nose, agreeing with him.

"Me neither," Lise said. "I heard they're going to change back to Old Coke like, any day now." When Jen wasn't around, Lise was more confident with Trish, more likely to speak up. When Jen wasn't around, Trish and Lise were *best friends*, and they hardly even talked about Jen.

But Trish shot Lise a warning look and turned the conversation to the new Schwarzenegger movie, *Commando*, which had a Galleria scene in it. "Like, all the security guards get mowed down," she giggled.

Lise hadn't seen *Commando*, which wasn't even out yet *and* was R-rated. Trish had seen an early screening because her mother had dated the director and Trish's mom *always* stayed friends with her ex-boyfriends, especially when they were important. They were *always* important. Trish could always see an R-rated movie: she had her sister Alexis's old ID *and* her mother loved to have a mother–daughter movie date. Lise's parents didn't go to the movies. They just didn't go to the movies. They had taken her once, when she was a little girl, to see *Mary Poppins*, and she had worn her pajamas to the show—but she didn't fall asleep, no way, she was too excited about that treat. Lise didn't understand why her parents didn't go to the movies like everyone else. She thought it might have something to do with morals, with nudity and violence and bad language—why they said they wouldn't get cable TV at their house.

"Yeah, I saw it," Romeo said.

"You did?" Trish's blue eyes brightened—her radiant beauty was almost impossible to believe, except that Lise was seeing it. When had she last seen Trish so happy? Trish was never happy, not like this. Lise's mom said it was because of the divorce, that divorce was such a bad thing for children, but Lise wasn't so sure. If Lise's parents got divorced, then Lise would be happy.

"My dad knows Lester."

"That's so weird, because my mom used to go out with him. You and me, we're practically cousins or something," Trish giggled.

Romeo smiled. "Yeah, that's right."

"Can you imagine having Arnold Schwarzenegger as your dad? That is totally unbelievable. I didn't believe it for a minute. But like, the Galleria scenes were so real. I mean, I could have been shopping that day, you know? Like, it could happen. And you can see Hot Dog on a Stick in the background." Trish was laughing, still talking about *Commando* when she knew Lise hadn't seen it. "You can see the guy that works there all the time. He's been there forever. I swear he doesn't get any older. And he smells like he's been deep-fried. I know this girl he tried to kiss and she was like, 'Get away from me, Fry Baby!' It was so funny."

Lise drifted from the conversation and began to watch a woman with frizzy, marmalade-colored hair and purple-framed glasses move among the tables of the food court, conspicuously older than the crowd she mingled with. Her scrutiny was exacting: she looked harder at the teenagers than they looked at each other or perhaps even studied themselves in the mirror. Her eyes burned through clothes to take a body's measure, feasting on one, then another. She made Lise nervous.

Romeo was saying he could get them into the Fetish if they wanted, instead of Phazes as usual. The Fetish stayed open all night, while Phazes closed at two.

"I know," Trish said.

"How come I've never seen you there before?" Romeo asked her.

"Um, because we usually go to the Zero." Lise didn't say anything. They had never been to the Zero, or the Fetish. They weren't old enough to get in—even Trish, with her sister's driver's license, couldn't get into the Fetish. Besides, she always said that place was full of weirdos.

"It's really dark in there," Romeo said.

"Yeah, *really* dark," Trish agreed. "Like, you can't see *anything*."

"That woman keeps staring at us. For like, the last five minutes," Lise said, consulting her Swatch. "Do you guys know her?"

"Who?"

The woman with the glasses started toward them. Her smile seemed too big, so glad to see them, almost *relieved*, as if she had been lost for some time. "Do you know her?" Lise asked again.

"No way do I know her," Romeo said.

"She's a total freak," said Trish.

"I don't think we should talk to her—" Lise started to say.

But the woman with the glasses had reached their table. "Hi guys! My name is Carol."

"Um, hi," Lise mumbled. Trish and Romeo didn't say anything.

"Can I talk to you for a minute?" The woman touched the back of the empty chair at their table for four. "Or are you waiting for someone?"

"Kind of," Trish said, looking at Romeo. "I mean, yeah, we're waiting."

"This will only take a minute." Carol shook her orange hair and straightened her glasses. "OK, I think you guys, I mean girls," she said, winking at Romeo, "because—sorry—I'm only interested in the girls here. But I think you have a really great look. Totally Valley, very pretty and fresh and, you know, *funky*."

"We're not *Valley*," Trish snorted. "That's so two years ago."

Carol just smiled, showing her buck teeth. "OK, whatever. Trendy, you know? You look great. And those haircuts are *great*."

"Thanks," Trish said. "Vidal Sassoon. I'm a hair model for them. They *invented* this haircut for me."

"Yeah," Lise said. She didn't get her hair cut at Vidal Sassoon, but she had a copycat cut from MJ's Studio in Van Nuys—she and Jen both. MJ was a friend of Jen's mom and gave the girls a discount.

"Oh really? You have modeling experience? Because I'm casting a show and I need models. I think you guys would be *perfect*."

The magic word. Lise had always wanted to be a model. Trish had been modeling since she was a baby, when she starred in a Pampers commercial, and she still did the occasional catalogue shoot for Bullocks and Bloomingdales, plus regular hair shows at Vidal Sassoon. Her sister Alexis modeled, too, and their mother had been a model in the Sixties. It was in their blood; posing and poise came naturally to the Blues. Lise had looked into modeling school, where they taught you how to walk in heels and widen your eyes so they didn't bulge, how to make up your face so you looked more adult and what kind of clothes suited your body type (there were two: pear or apple). But modeling school was expensive, hundreds of dollars for a four-week course, too expensive for Lise to afford on her own, and she couldn't ask her parents—definitely not her mother, who forbade fashion magazines and Barbie dolls in the house, and makeup, of course, and midriff-baring tops, or any kind of tight clothing that might expose the developing geometry of her daughter's body, not yet paved in curves, but soon, Lise hoped.

"What kind of show?" Trish asked.

"A fashion show representing the Galleria stores. Next Thursday night at eight, just a few trips up and down the catwalk, really easy, and you'll get to keep something, so free clothes!" Carol's enthusiasm was a bubbling source very close to the surface, a geyser that blew every few seconds, causing her to spit when she talked and clap her hands for emphasis.

"I'll have to check with my mother. She acts as my agent," Trish said.

"Me too," Lise said, although she would never dare ask; if Trish was doing it, she would just do it, too.

"I'll give you my card and your mothers can phone me. But believe me, I'm totally legit. Ask any store here—they all know me. I've been doing this for years."

"Really?" Trish said. "I've never seen a fashion show here. And I'm *always* here."

"Well, the last two years," Carol said, still grinning shamelessly. Lise smiled back, so happy, but Trish took Carol's card without looking at her.

"Modeling agents always look the same," Romeo commented when Carol had gone. "Total nerds. You should see the geek that takes care of *me*."

"That's because they can't be models. But they want to hang around us. It's like, *vicarious*," Trish said, emphasizing the big word.

Us, Lise thought happily. She was included. She was pretty enough to be a model.

"What time is it?" Romeo asked.

"It's seven o'clock," Lise answered. Romeo looked at her as if for the first time, Lise suddenly rising to his line of vision like a new toy brought forth from its hiding place and presented in a tangle of shiny paper and ribbon. He smiled. Lise beamed back. Their little exclusive group flamed with glory to near-incandescence, beyond even the brilliance of the food-court lights, with all its gaudy neon. Trish reached over and squeezed her hand, smiling, but not too much, the corners of her mouth lifted in a practiced, benevolent curve that hid her braces.

"I know a party we could go to," Romeo said. "It's like, a pre-party."

"Let's go," Trish said, squeezing Lise's hand again, her charge surging through Lise so that she wasn't sure, at that moment, where she ended and Trish began.

Eight

Driving back from South Pasadena, the Malibu's fog lights—the only lights that worked—were obscured by the bleary nighttime smog, so that other cars veered into their path or nipped at the bumper, causing the rallied Rats to reach their fists through the open windows and rumble the car's scraped-up side panels. They were on the warpath, the Malibu's exhaust pipe blowing smoke rings. Black Flag never showed, but four other bands had played and, in the hour before the cops turned up at the block party, managed indistinct fifteen-minute sets, while punks blowing whistles diverted traffic from the makeshift stage of milk crates spread with plywood (the remains of some skater's half-pipe). Most of the crowd had then adjourned to a nearby Dempsey's for cheap, hot food. Inevitably a food fight broke out (they were always having food fights) and the cops were called. No one got to finish their meal, but Dempsey's manager stood at the door, flanked by four police officers, making sure each bill was paid on the way out.

Ed Valencia suddenly said, "I think we should form a band." Everyone had bands; it was a natural teenage situation. There was nothing to stop the Rats, apart from the obvious: they had no instruments, no money to buy instruments, nor did they know how to play any instruments or, for that matter, write songs. Singing could be shouted—the one thing they knew how to do.

"For sure we should have a band," said Bones.

"It'll be total DIY. Just pick up a guitar, play G, C, D, and there you go. That's a fucking song right there," Ed Valencia said. "Dude, look at the Dickies. They were only together three weeks before they played the Whisky. We can do that. We can move that fast. We don't need a million fucking dollars' worth of equipment and lessons to make it. *We* could play the Whisky."

"Definitely," the others agreed.

"What would we call ourselves?" Pellet Head asked.

"Something to do with rats. The Ratpackers, or something like that," Bones suggested.

"Dude, that's a terrible name. People will think we're into Dean Martin and Sinatra," said Jeff Air.

"Yeah, nothing to do with rats. Rats is our *skater* identity. This band should stand for something," Ed Valencia said.

"I don't want to be political or like, social-minded," Bones said. "I don't know anything about that stuff."

"Yeah, but Valencia's right. We shouldn't just be an anarchy band, messing around," Cashdollar said. "We should be serious. We should take a stance against something. We should be, you know, leaders for other kids."

"Like Minor Threat."

"Yeah, but none of that 'Don't smoke, don't drink, don't fuck, at least I can fucking think' political stuff. I still want to do what I want, like a normal guy," said Cashdollar.

"Like anyone normal wants to fuck you," Jeff Air said.

"Fuck you," Cashdollar said.

"You're straight-edge anyway," said Jeff Air. "You don't drink and you don't smoke."

"I might want to someday."

"You look like you're twelve. Who'd give you anything to drink?"

"Fuck you," Cashdollar said. "All I said was I don't want to be political like that."

"What's political about straight-edge?" Pellet Head asked. "It's *personal*. A personal choice."

"All those guys with X's on their hands—they're totally making a political statement, resisting peer pressure and that kind of shit. It's a challenge," said Jeff Air. "It's a philosophy. And the philosophers are always the guys the government hates."

"I don't get it," Cashdollar said.

"Just standing for something is political. We could stand for like, not wearing underwear. Feeling the breeze on your balls. Keeping sperm happy for future generations," Pellet Head grinned. "We could play naked, make a fucking statement like *that*."

"No way am I getting naked in front of *anyone*," said Bones. "Not even my mom."

"Dude, your mom still gives you a bath," Jeff Air said.

"Fuck you," said Bones.

Cashdollar said, "I think we should be a unity band. You know, like positive force."

"Dude, I think we should sing about like, the Salvadoran

fucking death squads shooting up nuns and shit," Jeff Air said.

"What the fuck are you *talking* about?" Cashdollar said, whacking him on the side of his head.

"We just need a good name. That's like, the most important thing. Doesn't matter if we can't play, if we have a good name," said Ed Valencia.

"Something like the Germs—'We're called the Germs because we make people sick.' Something cool like that," said Pellet Head.

"Malibu Butchers."

"What?"

Bones shrugged. "OK, the Anti-Parents."

"Not bad," said Pellet Head.

"The Sandinistas," Jeff Air said. "The Dead Nuns. FSLN. The Sugar Daddies. Reagan's Soldiers. Contras. The Death Squad."

"The LADS already took that. Los Angeles Death Squad, duh."

"Yeah, but they're a gang, not a band."

Ed Valencia knew what to call the band. He had known right away. It was obvious. "The Latchkey Kids."

"The Latchkey Kids," Bone repeated. "Yeah, that's good."

Jeff Air looked dubious. "It's a stupid name. It doesn't stand for anything."

"No, that's us," the others said, agreeing with Ed Valencia. "The Latchkey Kids."

"Our first record can have a picture of a front door with 'Gates of Hell' written above it," Pellet Head said, excited.

"Yeah, and a fucking shotgun barrel poking out of the mail slot," Cashdollar said.

"I have the goddam right to defend myself!" Bones squeaked in a falsetto.

"But it doesn't stand for anything good. You said you wanted to stand for something," Jeff Air insisted. "The Latchkey Kids sounds like a bunch of kiddies."

"It stands for something," Ed Valencia said. The Latchkey Kids: they had homes, but their real families were their friends. They came and went as they pleased, keys around their necks like medals to protect them—St. Agatha, St. Ambrose, St. Jude Thaddeus, pray for them, unsupervised, harassed, luckless, doing God-knew-what. Lying on the phone to whoever called, "My mother said to take a message and she'll call you back," like she was just around the corner with her hands full of flour. The Latchkey Kids: exploding eggs in the microwave to see how long it took. Hoping against fire, or earthquakes, or nuclear war.

"Hey, where are we going?" Pellet Head asked. Bones was driving, careering downhill with the Malibu in neutral to save gas. The Valley sky was darkly alive—good water for fishing, Ed Valencia's dad used to say. The suburbs were quiet at midnight, a few house lights fidgeting here and there as residents made their way upstairs for the night, then down again to check the windows and doors, then back upstairs, then down for a glass of water, a last bite of ice cream right from the carton, fighting the urge to over-eat—one more, just one more, not bothering to wash the spoon between bites.

"The river. Let's go skate the river," Cashdollar said.

"Dude, we can't. It's too dangerous at night. That's where the Night Stalker lives," said Bones.

"The Night Stalker is only interested in girls," Cashdollar said.

"You better watch out, Cashdollar," said Jeff Air.

"Fuck you," Cashdollar answered.

"We'll just drive around, see what's happening," Ed Valencia said.

"I got like, no gas and no money," Bones said. "I can't afford to drive around."

The Rats took up a collection: three dollars, mostly in change. "I'm so sick of being broke," Ed Valencia groaned.

"I'd almost get a job, except that working would be worse than being broke," said Jeff Air. "Mass production killed the self."

"Like anyone would hire you, dude," Cashdollar said.

"We're all completely unemployable," Bones said.

"Always," agreed Ed Valencia: the last word on the subject.

When he arrived home just after two o'clock and inserted his key in the lock, his mother was waiting up. She had wrapped herself in a blanket, even though the apartment was stuffy and hot, and her hands leapt crazily in her lap, twisting the blanket's fringe. Her eyes were heavily shadowed, pupils stark with exhaustion, her nose a raw, dripping stub. Seeing her son, she sobbed harshly, more barking than crying, one hand now at her throat, pinching the skin, plucking it pink, then red, until it bled. "Where is she? Is she with you, Ed?"

"What are you talking about?"

"Where's Kelly?"

"She's here."

"No, she isn't!"

"Where is she?"

"That's what I'm asking, Ed. You stayed home with her."

Ed Valencia didn't understand. "I told you, Mom. I told you at breakfast that I couldn't. I had plans."

"I was counting on you. I needed a night off, and now look what you've done. She's gone! She's been kidnapped! She's never coming back!" His mother, huddled on the couch, didn't look well. She clung to the blanket's fringe like a rope, like it was the only thing that kept her from dropping down a hole.

Ed Valencia thought fast. "I know where she is. She's at *Rocky Horror*, Mom. I bet that's where she is."

"She's at what?"

"*Rocky Horror*. You know, that record she listens to all the time."

"I *know* what she listens to. She wears those clothes. I'm not that out of it," his mother said, rubbing her eyes. Her hands were bonier than Ed Valencia remembered. Her cheekbones stuck out like window ledges. She was tired. He knew she would say that if he asked. Tiredness at the end of a long work week made her pass out every Friday night, sleeping so soundly that Kelly could slip from the apartment and sneak back in again before morning.

"She probably went to the show," Ed Valencia said.

"What show? What are you talking about?"

"*Rocky Horror*. You know, it's a movie."

"She's at the *movies*? At this hour?"

"It shows at midnight at the Nuart. All the groupies go on Friday night."

"She's at the movies?" his mother repeated helplessly. "How did she get there?"

Ed Valencia shrugged. "I think she takes the bus."

"How many times has she done this?"

"I don't know. A bunch of times."

"How?"

"I don't know. Takes the bus, I guess," Ed Valencia said, trying not to sound impatient.

"I mean, *how*? How does she get out? Where am I when she's going to the movies at *midnight*?"

"You're sleeping or something. How should I know?"

Ed Valencia's mother began to talk very fast now. "I went to one meeting. One meeting—is that too much to ask? I had a cup of coffee with some people I met there, and then I drove home, thinking my children would be here, thinking my children were safe at home. I got home at eleven o'clock and no one—I didn't even know who to call! I don't know, do I? I don't know your friends' numbers. I don't even know their real names. I called the police, but they can't help. They told me I had to wait twenty-four hours. Twenty-four hours! Kelly could be dead by then," his mother sobbed.

"She's at *Rocky Horror*, Mom. I know she's there. She goes every week. How many times do I have to tell you?"

"You told me you were going to stay with her!"

"I told you I was going out with my friends." Ed Valencia knew what he had said, yet doubt was seeping in, devouring his conviction like acid indigestion wrecked his sleep. Was Kelly OK? Was she really? Shouldn't she be home by now? How long was that fucking movie?

"At breakfast. You told me at breakfast that you would babysit Kelly tonight. That's what you said." His mother was ranting. Her screechy voice and twisted fingers, the way her eyes didn't seem to focus—she filled the apartment with ominous electricity. A fluttering sound came from her lap. What was that? Sounded like a nest of something, a rustling nest of rats. But in his mother's lap? Ed Valencia was scanning the apartment, looking for Darby Crash. Had he escaped? His mother would freak if he had, she would really—

There was the noise of a key at the door, startling both of them. One by one, all five locks flicked open, before Kelly stepped into the room, carrying her tap shoes. She saw Ed Valencia and her mother and froze. Their mother was struggling to free herself from the blanket, then she ran to Kelly and embraced her, weeping, before she pulled back and slapped Kelly hard across the face. The next blow knocked Kelly down, shoes flung from her hands, marking the wall with dirty divots, the taps dinging when they hit. Their mother crouched and shook Kelly so that her head rattled against the floor before Ed Valencia grabbed her arm to make her stop. "That's enough! You'll hurt her."

Shamed now, their mother crawled into the kitchen,

where she collapsed in a heap, whimpering, immobile, no matter how Ed Valencia cajoled her to get up—she growled until he backed off.

"Come on, Mom. It's OK. Kelly's OK. Please, Mom. You can see she's OK." But Kelly was wailing, putting on a great show of being hurt. "Mom's just tired," Ed Valencia told Kelly, wanting her to stop. "We should go to bed and let her rest. Mom, we're going to bed." Ed Valencia heard the tremor in his own voice. We're all cracking up, he thought. He wanted to go back to breakfast and start the day over again, with a fresh bowl of corn flakes eaten at just the right pace so they tasted great. He wanted to do what his mother had asked of him in the first place. "Mom? Mom?"

There was no reply, no movement, just a drab, hunched figure.

"Go to bed, Kelly," Ed Valencia said. His sister's crying was spiraling down, becoming the smoke after the fire has been put out, and finally she went. He left a light on for his mother, then he, too, stumbled off to bed. He tried to sleep, but couldn't. For a long time he huddled with Darby Crash. The rat, as if sensing his need, clung to his breast, his claws gently pricking through T-shirt to skin, just where Ed Valencia's heart beat. It was like Darby Crash was trying to hug him, he thought, taking comfort. When, hours later, still sleepless, Ed Valencia got up for a drink of water, his mother lay curled on the kitchen floor, as before, and he didn't dare disturb her to reach the cupboard where the glasses were. He drank from the bathroom faucet instead, pausing again in front of his mother on the way back to his room. She didn't stir, didn't even seem to sense him staring at her. The light shone all night and she didn't fuss about the electricity bill, just let it burn, a cheap lamp from Kmart that scorched its shade when left on too long.

Ed Valencia finally slept just after dawn, with Darby Crash curled on the pillow by his nose. At noon, when he woke, his mother was gone, a ten-deep stack of cold pancakes in her place at the table. The note she left said she was at the grocery store and would be back later. Ed Valencia and Kelly were to stay put until she returned.

Nine

Early Saturday afternoon, Lise, Trish, her Romeo, and two of Romeo's friends (not Romeos themselves, but cute) woke in Trish's room. Sleeping bags snaked across the floor where Lise and the two non-Romeos had slept, while Trish and Romeo cuddled in her lace-canopied double bed, smoking cigarettes. Lise wondered if they had just done it.

Trish spoke first. "How's your hangover, Lise?"

Lise didn't get hangovers; she was only thirteen. "OK. I feel OK." She wondered what had happened last night, remembering only that first golden beer (and the toast before, the girls' usual, a pact to meet again in the year 2002, in the lobby of the Beverly Hills Hotel, on the eve of Trish's thirtieth birthday) and how it had warmed her throat and belly like a cook stove does a log cabin. Then the obvious loosening in her middle where she held herself tightest, her stomach a calcified knot, a *pearl*, her thin skin breached daily by irritants and fears. Around Lise, everything began to run together, the edges of things indistinct, no matter how she squinted to see, and she had a feeling of intense light *somewhere* that made her shade her eyes when she talked to people, as if the light came from behind them. At one point she had gone in search of this light, insisting on what she knew was there but elusive to her. She had asked *everyone*. Lise forgot her shyness when she drank.

Then, nothing.

Flashes of the night came back: climbing into a hot tub with her clothes on, where she sat for a long time before noticing that the two couples with whom she shared the tub were having sex, the girls bouncing in the boys' laps. Later, she had broken something, possibly valuable, felt the splash of glass around her ankles. She had briefly gone to bed, thinking if she just slept . . . but people kept walking in and laughing. What was so funny? She tried to laugh with them, keeping her eyes closed but still laughing, then drifting off until the door opened and the laughter began again. Now one question repeated like the hiccups: what else she had done? The night, on the whole, was a blackout, and she waited to hear about it. But wasn't Trish taking her time? Smoking, nuzzling her Romeo, while the pearl in Lise gained sustenance—it was becoming huge, at least the size of a golf ball.

Trish wouldn't peep. Worry made Lise feel hopped-up, like she needed to move, and she began to fuss with her sleeping bag's zipper, moving it forward two inches and back again. Trish flicked ash in the direction of the ashtray, spattering the bed sheets, and finally said, "You passed out. In some guy's lap. Like, I don't even know who he was. Don't worry, he didn't take advantage of you. We would never let *that* happen. Excuse me, could you stop that noise please? It's totally annoying. You're giving me a headache."

Lise was too agitated to stay in bed. Checking first to see that she was decent (still wearing her clothes from the night before, she found, including her red Reeboks, the laces double-knotted against tripping and prickly with broken glass), she unzipped the sleeping bag completely, the metal zipper gunning its length like a punctured muffler in a street race. She stood up too fast and the room whirled, a twister of pastel shades. "Um, I think I need a shower."

"Use Alexis's bathroom. She's away with her dad this weekend. Palm Springs." Trish wrinkled her nose and glanced at her Romeo. "*So* boring. At least my dad takes me to Maui."

"Yeah," Lise said. The world was steady now. "Your dad's cool."

"He's not, he's just rich. But he's better than Alexis's dad—richer, too." Trish lit another cigarette, dragged and exhaled, as if blowing Lise out of the room.

The house was silent except for the housekeeper's rubber-soled shoes squeaking on the tiled floor downstairs (Mrs. Blue slept late every day of the week—not just on Saturdays). After a long, hot shower, Lise felt calmer, her worry washed down the drain to the ocean. She blow-dried the long half of her hair (she liked the short side to have a spiky wet look) and dressed in last night's smoky clothes. Returning to Trish's room, she found everyone gone, the three sleeping bags balled in doughy-looking lumps on the floor. Hurrying now, Lise picked a fresh outfit from Trish's closet and changed, hoping the boys hadn't left yet. She wanted to talk to them, to meet them properly, show them she wasn't a total loser who passed out from a couple of beers. It was because she didn't have dinner last night, she would say, just some fries at the Galleria food court that

Trish wouldn't let her finish. Trish never let them eat dinner if they were going to drink because it was too many calories. Every beer was a slice of buttered bread, she said.

But Lise found only Trish in the kitchen, telling the housekeeper what to cook. "I'm having pancakes. What do you want?"

"Pancakes." Lise's stomach rumbled, she was so hungry. Had she thrown up last night? "Um, did they leave already?" she asked, trying not to show her disappointment that they hadn't said goodbye to her.

"They had to go somewhere."

"Where?"

"Home, I guess," Trish shrugged.

"Do you ever meet people and think they don't have parents? Like, they're too cool to have parents, or maybe they have the coolest parents ever, so cool they're not like parents, but more like kids. Maybe they party with their kids, like your mom does."

"Huh?"

"I guess I mean . . ." Lise paused. "Those guys just don't seem like they have parents. They're too *cool* for parents."

"I don't know. That's a weird thing to think about. I mean, of course they have parents. How else did they get born? Anyway, only *one* of those guys was cool. The other two were wannabes."

"Total wannabes," Lise agreed, even though she had thought they were cute. Wannabes were the worst. Wannabes wore and said what they thought was right to suit the people they were with. Wannabes hung around too long, even when the joke being told was on them. Wannabes pretended they took acid, but flushed it down the toilet instead, faking their trip in a way that was totally obvious—like, no one actually saw bugs crawling all over their skin and halos on everybody's head. "So what happened last night? Are you and Jason going together now?"

Trish nodded, smiling, showing her braces *totally*. "Second base. I went to first with him and he went to second with me. We didn't go to *sleep*! We stayed up all night, just talking. I think he's in love with me. I'm totally in love with him. He's *so* caring and sensitive. Like, at that party, he just sat with me the whole time, holding my hand. He really *listens*. I could tell him anything, I just know it."

"Really?"

"Really. Guys like him don't come along very often," Trish said knowingly. "Wait until I tell my mom. She'll probably like, try to steal him from me."

"Yeah, he seems really, really nice. You're so lucky, Trish."

"We're going to the Galleria later this afternoon. He's taking me shopping. He says he wants to buy me some perfume. He says I should have a perfume that I wear just for him. Isn't that romantic? So what do you think, should I get Poison? Poison is my potion," she intoned, like on TV.

"I want to get those ankle socks we saw yesterday. Remember? With the little black hearts all over them? They were so cute."

"You're not coming."

Lise didn't miss a beat. "Do you think your mom can take me home when she wakes up?"

"Sure. Probably," Trish shrugged.

The housekeeper set down a stack of pancakes on a hot plate between them, licks of butter from her generous knife sucked into the air bubbles that clustered in each cake, light as Styrofoam. Lise's mouth watered. "Yummy," she said.

"Now we'll only have one each, and no more butter, and only a little bit of syrup," Trish instructed. "It's a special occasion. I thought we should celebrate."

Lise spent the rest of that weekend in her bedroom, grounded for not calling to say that she would be late. She tried to tell her mother that Trish's mom didn't rise until four in the afternoon, but Mrs. Anderson only repeated herself: Lise could have called. She *should* have called, and she shouldn't blame her mistakes on other people. If she had called, she might have saved her mother another migraine. Mrs. Anderson had to lie down on the couch with a washcloth over her eyes while she yelled at Lise. "Get yourself something to eat and get moving up to that room," she ordered her daughter.

Lise turned away from the exposed, abundant cellulite of her mother's thighs, the knuckled veins deranging her legs, before she lost her appetite. Her mother's fat was always there for Lise to see, revealed by terry short-shorts left over from the Seventies and stretched beyond shape. It made her think of the cat they dissected in science class, the yolk-yellow fat slopping from the open seam, a spill on the table like curdled cream.

Her father sat in the kitchen with the Saturday paper and a drink—what looked like Coke but probably wasn't just Coke. When he looked at Lise, his eyes were vague, only one eye fully open so that he surveyed the news, and his daughter, telescopically.

"Hello, stranger," he said. "Where have you been all my life?"

"Um, I was at Trish's."

"The beauty Trish. How's her mother? She still single? I was thinking I should give her a call sometime."

Lise didn't reply. Her dad thought he was so funny, but really he was just gross. She set about making herself a ham and cheese sandwich, found a bag of potato chips and a liter bottle of Diet Coke, then approached the table. Her father, who had begun to doze in his chair while she bustled around the kitchen, woke. Lise pushed aside a section of the newspaper, creating a tiny square of space for her plate, and sat down, strangling herself not to snap at him to get a life.

"You must be taking final exams soon," he said.

"I already took them, Dad."

"Did you do good?"

"I don't know."

"What do you mean, you don't know?" If Lise were her mother, he would be at her throat now, citing her sulky tone, her answers that weren't really answers, but Lise was his little girl and he had always been soft on her—soft, yet indifferent, like she was a piece of fruit without much taste.

Lise shrugged.

"What's your favorite subject?" Her dad was wide awake now, his eyes hard and bright in the red woolly mush of his face.

Lise shrugged. Shrugging showed she was bored with his questions and wished he would shut up: a refusal to exert herself. But her father was persistent, or not perceptive enough to see that he should leave her alone, or just damn drunk.

"Come on, Lise. Stop acting like a turkey."

"Um, English, I guess." English was easy. You read the story and wrote down how you felt after reading. Lise did OK in English, better than she did in math or science or social studies, making Bs without really trying. Mostly she liked the stories, although she didn't understand some of the questions Mr. Feltman asked about them. He tried to be so deep, Jen complained. Lise usually forgot the story within a couple of days, plus she could never remember who wrote what. It just didn't seem important.

"You won't go far with that," her father snorted. "I mean, who gets paid to read? Nobody does." He yawned. Lise waited. She thought there was a name for what he had, the thing that made him fall asleep all of a sudden, in the middle of talking, sometimes.

Quickly, before he woke, she ate the insides of her sandwich, leaving the crust. She managed four potato chips and a few swallows of Diet Coke before she stopped herself; she had to model in a few days, after all. Model! Lise was going to be a model! She sucked in her breath. Oh, wasn't life beautiful suddenly? Wasn't it crazy how a dream could jump from where it lived inside her head and become the stuff of the real? How Lise could go from being an ordinary girl to a *model*?

"What's your mother doing?" Her dad was awake, interrupting her thoughts, his voice ugly and rough.

"She has a headache. She's lying down."

"She always has a goddamn headache. She has so many headaches, it's a miracle we had you," he cackled.

Lise blushed and escaped to her room, where she threw herself onto the bed, pulling a pillow over her head. She tried not to picture her mother's massive thighs, dented with effort, squeezing her father's head until his toupee popped off like the lid to a jack-in-the-box, blood pouring from his eyes; her mother's thighs forcing her father's head into a purple blot that blackened, deprived of oxygen, his pulpy nose exploding like a bomb test in the desert sand; her mother on the couch, knees spread like a gaping bear trap, calling to Lise, "Next!"

Ten

Did it matter where their father was? Not really. What mattered more in L.A. was *who* he was, or what he did, but Ed Valencia wasn't interested in those answers; he didn't have a father worth mentioning, nor did his friends. The kids who did stuck together, lived in the same neighborhoods, wore the same kinds of clothes, and drove the same cars—likewise the kids who didn't. Ed Valencia's father was a carpenter who lived like a hermit in a primitive burrow dripping stalactites of candle wax in Big Sur, or something like that. You had to be crazy to live year-round in Big Sur, his mother said, stranded in winter when landslides clobbered Highway 1, the road likewise clogged with summer tourists terrified of the blind bends, inching along. Their dad was a hard man to live with, a man who couldn't control himself, she told her kids. It was better that he lived alone, perched on the edge of the world, California's perilous, crusty coast, which, at any moment, might slide into the Pacific, courtesy of the fickle San Andreas fault.

Ed Valencia spurned romantic ideas about family reunions, going to live with his dad, or his dad's return. Ed Valencia didn't care if he saw him again; his dad had *walked out* on them. Kelly only knew the divorce part of the

California dream, but she had been the hope that might cement her parents' marriage. They were separated by the time she was born. Another kind of life never occurred to her, as Kelly hadn't been promised anything—no dog, no pool, no weekends in Monterey, no Valium addiction to keep her mom at peace, no convertible to drive them to school. Instead, Kelly was a bed-wetter who wasn't invited to the regular sleepovers that constituted the social world of girls her age. She had leached on to a cult film, rice for an onscreen wedding party seeping from her pockets, welcomed every Friday night to the midnight show by the faithful to whom *Rocky Horror* had spoken: "You're weird, but you belong somewhere. Let's all be weird together."

When Ed Valencia's dad left, no one knew where he was for two years, until divorce papers suddenly appeared in the mail with his new return address, Hwy 1 Big Sur. "There's going to be a lot more happiness in this house from now on," his mother announced. "A happy mother makes happy children and I'm *happy*. Your father was like a bad cold that I'm over. I'm focused on two things: my kids and my career. I'm going to have a career. And my kids—you're already great. You're just great," she said, reaching for them. Kelly hugged her mother's knee, while Ed Valencia, already to her shoulder and growing like a sun-soaked weed, embraced her awkwardly, his kiss landing on her nose instead of her cheek.

A career was better said than done. The new hard times of divorce had reached plague proportions: half of all families in America broke apart. Divorce had become a collective childhood experience, like chicken pox, and all over the nation, stimulated, energized mothers marched out to look for jobs. Survival was what many of them discovered—survival, not careers, and it chilled their souls until some of them said they couldn't feel. Over time, their souls blanched; bodies were exhausted, features dulled. Moms, someone said, weren't pretty anymore.

At first, Ed Valencia's mother worked nights, then days, then both. Nine years later, she had only just finished her secretarial course and found a full-time job. At her boss's request, she had her hair restyled with a bubbly permanent and her colors analyzed in Bullocks' cosmetics department: she was autumn, wearing a golden leopard-print scarf pinned to one shoulder like a beauty pageant banner, to bring out the mood and attitude of her eyes. For her thirty-ninth birthday, she treated herself to contact lenses and developed a new, coquettish tic, blinking rapidly to keep the difficult disks from escaping.

Ed Valencia heard other mothers bawling to the cops who pulled them over, "My husband wasn't sweet to me!" His mother drove cautiously, arms locked against the steering wheel; it was the other drivers she worried about, she said, wild-eyed men like his father in pickup trucks bearing down on her bumper. Some mothers sped, trying to make up the time they spent away from home at work, raising enough cash for rent. Bones' mother, having conquered Freeway Phobia, had recently lost her license for drunk driving, while Pellet Head's mother bitterly recalled the days when she drove a Trans-Am instead of a Pinto.

Ed Valencia emerged from the settling ash of his mother's

breakdown dressed in blue jeans and a well-pressed long-sleeved dress shirt that covered his tattoos, his Mohawk combed flat, and the assorted trinkets and earrings he usually wore stowed in a cereal bowl on his dresser. Saturday afternoon, his mother had taken him and Kelly shopping, Mrs. Costello decreeing that both children would wear "normal" clothes that would make them act right as well. Kelly, dressed in a plain red mini-dress and white Reeboks for school, was no longer speaking to her mother, despite pancakes for breakfast three days in a row; her *Rocky Horror* records, hot pants, bow tie, and tap shoes had been hidden in Ed Valencia's underwear drawer. Pancakes reminded Ed Valencia of the days just after the divorce, when meals came at odd times, depending on Mrs. Costello's work schedule. Pancakes for breakfast and lunch or sometimes brunch (that sophisticated word they loved to use, almost as tasty as the meal itself), boxes of Bisquick lined up in the cupboard, ready to mix. Pancakes in the middle of the night when his mother got home. Cold pancakes to snack on, spread with peanut butter and jelly, and pancakes in the freezer to microwave after school, pretending like they were fresh-cooked.

"Mom's crazy," Kelly had whispered to Ed Valencia early that Monday morning, poking at her syrup-sodden breakfast while their mother made up her face and teased her perm with a lethal needle-tooth comb.

"She's not. She's just overtired, like she said." Ed Valencia didn't know why he was defending his mother, who had threatened to put Darby Crash in the Dumpster where she said he belonged. Normal people didn't keep rats as pets, she said. Rats weren't *supposed* to be pets; they should be drowned like kittens in sacks when born.

"She's crazy," Kelly repeated, then added, "I wish I could go live with Dad."

"What? What did you just say?"

"I'm going to live with Dad."

"You don't even know him. He left Mom pregnant with you," Ed Valencia said. He pressed his head into his hands, eyes cupped in his palms as if peering at what he didn't understand. "I remember. Dad's an idiot. You can't take his side, OK? *He's* the one who's crazy."

"They both are," Kelly had said miserably. "I can't wait until I'm eighteen."

Ed Valencia, eighteen the next year, felt the same. As soon as he had his diploma, he would escape, maybe to Washington, DC, where the hardcore scene was good. He and Bones in the Malibu would travel slowly across the country, taking in the sights. Ed Valencia's mom had always said she wanted to show her kids America before she showed them Europe, if she could, but he was running out of time, waiting for her. Plus the thought of driving in a small car for hours on end with her and Kelly—no way, Ed Valencia thought. No way.

Now they were parked out front of North Hollywood High School. Their mother had arranged to be late for work in order to drop off both children. "And I'm going to call today to check on your attendance," she warned.

"Mom, it's the end of the school year," Ed Valencia complained. "No one cares if I'm here or not."

126

"I will see to it that you finish out the semester. Every last day."

"That's five days, including today. It's nothing." Ed Valencia slammed the door of the misshapen Ford Tempo, its side dimpled as if an asteroid had crashed into it.

His mother had her window down. "I'll be home by five," she said, but he wouldn't look at her; he was trying to pretend she wasn't there, that he wasn't related to her, that she was talking to some other kid, or to herself—that's right, she was crazy, just like Kelly said. He could believe that right now.

There was no time for him to meet the other Rats at Taco Bell. Instead, he stopped in the lavatory to change his dress shirt to a T-shirt ("Fuck the Mods"), wet his hair, and get his Mohawk upright using the hand dryer. But without glue (Ed Valencia's mother had taken his glue, too, claiming he might be a huffer), it was no use, and there wasn't time to swipe some from the art room. As the bell rang, Ed Valencia strolled to his locker, scowling (his usual school look), elbows out, pushing back at anyone who brushed against him, like he did in the mosh pit. He hated school. He was smart, but overlooked, and bored. There was no girl that he was secretly in love with to draw him to those neon-bright corridors, no teacher to fall in love with him and offer direction. There was no point in being there.

At his locker, he was joined not by Bones or any of the other Rats, but his homeroom teacher. Flanking Mrs. Butcher were the aphoristic fool who served as his guidance counselor—Ed Valencia couldn't remember his name—and

North Hollywood High School's discipline-hungry principal, Mr. Dodge, as well as a grinning janitor who held up oversized bolt-cutters like the catch of the day.

"Good morning, Mr. Costello. Glad you could join us." The principal rocked back on his heels, arms crossed, the corners of his mouth teased into a vinegary smile that cracked the arid crust of his face. Mr. Dodge's dazzling golden hair was speckled with flakes, while the skin still attached to his skull was a furious pink. Shaving was no doubt misery for Mr. Dodge, but Ed Valencia didn't hate him less for his suffering. No one did.

"Hey," Ed Valencia muttered. "What's going on?" He had nothing to do with any of these people if he could help it. He regularly skipped his guidance appointments—no-future was nothing a guidance counselor was interested in hearing about, while Ed Valencia didn't want to discuss his unadorned transcript nor give his reasons for not taking the SAT—and poked his head into homeroom only when he heard Mrs. Butcher take attendance. He had met Mr. Dodge just once before, the day Darby Crash came to school riding proud on Ed Valencia's shoulder. Darby Crash ended up spending the day in the biology lab, poked with pencils and decorated with lanyards made from drinking straws like a derby winner—until he began to snap, drawing blood from half a dozen fingers. Then the shoebox's lid was taped shut. At the end of the day, when Ed Valencia reported to collect his rat, Darby Crash was unconscious, oxygen-deprived; revived, he wept red tears of distress, trauma that required an expensive visit to the vet and weeks of the most tender care.

"We'd like to take a look inside your locker," Mr. Dodge said.

"Why do you want to do that?" Ed Valencia asked.

"We have reasonable grounds to suspect that our search will turn up a weapon." Mrs. Butcher cowed behind the janitor, fingers plucking at her cardigan buttons. Ed Valencia thought she marked him present even when he was absent or late, that she was afraid of him—Mrs. Butcher, with her gloomy face and tissue-soft voice, was afraid of most people.

"What? Like what? What kind of weapon? Because I don't carry weapons. No way. I'm the last guy who would carry a weapon." A crowd had gathered, listening in, already passing on their own version of things, the hallway a whispering alley. Ed Valencia, nervous now, was in the principal's power, and Mr. Dodge was not his "pal," as he had been taught in third-grade spelling.

"We have received information saying that you carry a gun. That you keep a loaded gun in your locker during school hours," Mr. Dodge said.

"Who said that? Who would say that?" A tremor passed through Ed Valencia's body—a sheen of perspiration was all over him. "No fucking way do I carry a fucking gun. Do you think I'm fucking stupid?"

"Mr. Costello, I think you have enough on your plate without resorting to foul language," the principal answered mildly.

Ed Valencia tried to keep his voice steady. "I'm telling you, I don't have a gun in there. I don't have a gun, period. This is crazy. You can't search my locker just because someone says I've got a gun. That's not fair—I know my rights. I have a right to privacy."

"If we suspect that a student has violated either the law or the rules of the school, then we have the privilege to search your locker or person, as designated by the Supreme Court in January of this year." Mr. Dodge's smile cracked his dry lips until they bled. He licked his lips, seeming to savor his own blood. Yes, he took pleasure in this, Ed Valencia thought. He loved his power, his tiny slice of kingdom. "Now open up."

"Wait, what? What did you just say? Supreme Court what?" Ed Valencia tried to remember which amendment gave him the right to privacy. Why couldn't he at least remember that *one* fact from history class?

"This is a public school, ultimately subsidized by the federal government. As far as I'm concerned, you gave up your rights when you walked through my doors this morning," Mr. Dodge replied. "Now, would you like to open your locker, or will Arthur open it for you?"

Arthur the janitor flexed his bolt-cutters and grinned, and the gathered students transmitted this last statement, already distorting it: "Now will you open your mouth, or will Arthur open it for you?" It seemed everyone smiled at Ed Valencia's misfortune, pressing in for a better view, intensifying the claustrophobia he'd always felt in school, locked into a classroom, a schedule, the eyes of his classmates upon him as he read aloud and stumbled over easy words that he *knew* how to pronounce. Ed Valencia listened to the expectant breathing, inhaled the reek of people—he smelled himself, especially, his fear. What was he afraid of? He thought of the banal stuff of his locker, the schoolbooks stained with burrito ooze, his secondhand gym uniform, black Converse All-Stars Duck-taped to keep water from leaking through the holes in their soles, the booger collection inherited from last year's tenant, photos of Darby Crash—both his rat and the singer of the Germs—taped inside the door—but Ed Valencia wasn't sticking around to face that humiliation, even if running made him look guilty. He wouldn't hand himself in, not to Mr. Dodge, or the counselor for talking things over, or FFF, or whoever. What more did he have to lose? He was the kid who had *nothing* to lose.

"Mr. Costello! Mr. Costello!" he heard the principal calling after him. Ed Valencia pushed on, bellowing through jammed intersections, his mouth a horn, past the auditorium where practicing cheerleaders—winners all—handed off the spirit stick like a golden baton, then on through the doors of Kennedy Hall and out into the acetic sunshine he had left just fifteen minutes before. He aimed his thundering feet along Colfax, turned the corner, and recklessly crossed wide-ass Magnolia, not even looking to be sure it was clear. Ed Valencia darted and feinted to avoid a dozen or so of the 4.7 million vehicles making 25 million trips daily among the 84 cities of L.A., hustling between cars that tailed each other to make the lights and make good time on their morning journey to work. He straddled the double yellow lines for a perilous minute before a gap in traffic opened (the kind of interstice that called out for a skateboard to shoot the chute), finally reaching Taco Bell, where he hoped at least one of the Rats might be lingering over a Breakfast Burrito.

Sure enough, Bones, loyal friend, sat alone at a table at the front, reading the new *Flipside*. "Where you been, Valencia? I was just getting ready to go. Everyone else left already, but I figured I'd skip homeroom and see if you showed."

"It was a fucking set-up!" Ed Valencia shouted. "FFF set me up!"

"Did they get you? Are you hurt, Valencia?"

Ed Valencia shook his head. "They told Dodge I had a gun in my locker. He's going through my shit right now."

"No way. No way they fucking set you up." Bones leapt from his seat to pace the restaurant, whacking tabletops with his rolled-up *Flipside*. "They set you up. I can't believe they set you up like that."

"This is fucking war. We're fucking going to war with FFF."

"I can't believe they did that. I already told them we didn't want to fight," Bones said.

"What do you mean, you told them?"

"Yeah. I told you."

"You didn't tell me. You don't tell me shit. What did you tell them? When?"

Bones looked panicked. "We saw a bunch of them on Saturday night. They asked where you were—your mom kept you in, remember? We were hanging around Oki Dog and they like, surrounded us. Dude, they're multiplying, I swear. There were like, fifty of them there. So we said you had some family business to take care of, like your mom was going mental and your sister tried to run away."

"You told them that?"

"Yeah. They totally understood. Everybody has family shit going on. Yours like, isn't that bad compared to some people."

Ed Valencia took a big breath. He couldn't believe what he was hearing. He wanted to punch Bones. "You told them I didn't want to fight?"

"They were cool, Valencia."

"What did they say?"

Bones paused. "Nothing. They were cool."

"What did they say?"

"They laughed. That's it. They were like, 'OK, thanks for telling us.' They were totally cool. We were all laughing about it."

"You fucking idiot! I can't believe this! I can't believe how stupid you are," Ed Valencia roared. He grabbed the rolled-up *Flipside* from Bones and lunged at his head with it. Bones ducked and Ed Valencia caught him on his back. Bones yelped.

"Hey! Not in here. Take it outside, boys." Taco Bell's manager—you could tell because he wore a tie—was leaning over the counter, pointing at Ed Valencia and Bones and then jerking his finger toward the door.

"We're fine," Ed Valencia answered back. "We're not fighting. We're having a discussion. A *private* discussion, if you don't mind."

"Outside, or I'm calling the cops," the manager threatened.

"Let's just go," Bones said.

"Fuck you," Ed Valencia said to the manager. "I'll never eat here again."

"Good. Kids like you are bad for business. You scare the customers," the manager said.

"Come on, Valencia," said Bones, holding the door for him.

The heat outside was stale and had been forever, and always would be: just another trap to walk into, thought Ed Valencia. It was too fucking hot in California. No wonder people moved east. Ed Valencia was definitely moving to DC, away from his friends and family, from school, from all this bullshit—from FFF especially. He might not wait until he graduated to leave. As soon as he was eighteen, he was going for sure.

"Dude, I'm sorry. I didn't think they'd set you up."

"I told you, FFF don't forget shit. They always get you back," Ed Valencia said. "We're going to call them out, that's what we're going to do. That's what they want us to do. They're *laughing* at us, Bones. We're not some big happy family, everyone getting along. You're a fucking idiot if you think that."

"Dude, you're wrong. I was there. I know what they said. They don't want to fight us," Bones insisted.

"They want to fight," Ed Valencia said. "We're going to fight."

"They'll *smear* us. They fight like fucking Marines. We're dead if we fight. We got no chance against those guys."

Defying the sun, Ed Valencia met Bones' eyes, which were terrified, the eyes of a hypochondriac, a teenager who complained of chest pains, whose mother didn't drive on the freeway for three years because she thought she would die on it. "Have they killed anyone yet?" Ed Valencia asked.

Bones shrugged. "People say shit. Like, there were all those gay guys who got beat up in the park and maybe one of them died—I can't remember."

"Was that FFF?"

"I don't know." It didn't matter. They knew what they were up against.

Eleven

Two girls, one in love, sat before a mirror. The one in love stared at her own reflection, loving the way she looked, while the other one watched, wishing she looked like her.

"After we do this, there's a party in the Donas. Jason will take us." Trish's gleaming sapphire eyes set in gold eyeliner and eye shadow had the sparkle of the real. The flush of her cheeks was centered appealingly in two bright spots. Her pretty mouth smiled, but not too much. "Jason says Tatum O'Neal might be there. I totally want to meet her."

"The Donas." Lise was impressed. She had never been to a house in the hilly Donas, but she heard they were huge. Only rich people lived in the Donas. Only rich people had views.

"Jason says all the Romeos are going. It's supposed to be like, a big party. Drew Barrymore is going to be there. Jason knows her. They grew up together. He says she's totally wild and she's only like, ten. Did you tell your mom you were sleeping over?"

"Yeah." Lise had lied to her mother as usual, saying that Trish's mother was away and Trish needed someone to stay the night with her because she got scared. The girls would take a taxi to school in the morning, and Mrs. Blue had left enough money for Lise to get to Millikan, too. Once Lise started a lie, she couldn't help but pile on the detail, her stories ballooning, becoming great, desperate escapes from the facts. As a little girl, her eyes had popped when she told whoppers, giving her away, but now she could tell a lie as smoothly as she could tell the truth.

"Where is Trish's mother?" Mrs. Anderson had asked.

"She's on a date. In the desert." Lise didn't know where the lies came from; they just appeared on the tip of her tongue, flowing like poetry, and she knew they were pleasing to her mother's ear.

"That woman never thinks about anyone but herself," Mrs. Anderson sniffed—but she didn't say no. She simply closed her eyes against the glare of the TV and shifted her colossal cauliflower-stalk legs to a more comfortable position. Sometimes, when Lise came in late at night and found her mother soaking up sunshiny sitcom reruns on the couch, utterly dazed, she would lay a hand on her shoulder, making sure she was alive. It was the only time Lise willingly touched her anymore. If Trish and Jen ever saw her mother like that, more vegetable than animal, a real couch potato—Lise shuddered. They would joke and laugh about it, but not in front of her. They would wait until Lise was gone, which was worse.

The dressing room in which the girls sat was improvised: a large canvas tent stocked with summer clothes on rails and mirrors propped up everywhere (Lise had tagged them all by now with fuchsia lips, to match her nail polish). A professional makeup artist and hairstylist dominated one table, ready to brush, twist, paint, and dust between sips of coffee from white foam cups, lipstick smiles in a chain around the rims. The girls had been told to take their pick of outfits, while a seamstress stood by to make sure they fit, tacking with pins, warning the girls to be careful when they sat. Trish had no pins in her outfit; Lise had ten, around her bust and hips.

"It's like being part of a real fashion show," Lise said, trying not to sound too excited. "She even plucked my eyebrows. That *kills*."

"You look so much better, though. She like, opened up your face. Your eyes are kind of close together, you know. Kind of like pig eyes, all squished up and piggy-looking."

"Pig eyes?" Lise looked in the mirror. Her eyes seemed smaller than she remembered, and now they were full of tears. She reached for some tissue and eyeliner. Her eyes weren't Trish's saucers, but they were fine, normal-sized eyes. Not piggy. They *were* brown, and she had a habit of squinting when she looked at things in the distance, things not quite distinct until she got up close (but she didn't need glasses. No way. If she squinted, or even tugged at the corners of her eyes, she could see just fine). But she didn't have *pig* eyes.

"Ohmigod, are you *crying*?"

Lise shook her head and blinked, expertly blotting with tissue. She lined both eyelids heavily in blue. That looked better. Bigger. She just needed to wear more eyeliner. She wished her mother would let her wear makeup all the time. "I don't have pig eyes. I really don't have pig eyes."

"Not *exactly* pig eyes. They're just close together. I

didn't mean *pig eyes*. God, you're so sensitive! It was just a thing to say."

"I mean, they wouldn't have asked me to do this show if they thought I had *pig eyes*, that's all. I'm not *crying* about it or anything." Lise would ruin her makeup if she cried, and she had just had her makeup professionally done for the first time in her life!

Trish surveyed the dressing room in the big mirror. The other girls, some their age, some older, twittered and preened, chattering constantly. "When I do shows for Vidal Sassoon they give me a glass of champagne *and* I can smoke. I don't know why they don't do that here." The girls had been offered soda pop, potato chips, and brownies, none of which they'd touched, opting for twin bottles of Evian instead (Lise always following Trish's lead). When Trish lit a cigarette a few minutes after they arrived, Carol—recruiter and producer of the show—rushed over, squawking about fire hazards. She listed the various flammable materials in their immediate vicinity: rayon, acrylic, polyester, fast-moving clouds of hairspray, gallons of nail polish remover. "I'm like, the only professional model here. You can tell just by looking that none of these girls have done this before."

"I know. Totally," Lise said. She scratched the soles of her white pumps on the floor, trying to rough them up like Trish had showed her; she was worried about walking in new shoes in front of so many people. She might fall. What if she fell in front of everyone?

"I can't believe they picked that one girl over there. The

one with the curly red hair. She looks like a complete loser. I'm like, embarrassed to be seen with her. Did you see her hair close up? It's like, split-end central. *And* she's totally fat. She came in wearing *boxer* shorts. I bet they're her dad's. I bet they have *skid* marks."

Lise nodded. Then, taking up the eyeliner again, she flared the lines straddling her lids, so that her eyes looked bigger yet.

"Are you ready, ladies?" Carol clapped her hands to get their attention, pumping her arms like pistons. "Let's get psyched. Let's get hyper! I want you to go out there and wow that audience. You should hear them—they're cheering and clapping! They can't *wait* to see you!"

"Ohmigod," Trish muttered. "This is like, too much."

Lise stood up. She was as ready as she ever would be. She fixed her eyes to the floor in front of her, to be sure where she stepped. The pink jersey dress she wore clung to her sweating parts (was she staining it, she wondered?) while Trish looked comfortable and cool in a red-and-white sailor suit with cropped trousers—the nautical look, which was supposed to be hot that summer. "I want you to have a good time," Carol hollered as the girls filed on to the makeshift runway, gathering just behind the curtain. She held them back while the applause built up, before letting them loose, one by one. "Give it everything you've got! Sparkle, sparkle!"

"Sparkle, sparkle!" Trish mimicked in a squeaky voice.

Lise, just behind her, giggled nervously. "I don't know if I can do this." Her knees felt unreliable, never mind the slippery soles of her new shoes. "Seriously, Trish. I don't know—"

But Trish was already gone. Three beats, Lise was to wait three beats before following. She stepped forward tentatively. What if her mother was there, she suddenly thought. Her stomach dropped and she stalled. God, what if her mother was shopping, inexplicably drawn to the mall? What if she had decided to buy some new clothes or shoes or something? But that was impossible. Her mother had never been inside the Galleria that Lise could remember. Why would she come now?

"Go!" Carol barked. "Keep moving! Don't stop! Three beats, I said three beats!" Carol was holding a poster that read "Smile and Be Happy" and she rattled it furiously. Lise jumped. It was too late now. Copying (she hoped) the swing of Trish's hips, she set out on her first lap, heels slipping like they were greased, ankles threatening to crumble and cause a landslide of the rest of her. At the catwalk's end, where the audience converged and a few photographers snapped—mostly mothers, Lise saw out of the corner of one eye—she overturned and had to compensate with a quick two-step before marching back to the changing tent. Had she really just done that? There was no time to think; the girls were tearing into their next outfits—for Lise, a maxi-shoulder yellow blazer paired with tropical-print clam-diggers. This time out, she managed to look straight ahead as she walked, wobbling only at the turn. She saw Mrs. Blue and Jen and Trish's Romeo and his friends and a handful of kids from Milliken, a noisy group, possibly the

Crew-Cut Crue—she had a glimpse of flattop haircuts. But really, there wasn't time to look.

Her last run, dressed in a black taffeta sheath splattered with white paint, Lise felt the beginnings of triumph and it showed in her assured step, legs kicking out like a majorette's bobbing baton. She could *do* this! Following Trish's lead, she paused at the end of the catwalk, hip cocked, one beat, two beat, no spin, just a simple stance, reveling in the gaze of the audience. Three beats and she finally moved on, wiggling in the tight dress as she walked.

Back in the tent, the girls shrieked and jumped around, clinging to each other in their excitement, hearing the applause. "People, you were *great!*" Carol yelled. "I'm so proud of you!"

Lise wanted to hug Trish, but Trish was already at work on her face, seated before a mirror, gazing at herself again. "Now is when we should get a glass of champagne," she said. "At Vidal Sassoon we always do."

Lise did as Trish, quickly and expertly toning down her makeup, leaving just enough to show that she had been onstage that day. They didn't change their clothes; as payment, they were allowed to keep one outfit, and both had already decided on the last. Lise's mother would never buy her a dress like it.

"Everyone's acting retarded, like it's the Miss America pageant or something." Trish spoke loudly enough to be heard. "They're total losers. They think this is such a big deal."

"I know," Lise agreed, feeling above it all, too. She had proved herself: she was a model. She had worked as a model. She could tell people. She had been good, not as good as Trish, but still good. Better than those other girls, those *wannabes*.

Lise hurried after Trish, in a rush to join the Romeos—and maybe there was a Romeo for her now. But on her way, someone grabbed Lise's arm with a kind of violence so that she almost fell in her high-heeled shoes.

"No—" she gasped. Her mother had seen her after all. She had somehow known what Lise was up to and had come to take her home. Lise was in big trouble. Her mother would freak, her shrill voice traveling like one of those whistling fireworks up the three tiers of Galleria promenade, so that everyone would look out over the concourse rail to see what was happening, alert for a victim in the sea of bodies. Mrs. Anderson was not above slapping her daughter—in fact had slapped her already this week, when Lise cursed two slices of burnt breakfast toast—and as Lise turned to face her, she reared back, anticipating the blow.

"Hey," a boy's voice said. "I'm not going to hurt you."

Lise's heart flared as if it would burn through the bodice of her dress: Mikey from FFF. The arm he touched warmed, then her shoulder and her neck, spreading across her face like a rash.

"Did I scare you?"

"No." But Lise knew she had jumped.

"You were really good in that show. I thought you were the best," Mikey said.

Lise blushed more deeply and wished she wouldn't. Her body had fixed itself at an awkward cant, her back twisted as if she had a crooked spine, one leg coiled around the other. She didn't know what to do with her arms and so let them dangle—they seemed to go on forever, hanging all the way to her knees like an orangutan. She tried to ease herself into a less grotesque shape without Mikey noticing: chin lifted, tummy sucked in, chest thrust forward, teeth wet, her tongue traipsing over their ridges like she was tasting them. And her eyes—she spread them as wide as she could.

"I like your hair," he said. He reached out like he would touch it, but didn't quite.

"Thanks," Lise mumbled.

"Come on, don't you like me? What's your name?"

"Um, Lise." She smiled, wishing she could dazzle him with a smile the way Trish did, kindling immediate devotion in boys.

Mikey grinned back. "I'm Mikey."

"I know."

Mikey looked pleased. "You know who I am? How do you know?"

"I've seen you around," Lise admitted.

His grin blazed like the hottest day, his hand racing through his flattop to make it stand on end—the same hand that had touched Lise's arm the moment before. Just like that, so casual, the two of them mixed up together, his hand, her arm, his hair. "You've seen me around? Were you like, spying on me? Because I'd remember if I'd seen you."

"You would?"

"I'd *totally* remember you."

Lise blushed. Stop blushing, she told herself. You're *so* not cool.

144

"I have a question," Mikey said, leaning in close enough that she could smell him. He wore some kind of cologne that wasn't Polo, the usual scent of teenage boys, and his white T-shirt was laundry-fresh. His skin was clear and smooth, his left cheekbone slightly reddened, like he'd knocked it against something. But it was his eyes that were amazing: brilliant blue, faceted like those mirrors that showed a thousand deepening reflections, as if they went on forever, all the way to the end of the hemisphere. "Are you ready for my question?"

"OK," Lise nodded. She was holding her breath.

"Actually, I have two questions. The first one's easy. Are you ready?"

"Yeah, I'm ready." Lise laughed nervously, a little too loud, the held breath snorting out her nose. I've blown it, she thought.

"If I asked you, would you go out with me? I mean, I'm seeing someone right now, but we're about to break up. And I'd like to ask you out. Like, maybe tomorrow night we could do something. We could go to a party, or we could go somewhere else. Or maybe we could get together later tonight."

"Um, I'm staying at my friend's house tonight. We're going to this party in the Donas," Lise said. "Do you know about it?"

His smile disappeared. "I don't hang out in the Jewish Alps, and neither should you."

"What?" Lise was startled; she hadn't expected him to say that. It wasn't the kind of thing she was used to hearing, and at first she didn't understand. But then she did.

"Listen, I have to go. My friends are waiting. Let me give you my number and you can call me later," Mikey said.

"I don't have a pen," said Lise.

He shrugged. "Me neither."

Then Lise remembered. "Wait, I have this." She produced the eyeliner pencil with which she'd made her eyes look bigger for the fashion show.

Mikey smiled. "Girls," he said, taking her hand to write on it. She saw then that his hand was damaged, the knuckles bulging, doubled in bulk, and towards his wrist was a tooth-sized divot, freshly scabbed. When he saw her looking at it, he pulled his hand away. "Gotta go," he said.

"What was your second question?" Lise called after him. But Mikey didn't look back. Just like the movies, she thought.

Twelve

The Rats skipped school to celebrate the last day of it. They hadn't been in all week, lingering over breakfast in Taco Bell until rush-hour traffic dwindled to the privileged, non-working moms and step-moms on their way to aerobics class. Then the Rats skated to Cashdollar's house, where they watched TV and listened to music, as usual, waiting until three o'clock when they could be released. School hours were the only freedom Ed Valencia had that week, and he wasn't about to spend them pent up inside North Hollywood High, watching his back for Mr. Dodge or FFF. Instead he pretended to go to school, observed a 5 P.M. curfew, ate a home-cooked meal followed by a little TV (sitcoms he didn't find funny), and then bed. He did it so that peace would return to his mother.

Her voice sounded the same when she addressed her children—calmer, even, than it had been for a while—but something was missing, some integral element of being, the fuse to which the lights connected. His mother's eyes looked straight out of their hollows, clicking to her children and back, skimming her ill-fitting business suit for lint and stray hairs and dandruff, her eyelids rolling up and down as she woke and slept, woke and slept and polished her shoes in front of the television so they would look new. A secretary really should buy new shoes every Saturday, to wear on Monday; all the young ones in the office did, she said.

Ed Valencia wanted his mother to scream and show her pain, slap him when he used bad language, to slam doors, hurl crockery at the walls, anything but this suffocating in her own skin. He told Kelly she should sleep on the couch and let their mother get some rest. Rest was a cure; everyone knew that. Kelly, surprising him, did, and in the morning turned over the cushion she had wet in the night. By the end of the week the living room reeked of urine and still his mother didn't react. Ed Valencia opened the windows that weren't painted shut, bought cans of air freshener with money from his own pocket: Bridal Bouquet, Kelly's favorite scent, and she sprayed it lavishly. Still not a word was said. Their mother's sense of smell had disappeared with everything else.

A whole week passed like that and then he arrived home to find Kelly dressed as Magenta, listening to *Rocky Horror* full-blast—the finale, he knew, although he wished he didn't. His bedroom had been ransacked before the record was discovered, bedclothes disturbed, drawers turned out, his own record collection rummaged, sleeves jutting at every angle, some missing their plastic dust covers. Darby Crash was frantic, sprinting in his wheel, and Ed Valencia cupped the rat carefully, smoothing down the raised hairs on his back. When Darby Crash was settled again in his nest, Ed Valencia stormed into the living room. "Jesus, Kelly, you could have just asked me for your fucking record. You didn't have to wreck my stuff. You made Darby all upset."

Kelly said, "Mom called. She has a date. Some guy from the other night, when she went to that meeting. She said don't wait up. We're supposed to order pizza or get McDonald's or something. There's money in the cookie jar. You should have heard her, Ed—she was freaking out about this guy. She's really excited."

Ed Valencia took it all in: *Rocky Horror* on the stereo, his mother out. So things were back to normal, then. Their mother had a date. She would be out late—she might not be home until morning. Ed Valencia had a vision of her getting ready for previous dates, always giddy, piling on the makeup and perfume, her swollen feet trussed in high-heeled sandals. He didn't feel much either way about his mother's dates; they never became her boyfriends.

"Are you going to *Rocky Horror* tonight?" he asked Kelly.

She shrugged, ignoring the question, concentrating instead on Frank N. Furter's final ascent to the stars and oblivion. "And crawling on the planet's face," the record said.

"Kelly, I'm talking to you. I want to know, are you going to *Rocky Horror* tonight?"

"Maybe," she answered coyly.

"Lost in time, and lost in space, and meaning," the record said.

Ed Valencia waited for the wild cheering and applause to subside, and the jokey voice that came at the end to ask, for the millionth time, "You mean I got to go home?" Kelly reached to change records, swapping side four with side one, ready to do the whole thing all over again. "Maybe you shouldn't go. Make sure Mom's OK, you know? She really went for you. It was scary. Weren't you scared?"

"She didn't hurt me. I'm not scared of Mom."

"I'm just saying she's had kind of a rough week. I want her to get better, not worse. So maybe you shouldn't upset her."

"If she's going out on a date, she's OK," Kelly said. "She couldn't go if she was sick."

"She's not *sick*."

"That's what you said."

"No, I didn't."

"That's what you *meant*."

"I meant she was upset. I just think we should, you know, behave right now. Do what she wants us to do."

"You haven't been going to school."

"What?"

"I saw you," Kelly said.

"What are you talking about? Where did you see me?"

"I saw you skating. At the river."

"What the fuck were you doing at the river, Kelly? That place is dangerous and you know it. Crazy, fucked-up people hang out there. You'll get killed."

"*You* hang out there."

"I *skate* there. It's different."

"Mom thinks you're bad. She thinks you're in trouble all the time. She thinks you and your friends make trouble and that you hide it from us. She thinks you're going to end up in jail." Kelly's face was screwed up tight, rodent-like: her mean look.

"You're full of shit."

"Am not."

"Is that what Mom thinks? Is that what she said? Well, the next time you two are talking about me, tell her I'm not going to end up in jail. Tell her she doesn't have to worry about me. Tell her I'm doing just fine. And don't forget to tell her," Ed Valencia said, his voice thick with rage, "what you've been doing at the river."

"Why don't you stick around and tell her yourself?" Kelly huffed. "You're supposed to stay with me anyway. That's what she said. She said we're both still grounded."

"Curfew. We have a curfew, we're not grounded." Grounding was for little kids.

"You're supposed to stay with me and we'll get pizza. Or McDonald's. Whatever you want," Kelly insisted.

But Ed Valencia had no plans to stick around. He wouldn't risk another night homebound, the headache-making fizz of TV in the background, time a drain down which anything, anything at all might be dumped, just to be rid of the hours—*The Cosby Show*, with its false family exuberance, the repetitive humiliations of *TV Bloopers and Practical Jokes*. Even Darby Crash seemed bored after six nights indoors, his naturally curious nose tucked into his paws. Besides, it was the last day of school. For the next three months, the Rats were rightly entitled to spend their days as hard-working skaters and punks, and tonight they would slam hard to celebrate. Ed Valencia had heard that Black Flag were playing somewhere.

Kelly stood in front of him, her small fists clenched, waiting for an answer.

"You're a little liar," he told her. "You lied about the river. I haven't been there all week." It was true; he'd spent the week in Cashdollar's bedroom—but what Kelly was doing at the river he didn't know, and he didn't care right now.

"Where are you going?" Kelly screamed. "You better not leave. I'm telling! Mom said you're supposed to stay with me!" Her loneliness was there, in that room, in his face, the stench of her bed-wetting disguised in Bridal Bouquet air-freshener spray. She was friendless, sitting around at home, and he left anyway.

Thirteen

She was dancing alone in front of the wall of mirrors at Phazes. A harlequin mix of disco lights picked her out, dividing her face into fractions. Lightning bolts, puffs of smoke, strobe, strobe, strobe. She hoped Mikey was watching. He stood with his friends along one of the railings off to the side. Trish was somewhere with her Romeo—probably out drinking in the parking lot—while Jen had disappeared with a pretty Asian boy named Victor she'd just met that night.

Lise danced to Tears for Fears and Depeche Mode and the Thompson Twins and the Go-Go's. All her bedroom practice seemed to be paying off: the glimpses she caught of herself in the mirrors, illuminated now by a revolving blue-and-white police light, showed her moving naturally, as if the music had taken over her nerve center. Lise swayed, supple as a stalk, her arms making shapes, head snapping out the beats. She could feel eyes on her and she looked at Mikey, making an invitation with her body like the finger that playfully, secretly, strokes the palm in a handshake. But Mikey was gone. His wannabe friend stood where Mikey had been, staring hard at Lise. Voyd, he said his name was, spelling it out: V-O-Y-D. He introduced himself in the parking lot, where she was waiting to meet Mikey. Last night on the phone Mikey had said he would be there at eleven, but she waited almost an hour before Voyd came up to her. Voyd told her Mikey was one of his best friends and that he was on his way, but he had some business to take care of first. In the meantime, they would hang out, she and Voyd. He was Lise's age, maybe a little older—maybe fourteen—with the usual FFF flattop, blond hair, decently tanned, the wisp of a mustache glistening on his lip. He was cute, but not as cute as Mikey. Lise liked dark-haired boys best, plus she could tell this guy was a wannabe, the way he brought up Mikey all the time. How he stayed at Mikey's house—anyone who was anyone did, Lise knew that—and how he was Mikey's right-hand man.

It was 12:30 before Mikey finally did arrive, in a big group of boys and girls. Voyd pulled him to one side to talk, heads close together, both looking very serious. Then Voyd returned to Lise. "Let's go," he said.

Lise followed him past Wolf, who waved a bunch of them in for free, Mikey at their lead. They skirted the metal detector while Wolf pretended he didn't see: being with Mikey was like being with a celebrity. Lise tried to get closer to him—he hadn't said hi to her yet, or really even looked her way. There were other girls, who had arrived in the same car, who joked and laughed familiarly with Mikey, talking about things Lise didn't understand. She didn't like them. Once inside Phazes, the group scattered, leaving Lise behind with Voyd. He kept touching her—her arms, her back, her face and hair.

Dancing now, she held up an invisible compact and

154

pretended to powder her nose. She glanced over to where Voyd stood with a group of younger boys around him— more wannabes—hoping to see Mikey back, but he wasn't there. Voyd motioned to her. Lise hesitated. Maybe he had a message from Mikey, she thought. He lifted her up and over the railing. "Hey," he said, enfolding her from behind, shaking her to the music, his lips to her ear. "Are you having a good time tonight?"

Lise tried to pull away. "No," she said.

"You're not having fun? But it's like, the last day of school. You should be totally happy." Voyd hugged her tighter. "We have to make sure you have fun tonight." He held her with one arm as his other hand pushed a bottle of Coke into her mouth.

Lise drank. It wasn't Coke, but rum, and she swallowed greedily until Voyd took the bottle away. The warm, heady feeling was instantaneous. "Poison is my potion," she said, like on TV, trying to sound sultry, trying to sound like Trish when she doused herself in the perfume she wore just for her Romeo—but Lise giggled, hearing her voice like that.

"What?" Voyd said. His tongue flickered at her earlobe, making the dangly earring—a clip-on that looked like a pierced earring—swing.

"Nothing."

Lise thought that if a slow song came on, Mikey would reappear to ask her to dance, but so far no slow songs had played. She thought about trying to find Mikey. Maybe he was waiting for her outside in the parking lot, where she knew the FFFers always drank. She glanced at Voyd. "What is it?" he asked. His hand dropped below her belly and began to trace the line of her underpants.

"Um, I need something to drink."

Voyd looked around to place the bouncers. "Not here," he said.

It wasn't what Lise had intended; she meant to escape. But Voyd was proving an obstacle—or maybe he was the way to Mikey and she'd better go along with him. She followed him to the toilets that were, like everywhere in Phazes, jam-packed with kids: making out, throwing up, fixing makeup, drinking from shared soda-pop bottles. The mirrors were glazed with smoke and steam, not giving any reflection back. Voyd pushed Lise into an empty stall, locking the door behind them. They were forced to stand close, face to face, her bare legs chilled by the sudden cool of the porcelain bowl she bumped against. "Here," he said, thrusting the Coke bottle to her mouth so that her teeth scraped the rim.

Lise drank. She drank until he took the bottle away and kissed her, vigorously exploring the whole of her mouth with his tongue. Lise, obedient, opened wider. His tongue tapped her molars, then each of the four fleshy nubs that would become her wisdom teeth, sweeping the sides of her mouth. She had never been so thoroughly kissed in her life.

After a few minutes, he pulled back and asked her point-blank, "Do you want to go somewhere?"

"Like where?" Her legs were covered in goose bumps and tingled like they were asleep. Were they really? They might be; she was losing feeling the way she always did when she drank.

"We could go to my friend's place. He lives near here. He has his own apartment. I just saw him outside—I can get the key."

The rum had liquefied her shoulders and Lise shrugged carelessly. "OK."

Voyd opened the stall door and strode out. Lise, following, grabbed at walls and railings, feeling her way because the floor, instead of being flat, had been sliced into sliding plates, colliding at all angles. Phazes was a carnival fun house, mirrors distorting everything, not a surface she could trust. "You're totally wasted," Voyd laughed, but Lise denied it with a vehement shake of her head, even as her legs gave out and he had to lift her to her feet.

They left through a fire exit that opened onto the parking lot, a door Lise had never seen before—a portal, as far as she was concerned, for that one special night. Outside, she looked around vaguely for Trish and Jen, but her eyes were unfocused, seeing twins and triplets. She tried to stay steady and smile, clinging to Voyd's hand for balance, listening to him talk. She couldn't remember anyone's name or understand what they were saying, their language coded against her, peppered with Mexican phrases, and Lise didn't speak Spanish; at school, she was studying French like Trish and Jen—what all the pretty girls signed up for, in the hopes of going to Paris someday.

And where were Trish and Jen? She kept forgetting about them, and then remembering, and then forgetting.

"Maybe you just need to lie down," Voyd suggested when she pitched forward, slipping his grasp, to land hard on her knees. If she bled, she didn't notice, nor did the blow sober her up in the least. By then she wasn't even embarrassed. She was nothing.

"OK," Lise readily agreed. "Let's go."

The door to Voyd's friend's apartment met resistance from a trash heap piled behind it, extending down the hall. The walls were decorated with tags and pornography, carpet puckered on the floor like old skin, with litter running underfoot—magazines, discarded clothing, jars of Vaseline. Voyd ventured into the horrific, unlit depths, seeming to know where he was going, and Lise followed him blindly, bumping her shoulder along the sticky walls to the kitchen, where the open refrigerator door revealed a carton of leaking eggs and some Roach Motels. She moved toward its light. "No chasers," Voyd announced. He was brandishing the Coke bottle again, in which golden rum-butter churned. Lise's stomach tossed with the bottle, but she nodded anyway, forcing down the syrup—and keeping it down.

Voyd grinned. "That's my girl. You know how to party." He kicked shut the fridge door and left the room. She heard him saying, somewhere in the dark, "Everyone will be back here in a couple of hours, after Phazes. We always come back here. Pigpen's parents rent it for him. They live in Africa. His dad's a diplomat. He's like, related to Ronald Reagan."

Lise remembered Mikey then. He would be here later, she was sure. She could still talk to him. There was time, the rest of the night, because she was staying at Trish's house and Trish's mom didn't care. Mikey had a question for her. When they met at the Galleria, he told her he had two questions and he only asked her one. What did he want to ask? She would marry him, yes, of course, definitely, totally. She would say yes to anything he asked.

"Hey," Voyd called.

She found him in the bedroom, where a purple lava lamp oozed on the shelf above his head. The bed, when she tumbled down next to him, gave way like freshly dug earth, swallowing her. Too soft, Lise giggled, thinking of Goldilocks. Then Voyd was on top, and over his shoulder the room spun. She closed her eyes. Their clothes came off— she was surprised by how deftly her fingers worked the button-fly of his jeans and the strength in her arms when she lifted off his T-shirt. Now they were in their underwear, as far as she had ever gone with a boy. Voyd was lean, his limbs well knit, chest smooth as wax, with a deep bowl where his ribs and breastbone met. He unfastened her bra, his mouth a sucker on her nipples, first one, then the other, alternating until she was dizzy and not sure where the sensation was coming from. His fingers probed the elastic of her underpants, then dove inside and fastened on the curls of flesh, rubbing at furious speed. His breathing was regular but hers was ragged. Where was his underwear? Somehow he'd slipped it down without her noticing, and then hers was gone, too, floating around one ankle, marooned very far from the rest of her.

It was happening. Instinctively, Lise wrapped her legs around him to hold on. He was a rocking boat, a boat in which people were having sex, his rocking exaggerated, cartoonish, and yet this was very serious business: Lise was losing her virginity, fast, pierced by an isolated pain—and that was it. Voyd reached over the side of the bed and came up with a damp, foul-smelling towel he offered to wipe her with.

Next thing she knew, there was a lot of noise and she roused to see Voyd dressing himself. He told her to get dressed but she needed help, her limbs still dumb with rum. Sitting, she slumped; standing, she nearly fell. "Come on, get it together," he said, sounding impatient now, at her feet tying her Reeboks in clumsy bows. "Do you need to go home?"

Lise shook her head and tipped over, just missing the bed.

"Where are your friends?" he asked, roughly pulling at her arms.

Lise didn't know where her friends were. She squinted into the distance, as if she could see them there, emerging from parked cars, their lips inflamed from kissing, hair freshly brushed, eyes dreamy with pleasure. "Don't know," she mumbled.

"I'll find someone to take you home. What's your address?"

Her answer was automatic, like she had been drilled in kindergarten, and Lise rolled onto her side, wishing for sleep before she threw up. Voyd pulled the bedroom door shut behind him, sealing the room to cook in its own juices. It was hot in there, too hot. There was no window, only the door, behind which she could hear people passing back and forth. She must get up and join them. She would find Mikey—she had to ask him something. Who was the teacher at North Hollywood High who bought beer for kids? What was his name again? Mikey had told her last

160

night. That question was bothering her, she would say. She would get up in a minute. Lise rolled to her other side and found oblivion in three deep breaths of the fetid air.

The next time she woke, Voyd had a big man with him. He was telling the big man where she lived. "No," Lise said. "I don't want to go home."

"You're wasted," Voyd said.

"I'm not. I feel much better," said Lise. She felt a floating lightness, her legs fizzing where they'd fallen asleep because of the way she dropped onto the floor. She hit out at her legs, missing them completely, and laughed.

But Voyd didn't look happy—he didn't think she was funny. "You can't stay. I'm leaving anyway." He looked at the big man. "Come on, we're leaving."

The big man, who didn't say a word, picked up Lise and slung her casually over one shoulder. A car waited outside at the curb, into which she was folded. Voyd was coming in a minute. There was another party to go to, she knew that. Another party. FFF always knew where the parties were. Mikey was waiting for her there, and Voyd was coming now, he was on his way. Lise drifted off—and caught herself suddenly. She sat up. Something was not right. The big man was beside her now, behind the wheel, starting the car, and Voyd wasn't there. The big man was driving away with her. It was just like the newspaper said: she would be raped and killed. She would be left on a hillside for the coyotes. Her parents would never find her. She would be on the milk cartons at school. Lise began to shout, "Mikey! Mikey, help!"

"Shut up. You want to wake the whole neighborhood?"

"Help me, Mikey!"

"I said shut up," the big man yelled back.

Lise tried to open her car door, but it was locked. She fumbled the button, her fingers useless, drunk. She was so drunk.

"I'm taking you home," the big man insisted.

"I want to go home," Lise wailed. "Mikey, I want to go home."

"What the fuck do you think I'm doing?" The big man drove fast, tailing the car in front of him—he was too close, too close, and Lise felt loose in the car. She was flying around like a burst balloon. Then something clicked in her head and she was senseless again, her head lolling on the window frame. She woke—only just—when she felt the scrape of cement on her back, before her head found a softer spot in the crook of one arm, and Lise slept.

Fourteen

The hilly streets and canyon drives of L.A. were too profuse, too enticing to be ignored, with curves like a loop-de-loop, even if they were full of potholes and cars. Ed Valencia led the Rats slaloming downhill, imagining gates to slide through, catching air on curb-cut moguls. His black T-shirt was a billowing pirate's sail. Ed Valencia aimed for the lampposts that would illuminate the Rats to drivers, zigzagging between light pools the color of firefly guts. They joined a procession of black-and-white stretch limousines on the Sunset Strip, traveling the barrel of the pistol that was West Hollywood past the dollar-green acres of the Los Angeles Country Club, the blazing hi-rises of Century City (once a movie lot, now a pristine alternative to Downtown), then on past the Mormon Temple and its gold-leaf angel astride the temple's hilltop summit, more cocktail lounge than place of worship. Ed Valencia's legs burned with hard work; behind him the Rats were tired, calling out to him to stop and rest, get a Coke, maybe find a spot to try some tricks. But Ed Valencia was chasing something, every corner turned giving him hope that he was almost there.

The moment before he struck the curb outside the Nuart, Ed Valencia drove his foot down onto the skateboard's tail, pulling up short. Nevertheless, Kelly screamed like she had been struck, dropping her bag of props (rice, newspapers, water pistol, flashlight, rubber gloves, confetti, toilet-paper roll, unbuttered burnt toast, and party hat). "What are you doing here?" she demanded.

Ed Valencia didn't really know. Ever since he'd left the apartment that afternoon, he'd had a feeling, more like a headache, that seemed to have begun its brief career worrying about Kelly. She was too little to be wandering L.A. on her own, especially at night. He should have stayed at home with her. In the last week, something had changed—there was some threat to his existence, in which he'd previously ignored his family and gone about his own business. Now here he was to save Kelly. "What are *you* doing here? What did I tell you? Don't you ever listen to me?"

"I don't have to listen to you. You're not my father. You can't tell me what to do."

Kelly stood with a middle-aged Janet and Brad, flanking her one on either side, and Brad spoke up, crying in a high voice, "What do you want?"

"Come on, Kelly. We're going home," Ed Valencia said.

"No way," she said, glaring at him. "Leave me alone. Go away."

"Yeah, leave her alone," Brad echoed. He was scrawny and pale, like all the other Brads, dressed in a tuxedo and red plaid cummerbund, wearing old-fashioned horn-rimmed glasses. "Go on, leave her alone."

He was all mouth, thought Ed Valencia. "Kelly, come on. Let's get out of here." One by one, the other Rats were banging into the curb, swooping in like parachuters: one, two, three, four, enough backup for a war.

"What's going on, Valencia?" Bones said.

Kelly moved closer to Janet, who encircled her protectively with one arm. "I want to go to the show. You can't stop me."

"She wants to go to the show," Janet repeated.

"Yeah, she wants to go to the show," said Brad.

"She's not going. She's coming with me. I'm taking her home. *We're* taking her," Ed Valencia said—although how they would get there, he wasn't sure. He hadn't thought that far ahead. They would have to take the bus or something, he guessed. Bones' Malibu was stranded at his dad's place in Long Beach, where it wouldn't start.

"She's been waiting all week for tonight. We'll take care of her. She always sits with us," Janet said, her voice softer, more reassuring than before.

Ed Valencia studied the couple. He couldn't be sure how old they were. Janet's eyes were hooded with tired skin, her teeth flashing gold everywhere in their molars, one long front tooth chipped, gray and dead. Brad's cummerbund had wiggled to the gully above his paunch, his five o'clock shadow more silver than black, ventriloquist's dummy lines etched deep on either side of his mouth. Now Brad had his hand on Kelly's head and Ed Valencia saw a brand-new gold wedding band.

Kelly said, "These are my friends, Melanie and Sam.

They got married here a couple of weeks ago. I was the flower girl."

Cashdollar snorted, picturing this: Kelly in hot pants and tap shoes, gracelessly plowing down the aisle, gawky legs outrunning the rest of her, an accident waiting to happen—and Janet and Brad, dregs of the high-school marching band, united in matrimony under the winking eye of their god, *Rocky Horror*. All the Rats laughed.

"Your sister is like a daughter to us," Janet explained. "We've practically adopted her. We always sit together." Kelly looked pleased, hearing this.

"Our mom's waiting. She told me to get Kelly and bring her home," Ed Valencia said.

But Kelly smelled the lie. "Mom's not even there. She's out on a date." Her jaw squared stubbornly. "I want to stay. You can't make me go."

"We'll take care of Kelly," Janet said. "Really. You don't have to worry. She always sits with us. Don't you, hon?"

Kelly nodded and snuggled against Janet. "I'm not leaving. I'm staying with Melanie and Sam."

The Rats flanked Ed Valencia, skateboards dawdling at their feet. They were watching him to know what to do next—how far they should take things. "Kelly's coming with us. We came to take her home," Ed Valencia said.

"How? On your skateboards?" Kelly spat with all the outrage an eleven-year-old could muster. "I don't want to go with your weirdo friends."

The Rats laughed. "Weird? Who are you calling weird?"

"At least we're ourselves," said Bones. "Not dressed up like some dumb movie character."

"At least we listen to decent music," Cashdollar rounded out.

"We've given her rides home before," said Brad. "Someone always gives Kelly a ride."

"Is that right?" Ed Valencia said, looking at Kelly. She nodded. "You're pretty stupid, Kelly, getting in cars with strangers. You're a lot dumber than I thought."

"We're not strangers. Everyone here loves Kelly. No one would hurt her. She knows that, don't you, hon?" Kelly looked up at Janet and beamed her assent. Ed Valencia had rarely seen her smile so big and strong, and never at home. Never for their mother at home. "Kelly knows that everyone here is her friend. That's why she comes. That's why we all we come to *Rocky Horror*."

Brad looked at his watch. "Time for the late-night double-feature picture show, people." The line of moviegoers began to flow forward, undulating and bubbling, a colorful waterline that snaked inside the theatre doors and threatened to carry off Kelly for good.

"Kelly," Ed Valencia warned.

Janet hesitated. "I don't know. Maybe Kelly should go with her brother."

Encouraged, Ed Valencia reached out for his sister's hand. He hadn't held her hand since she was a little girl and afraid of everything—dogs, men with mustaches, the dark (begging him to her bedside when their mother worked the night shift), sea gulls, thunder, Pop Rocks, spiders. She had clung to him then, when the world was all new, almost all terrible, already lonely.

"No!" Kelly shrieked. "I won't go with him!" She

pushed for the front of the line and disappeared inside the Nuart, leaving Ed Valencia empty-handed.

"Help me," he called to the Rats, who pounced—too late: a human barrier had gone up, a surprise snarl of flesh and costumes and props to hold them back while Janet and Brad made their escape, joining Kelly inside. "That's my sister! She's my fucking sister!" Ed Valencia thrashed against his pinned arms, but the Rats were outnumbered.

"Better luck next time," a middle-aged Frank N. Furter jeered, while Rocky, his monstrous sexual creation, squirted a loaded water pistol in their faces, shooting all the way, the last to retreat inside the theatre. Then the Nuart doors were locked, the usher standing guard with an air of importance about him, like a thug.

Jeff Air wiped his face. "Thanks a lot, Valencia."

"What the fuck just happened?" Cashdollar asked, looking stunned.

"That really wasn't funny. Those guys were *tickling* me," Bones said, catching his breath.

"Those guys looked like a bunch of sissies, but they weren't. They definitely were not," Pellet Head said.

"There were girls in there, too, you know," said Jeff Air. "We just got beat up by girls."

"What the fuck did we come here for anyway?" Pellet Head said, sounding angry. "We skated a hundred miles for this?" Behind the Nuart doors, the usher grinned at them. Pellet Head gave him the finger.

But Ed Valencia didn't hear what his friends said; he was thinking about Kelly, sandwiched between Janet and Brad

168

in the dark theatre, near the back—in the back row, probably, at the very end of the row, by the wall, with no way
out, another wall at her back. He was imagining the worst
possible things.

Fifteen

As she slept, her mouth opened and closed on the words: things are all wrong. Things are all wrong. It was not a peaceful sleep; it was a blackout. One hand gripped the rough corner of the front step, wearing a burn into her palm that, in the morning, she wouldn't know where it came from, likewise the rasher stripped from her shin and the flag of skin lifted from her left elbow. But the soreness of other parts, specifically her privates, she would immediately understand. Lise had guessed how it would feel, grinding a stuffed animal (a seal, sometimes an elephant) between her legs at night. Finally doing it for real hurt, but was not so terrifying as she had thought. It wasn't *terror*. She would not let it trouble her, consciously. Her subconscious was another matter.

Cars streamed past, but not many, stirring a breeze for which Lise's hot sleeping skin was grateful. A nurse sped to a dawn operation, a night-shift worker returned for dinner—he ate breakfast at 3 P.M., when he woke. A handful of college students drifted in, home for the summer, all of whom made it upstairs to their beds without encountering parents, where they became mounds of bedclothes, piles of dirty laundry, smells, shed dead skin cells, knots of hair.

No one saw the girl asleep or heard what she had to say: all wrong, all wrong, words she chewed like gum.

The distant stars had begun to fade, never at rest, but withdrawn during the day. The few birds that roosted in the neighborhood trees roused themselves to a pathetic chorus that sounded like, "Coffee, more coffee, please." Lise didn't care about stars at her age (although she occasionally read, and believed, her star sign—Libra—forecast in two-dollar scrolls at 7-Eleven). She didn't care if the moon bloomed or waned, or if birds were driven out of the area by production-line-style suburban expansion. She had once cared, and would care again, but not now, not at thirteen, an age inspired by how she *felt* but contradicted by how she thought she *should* feel and what she wanted to feel now, not later, when she was old enough. *Now.*

The flow of blood to the hand that cradled her cheek had slowed, the hand numb, seemingly stubbed of fingers and touch, the skin puckered white where drool soaked it. As mattresses went, the step was not bad: hard, certainly, but familiar, and swept clean—not the worst bed she had slept on that night. At least the pillow, with its soggy case, was her own.

It was just after five on a Saturday morning. The paperboy's radio was telling him the day would be hot, at least a hundred in the Valley. The paperboy was also asleep, but soon his mother would come into the room and jerk back the covers, making him jump. They ran the air-conditioning so high in his house that he slept with three blankets, and the heat outside, where his papers awaited him on the driveway, felt hotter than it actually was.

171

If the paperboy, with his untidy bed-head, crusty eyes, constant wheeze, and potbelly (a baggy Lakers' T-shirt hiding its deep, distended navel), happened to deliver on time that morning, then Lise could be carried inside with the paper before her shame was discovered by the rest of the street. If the paper was late, as it more often was, neighbors would see her prone, strewn body, one leg here, the other there, like scattered pieces of seashell, and the surprise, the beachcomber's treasure: the pearly pink shine of her female secret, the blush-colored whorl, no longer whole.

The paperboy's mother had reached the door to his room. The hall light burned and he saw, through her thin nightgown, the twin rings of Saturn and the wild thatch of no-man's-land below where his father no longer traveled, having left the family some years ago. The paper boy turned away, not wanting to see, never wanting to face the day. Outside, a motorbike growled down the street, its driver chortling at the noise he made, and for a moment birdsong ceased. A lamp blinked on, then off again. Lise stirred briefly with a small sigh, a creak of her knee, and re-entered sleep at a new junction, slipping down a just-paved road in a foreign country that could not even be called a country. The signposted words crashed through her brain. She read them aloud, one billboard at a time: Things. Are. All. Wrong. What was reality and what was dream, she didn't know for sure.

Sixteen

Ed fingered the blade. He didn't particularly want to die. His jaw throbbed—he might die from this toothache, he thought. Carefully he touched his tongue to the broken molar, releasing pain meteor-bright, a flash of pain trailed by lesser pain, fizzling out. He cleaned his fingernails with the blade, cowboy-style, peeling off curls of dried blood, then set the knife aside before he made a promise he knew, deep down, he didn't really want to keep. His mother wasn't there to save him, and neither was his sister. Ed had been relieved, when he got home, for a kitchen in which to prepare an ice pack without drawing comment, a bathroom door he could leave open, too tired and sore to wrestle with the warped plywood, a poor fit for its ramshackle frame. For the first time in a long time, he had the apartment to himself, and all he wanted to do was sleep. He lay back on his bed and closed his right eye, the left being already swollen shut. His pain was a box around him, smaller than his room, much smaller—so tight.

After the scene at the Nuart, the Rats ended up at someone called Puppet's garage, whose parents were out of town. A couple of Valley bands had congregated there, just high-school kids messing around, borrowing each other's instruments, but a show was a show: a two-car garage with sixty bodies, plus a family of ten-speed bicycles and a lawnmower, was a show. Ed didn't care how bad the band was (the noise of a crowd could have a tune in it), he was ready to go berserk. The music was hacking at him and he was hacking right back, pushing for all he was worth, when he backed into a strong pair of arms which tightened around his chest. Even as he struggled and his feet left the ground, Ed thought it might be one of the Rats, messing around.

"You thought we forgot? Is that what you thought? FFF don't forget."

Inside his box of pain, Ed heard his own breathing loud in his ears, and felt it, too, in the ache of damaged muscle, the blood-thickened lining of his nose. To nurse himself, he would find an easy, safe place from his childhood and revisit it. Ed tried to remember the house they had lived in as a family, when his dad was still around. The house was supposed to be pink stucco, but he remembered it as gray cardboard and two-dimensional, a collapsed matchbox, small enough to hold in his hand. When he looked through the front door, he could see the backyard, the wire-mesh fence that should have been fifty feet back but was right there, with nothing—no family, no square of sunlit green, no paddling pool or sandpit for baby Kelly—nothing to pen in and protect. Really, there was nothing there. His hand was empty.

Was there another place he could go? A place like where his father lived, a hermit's hole? The pain in his jaw was incredible, a drill that went too deep. Quick, Ed thought, somewhere else.

He rode bikes everywhere as a kid, before he could skate. He didn't always have a direction; he just rode. He had a brown secondhand ten-speed from Kmart, its black vinyl seat cracked like the belly of a beached whale two days in the sun, with a rusty bell—more scratch than chime—and rainbow-colored straws in the spokes of his wheels that his mother put in to make the bike more cheerful. Ed, in his box, climbed onto the bike and pedaled off, looking around at the beautiful sights: the proud, well-kept houses decked with lights that had nothing to do with Christmas; the fountains that flung silver to the sky; plumes of bougainvillea and uniform grass spears, every last one at attention, awaiting further orders. The streets these properties flanked were safe and quiet, religiously policed—indeed, were everything promised their owners as buyers of dreams. Peace was there. Home was a mellow resting place, for those who could afford it, and riding those streets, Ed's breathing gentled, breaths coming at greater intervals from deep within. He began to feel he might sleep.

But he wasn't free. Someone else was in the room, standing over him, extending the blade. He was too afraid to look. "Who is it?" he asked the room, his voice muffled by the box, his toothache, the distorted lines of his tumid face.

"Ed? Eddie, is that you?" His mother's voice was shrill. She didn't sound like his mother, but a ghoul. If she was in the room, she was somewhere near the ceiling, perched on a broom. He opened his eyes. The blade flashed—who held it now? Half-dreaming, Ed saw the knife in his hand, and then it was snatched from him. "What are you doing? What happened to you?" his mother shrieked.

"Get out!" he cried, sitting up in bed. "Get out of here!"

Then she was gone, running from the room in terror, or excitement—Ed didn't know. Was he really trying to kill his own mother? Someone had tried to kill *him*, that's what happened. Someone beat him black and blue, and now he was back at home, where he should have been safe.

He needed to check the doors and windows. He needed to know his family were there before he could sleep.

In the living room, Kelly slept on the couch, still dressed in *Rocky Horror* regalia, her tap shoes in her lap. When had she come home? Ed hadn't heard anything. The curtains were drawn; the light inside was mud. The kitchen clock read noon. The door was locked, the windows sealed with paint, most of them.

He pushed open the door to his mother's room. "Mom? Okay if I sleep with you?" he asked, his voice ringing out plaintively, shuffling his feet while he waited for her reply.

She hesitated, but only for a moment, then opened up her arms. "Come here. Give me a hug. Tell me what happened. Your face—it's terrible."

"Just got beat up," Ed murmured. "It's not that bad." He slipped between the covers, snaking his hand underneath the mattress as he did, to be sure: no knife.

"Terrible, terrible." She stroked the hair away from his forehead, then circled the goose egg at his temple, daubing a scrape with the wet pad of her finger to lift out the grit.

"I'll call the doctor later. Did you use ice? Did you take an aspirin?"

Ed nodded. "My teeth," he said, wincing.

"I'll call the dentist. He'll see you first thing tomorrow," his mother promised, as if she really could do this, as if she were so important—as if she believed in magic. Ed hadn't had a dental checkup since he was twelve, when his mother deemed his teeth perfectly healthy, every one in its right place, to save on bills.

"Thanks, Mom." He was drowsy enough to sleep through the pain. He was thinking of nothing but how tired he was, how good to sleep. He would sleep for a long time, for days. It was summer vacation—school was out—and he didn't have to wake until he was ready.

Just before he drifted off, his mother whispered, "I think I'm in love."

Ed didn't think anything of it. She always said that after a date. She clasped his hand and held it tightly, humming a *Rocky Horror* refrain.

Seventeen

First Lise's mother threatened to call the police. Then she
wanted to take Lise to the hospital for an examination—
better yet, go straight to the rape-crisis center, as her
daughter had obviously been raped. What thirteen-year-old
girl would consent to sex?

Four hours had passed since the paperboy rang the door-
bell, alerting her parents to Lise asleep on the front step.
Now Lise, who had twice tried to abscond to her room, was
kept at bay by her mother endlessly circling the still life of
daughter, kitchen table, fruit bowl, and chair, making the
linoleum creak in the same place over and over. Lise wanted
to plug her ears; she was trying to think about Mikey. What
was he doing right now? Was he even awake? She wanted
to call him—but he was probably still asleep. It was only
like, ten o'clock in the morning. She could call him at lunch-
time, pretend she was just awake, tell him she went to
another party last night. That's right. That's why she left so
early. And his friend Voyd was really nice, but—or maybe
she wouldn't even bring up Voyd. Not unless Mikey did.

"You were supposed to be sleeping at Trish's," her
mother was saying. "You told me you were staying with
her while her mother was away. You said you and Trish

were going to the movies, but that was obviously a lie. So what else don't I know? What else is a lie?"

There were so many things. Modeling at the Galleria, to begin with. Hitchhiking with Jen, stealing from their friends, riding in cars with boys, wearing makeup. Every beer she had drunk in her life, every bong hit or joint smoked, the R-rated movies she had managed to see, tests she had cheated on, the rock star she promised to blow when he whistled at her from his limousine window. There were the dirty letters she wrote to Mikey, unsent, but sitting in her box of secrets under the bed, so easily found and read. There was a box of chocolate-flavored laxatives for when she felt fat. Lise even lied about what she ate for lunch at school, declaring a healthy ham sandwich and plain milk instead of the hamburger, corn chips, Coke, and ice-cream cone she usually had, except when she and Jen were on diets, when they stuck to Iceberg lettuce doused with Thousand Island dressing. And diets—her mother didn't approve of diets, so Lise had to lie about *that*. "So I lied. So what? I had to. You *made* me. You never let me do anything. Like, my friends can do what they want and I can't do *anything*."

"You see your friends more than you see your dad and me."

"I hang out with my friends because you guys fight all the time. I can't stand to be around you. Did you ever think of that?"

"Don't turn this back on me, Elise. You *lied* to stay out all night and get drunk, and for all I know, this isn't the first time."

Lise covered her ears with her hands; she couldn't take any more of this—this—this *harassment*. Her father had driven off with the paper to a coffee shop somewhere, to get away from the noise of their fight. She didn't blame him. Lise had already downed six aspirin. Her head *killed*, plus she was trying not to look at her mother's nose: a recurring pimple was back, nestled into the crack where nostril met cheek, a zit that looked like it was about to pop. If it popped, Lise would definitely barf. Once, in a restaurant, while ordering her meal—right in front of the waiter—Mrs. Anderson's nose had twitched and this zit, the same zit—but Lise couldn't think about it or she really would be sick.

"Whoever it was, they just left you there. They didn't care. They didn't ring the bell or knock at the door, just left you lying on the front step. Don't you know about the Night Stalker, Lise? You could have been raped. You could have been *murdered*. You were lying there for anyone to take." Her mother banged shut the microwave door, a damning blow, to reheat a cup of coffee. "And you weren't wearing any underwear!"

Lise flushed. Every time her mother said that, she went red in the face—and her mother had mentioned it at least a dozen times. It was true Lise hadn't been wearing underwear, or, for that matter, her own clothes. The shirt was too big, the skirt too small, both of inferior material and style to what she had borrowed from Trish to wear out last night. At least she had been wearing her own shoes, expensive Reeboks laced so tightly that even now, hours later, she still had shoelaces stamped into the thin, itchy skin on top of both feet.

"This is what I can't understand. This is what I keep going over and over in my head. I'm shocked, Lise. I think it's disgusting. Why weren't you wearing underwear? Did he want to keep it as some kind of sick trophy? Who was it, Lise? You've got to tell me. I need to know so I can *do* something," her mother begged.

"Um, what's the Night Stalker?"

"What's the Night Stalker? What's the Night Stalker? What's wrong with you? The Night Stalker has been raping and killing women in the Valley this whole year! The Night Stalker is the reason we lock our windows and doors! The Night Stalker is *hunting* women. Honey, listen to me: every woman is vulnerable." The microwave blared—beep— end—beep—and Lise's mother reached for her coffee cup, wrapping both hands around it as if it could warm her through.

Mrs. Anderson was at her best when she was on the warpath. She was generally frustrated and seeking revenge, but when she had reason, when she felt justified and was guaranteed a captive audience, her tirades were pure theatre. Caffeine possessed her, and Lise's mother loved coffee, especially on a Saturday when she could drink, at her leisure, a whole pot. This was her *second* pot, and Lise could see her mother's hands trembling and the coffee churning in the cup, could hear the tremor in her voice. Her mother picked up a kitchen towel and wiped her brow, her neck, her meager, neglected décolletage. Lise waited for her to speak. Her mother opened her mouth, closed it, opened it again. "I want to understand you, Elise. I really do. And for me to do that, you need to tell me what happened last night, OK? Did someone *hurt* you?"

Like Lise was going to answer this. Her mother had uniquely failed to understand her all these years, so to talk about sex now would be absurd, even if it might be the crux at which their relationship flowered: Lise finally old enough to understand the way men worked, the way her mother understood. She never stood a chance, her mother would tell her. Sorry, that's just the way things were, and would be, forevermore. Any woman who thought otherwise (her mother laughing by now, but her eyes were black ice, absolutely lethal), the old wives who said don't sweat the small stuff, or for that matter the big-time crimes, who said drink with a husband who drinks, and all that bullshit about the Sisterhood making things better—well, said Lise's mom, it was like giving to the Church: you think you're going somewhere with it, someplace great, but really, going nowhere. Nothing would change. No one was right about women—not the old wives, not the Sisterhood, not least Lise's very own self, sitting there like a target—the way Lise's mom was right about men. All men were bastards. Most men hated women anyway. Lise would learn. She would learn the nasty way. Life is shit—especially if you're a woman—and then you die.

"I wasn't raped," Lise finally answered.

"What do you mean, you weren't raped?"

"I like him. I wanted to do it. I liked it," Lise said, even though she remembered very little about last night.

"Who's *him*? What's his name? You have to tell me, Elise," her mother insisted, her hands shaking desperately. "I'm your mother. I have a right to know these things."

"I'm not telling."

"What?"

"Can I go now? Because I have a headache."

"I could have told you not to do it," her mother said, looking like she might cry. "I never thought you'd even be thinking about sex at your age."

"I'm thinking about it."

"If you won't tell me, then when he calls, whoever he is, I'm going to tell him you can't speak, because you're grounded, Elise. You're grounded *indefinitely*."

Lise was silent, taking this in. She was always being grounded, but now was different. Now she had a reason to go out: she had to see Mikey again. She couldn't be grounded on the first day of summer vacation, not when Mikey liked her—if he still did, that is, after she slept with his friend and passed out drunk and went home before everyone else. She had to see Mikey today or she would lose him; there were so many other girls he could choose, girls whose mothers let them do whatever they wanted. "I don't have to be grounded, you know. You can't force me to stay here."

"I can until you're eighteen."

"No, you can't. You can't make me do anything. Because I could just leave. I could run away." Lise had never said this before. She had thought it, certainly, and thought of saying it many times. The worst thing a kid could do was

183

make their parents wonder if they were alive or dead, with no word to ease their minds.

"The police will bring you back," her mother warned. "You'll only be grounded longer. You'll be grounded all summer, and that's not a threat, Elise. That's a promise. You can bank on it."

"Not if the police can't find me," Lise taunted.

"*I'll* find you."

"You don't know where I go. You don't know *shit* about my life." Lise stood up. "You don't know anything. You're stupid."

"Sit down! I haven't finished."

"Fuck you!" Lise yelled back at her mother—she was in so much trouble that swearing didn't make a difference anymore—and punched the kitchen wall, which gave way to her fist with an underwhelming "poof" and fluff of dust, nothing worth choking on. The wall was paper and air. Shocked, Lise's mother dropped her coffee cup, snapping off its handle, coffee dregs peppering her ankles, the linoleum, the white refrigerator door and cupboards. She looked like she didn't know what to do, and so bent to the mess on the floor, jelly thighs squeezing out of her shorts in purple lumps and marmalade swirls. Lise seized her escape, tearing off out the back door, around the side of the house, down the driveway, and on down the street—never mind her bare feet and that she still wore the awful clothes of the night before. She had no money, no bag of necessary things, no makeup or tapes or clean underwear or her favorite pillow. She was light, so light, with nothing to carry, her arms free to pump at her sides. She was running—she was running harder than ever, a five-minute mile, maybe four. She had trained for this moment all those weeks with Jen, running for Robo and his car. Her lungs burned, the soles of her feet tore on the tarmac, but she didn't stop, nor did she look back. She thought of neither future nor past. She just ran.

She ran to Milliken, the school desolate out of season, but no line for the pay phone, and there was her tag by the coin slot—hot pink lipstick—reassuringly familiar, the mark of who she really was. Trish answered on the fourth ring. She sounded sleepy when she accepted Lise's collect call at the operator's request. "Did I wake you?" Lise's throat was dry, asking.

"Not exactly."

Lise heard rustling sheets, murmuring. Trish was with her Romeo. "Um. I totally had a killer fight with my mom just now," Lise began.

"Hold on a sec." More murmuring, the double snap of a Zippo, then Trish dragged dramatically on a cigarette. "OK. Wait, like, where did you go last night? Jen and I waited forever at Phazes. You totally bailed on us. That's *so* not cool. We waited in the parking lot until almost three o'clock, way after everyone left. We thought something happened to you. I like, couldn't even call your house because your mom thought you were with me."

"I went to this guy's place. That's kind of the reason I'm calling—"

"You were so drunk, Lise. Everyone said. You know

what you're like when you're drunk. You just forget about everyone else. You totally zone out."

"Wait, what am I like?"

"You're like, a total space cadet. You don't know *what's* going on. You don't connect."

"I don't? Really?"

"Really. Really, really. It's sad."

"I don't mean to. I didn't know." Lise blushed, despite that she was alone.

"Well, you should work on it. It's totally lame."

Lise listened to Trish smoke for a minute before she said, "So my mom like, freaked out when I got home, screaming at me and stuff and saying I was grounded and that she was like, going to call the police because she thought some guy raped me."

"What?"

"I had sex with this guy but she thought he raped me."

"You had *sex*? I knew it! I knew you would do it! I knew you wouldn't wait!" Trish hooted. "Ohmigod, did you tell Jen? Wait, what *guy*? That guy from the mall?"

Lise's heart sank. She had always said she would hold out for Mikey. When she first woke that morning—when her mother dragged her from the front step to the living-room floor—she had even thought it was Mikey who had taken her underwear and left her for the Night Stalker. At least for a few minutes, she thought it was Mikey, but it was Mikey's friend, not Mikey. Blond hair. Smaller, younger. She couldn't remember his face, but his name had stuck, spelled out into her hand with his fingertip like she was blind. "It was just some guy."

"Who?"

"His name's Voyd."

"What?"

"Voyd. It's like, a totally weird name. He made it up, I think."

"That's so dumb."

"He's OK. I mean, he's cute and stuff. He's fine." Lise hoped she was right. She didn't want to talk about it now. She didn't want to celebrate sex with Voyd. Maybe she shouldn't even have told Trish about having sex with him, except she had to tell Trish—she needed her help. "Listen, can I come over?"

Trish didn't say anything, just dragged on her cigarette.

"Can your mom come get me? I'm at Milliken."

Trish exhaled loudly. "She's not here. She's with Alexis's dad in Palm Springs. You know, you can't just come over whenever you want."

"I ran away and I need somewhere to stay, Trish. I thought I could stay with you tonight, and then I'm going to ask Mikey if I can stay with him. His mom's supposed to be cool. They always have a bunch of kids living with them," Lise explained.

"You ran away?"

"My mom's totally nuts. You know what she's like."

"You really ran away? That's so not cool, Lise. I mean, it's going to change everything," Trish said.

"What do you mean?"

"You're going to be like, this homeless girl. You'll get all dirty and your hair will be horrible. You'll smell. You'll be like, wearing the same pair of Reeboks every day. Your

teeth will fall out. You'll have claws instead of fingernails."
Trish was laughing. Lise wanted to cry—she *was* crying.
Her feet hurt, shredded raw like hamburger from the street.
She thought she heard someone coming and she wanted to
hide herself. No one could see her like this. It was bad
enough what the paperboy had seen—he went to Milliken.
What if Mikey found out? What if he saw what she was
wearing? Trish would have to see, and her Romeo, if he
was driving, but she would make them swear not to tell
anybody. "Look, can you guys just come and get me? I
know Jason's there. He has a car."

"Did you call Jen?"

"No, I called you first."

"Good."

"So are you guys coming?" Lise asked for the last time.

Eighteen

Be cool, hang out, and don't say shit. Fuck social values. Be yourself, live your own life. Fight for freedom.

Voyd was Mikey's right-hand man, his little brother, the way Mikey was to Ranger when he was thirteen, when Ranger jumped him into FFF. Ranger was long gone—all the older, famous FFFers had disappeared, some of them in jail, others with the LADS now, some even married with kids. Now it was up to Mikey and Voyd to run things and keep FFF's ideals intact, calling out anyone who dared to challenge their authority on the punk scene, at school, on the street, at the mall, the clubs, the shows. Voyd, like Mikey and Ranger before him, was quickly becoming a hero to the younger boys joining FFF by the dozen.

He had been staying at Mikey's off and on all year, whenever he had trouble at home or just didn't want to be there anymore. Voyd's parents didn't really care what he did, and they certainly didn't want to get to know his friends. If they had cared, he couldn't hang. If they told him to be home by midnight, it was social suicide—not that his parents did try. It was the eighties, not the fifties, and they were busy living their own boring lives. They had other things to think about than kids.

If Voyd told his parents he was at Mikey's, they had a vague sense that this was fine, this was safe. They had met Mikey once or twice and he was a handsome boy, a star athlete, polite, and funny. He put parents at ease. Everyone knew it was cool at Mikey's, that his mom was cool and tried to look after the kids who stayed there. You could do what you needed to do at Mikey's, without hassle, but it was getting crowded now, with so many bodies needing space to sleep.

"Where were you in '42?" Voyd had a tape of Ranger singing FFF's fight song—a rare thing to have, considering the band hadn't played out in three years. "There was no place for Jews, people dying in the streets just because of their beliefs." He had a copy of former KKK Grand Dragon Tom Metzger's WAR book personally inscribed to FFF, telling them to keep up the good work, and when the Aryan Youth Movement distributed pamphlets in the schools in January, Voyd made sure he got one of those. He had lost his virginity to one of Ranger's old skinhead girlfriends, going skin himself for a while, his Doc Marten nine-holes laced with white, until he got picked up by the cops for fighting. From then on his parents demanded at least an inch of hair, as if hair could keep him from blowing his top. Voyd had taken a number of Mikey's hand-me-down girls as well (which, these days, was almost as good as going out with one of Ranger's), including Lise, who Mikey thought he liked for about five minutes. Mikey said Lise was a model. She was just a little kid, with about twelve pubic hairs and no tits, who cried when she talked about her mother. She was OK, nothing great—nothing like Jessica,

Mikey's new girlfriend, an absolute knockout. But Voyd knew something Mikey didn't know: Jessica had tainted blood. Her mother, who was dead, was a Jew. That's where Jessica's kinky hair came from—the very hair that Mikey loved.

"The time of the Holocaust is now—Adolf Hitler showed us how!" It was a song that stuck to his ribs. It was a song that gave him something to believe in. Voyd's parents didn't believe in anything that he knew of, beyond Ronald Reagan's happy tax policies and the possibility of an outer-space intervention of the Russian nukes (otherwise, when the bomb dropped, they'd all look like Ethiopians, their skin crisped up, black as sin). Voyd watched Tom Metzger's cable-access show, *Race and Reason*, and believed what those leaders and activists—the Holocaust-deniers, Aryan women's groups, Christian Identity, the American Nazi Party, and the World Church of the Creator—had to say. Voyd believed in free-speech rights, especially when people complained that *Race and Reason* should be taken off the air because it was offensive. He wanted to scream at them, "The First Amendment! The very first!" Voyd knew his amendments and rights. He was anti-Black, anti-gay, anti-Jew, anti-Hispanic, anti-Asian, and anti-immigrant. He was a frontline warrior for the revolutionary right, building white pride, and he would take the fight all the way.

Nineteen

As soon as she arrived at Trish's, and Trish and Romeo were safely upstairs, Lise dialed Mikey's number, which she already knew by heart. She really needed to talk to Mikey, especially after everything that had happened. Before she called, Lise rehearsed what she would say. "Mikey? It's me, Lise."

"This is Keith."

"Can I talk to Mikey?"

"He's not here right now."

Lise's stomach clenched. "Where is he?" Was he with another girl?

"I think he went somewhere with his mom."

"Um, can you tell him I called? This is Lise. I'll call back."

"Lisa. OK."

"Lise."

"What?"

"It's Lise."

"That's what I said."

Lise flipped through the TV channels, only half-watching. After fifteen minutes, she tried Mikey's house, but he still wasn't home (according to whoever answered), nor had Trish and her Romeo emerged from her bedroom. Time dragged. She tried Mikey's house again, only this time no one answered. Like a pest—insistent for what it knows it can get—she tried his number again, then again, letting the phone ring a dozen, then twenty, thirty times. Lise was convinced that Mikey was home, or at least *someone* was. She tried again: fifty-eight times the phone rang and still no one answered. They were all laughing at her. They were deliberately not picking up the phone, just to see if she would keep calling. She would. Lise was frantic. She had blown it with Mikey, obviously, and yet she couldn't stop herself picking up the phone and dialing his number until she lost count of how many times she called.

Finally a woman's voice answered—his mother, it sounded like, or somebody's mother. A grownup. "Hello?" she said, breathless.

"Is Mikey there?"

"He's right behind me. We just walked in the door. Hang on a sec."

Lise heard footsteps walking across a floor. "Hello?"

"Mikey? It's me, Lise."

"Hey."

Did he sound disappointed? Did he sound like he even remembered who she was? "I was just calling to say I got home OK last night. But I'm totally in trouble. I like, had to run away."

"Did you?" Paper bags rustled in the background at Mikey's end, cans of things thudding the countertop, a clanking of bottles, crackling cellophane, cupboards opening and closing on creaky hinges, the sound of ice cracking up like cabin fever, the hiss of a bottle top unscrewed, glug, glug, glug into a glass, then the snap-and-pop of soda on ice. Mikey gulped his drink, too thirsty, maybe, to speak.

"Yeah. I had a big fight with my mom. We always fight. She's such a bitch. She picks on me all the time about like, what I wear and what my hair looks like and like, makeup and stuff. I can't do anything right, you know? So I'm staying at my friend Trish's house. You remember her, the girl I was with after the fashion show?" Mikey didn't say anything. "She's my best friend. I think you met her before. I mean, other than me and our friend Jen, she mostly hangs out with older people. Like, a couple of her boyfriends were in college and stuff. So yeah, I'm staying here now, but I don't know how long I can stay. I don't know where I'll go."

She hoped that Mikey would offer for her to stay with him, but he didn't. He said, "That's too bad."

"Do you always get along with your mom?" Lise asked quickly, to keep the conversation going. She already knew about Mikey's mom: that she was young and understanding and *interested*, totally interested in kids. Like, you could talk to her about anything, even sex, and it wasn't embarrassing. That's what Voyd had said.

"Yeah, my mom's great. Everybody loves her."

"You're so lucky, Mikey. I mean, most people don't get along with their parents. Don't you think that's true? Like, almost everyone I know, practically, hates their parents, or at least they say so. But I really hate mine. My mom is totally evil. She never thinks I should do *anything*. I can't really talk to her about things."

"Listen, I got to go. There's a bunch of people coming over and my mom needs help with the groceries and cooking and stuff."

"Are you going to Phazes tonight?"

"I don't know."

"Because maybe we could meet there later."

"Yeah, maybe," Mikey said vaguely. "I got to go." He hung up.

Lise knew what she would do. She sneaked upstairs into Alexis's closet and borrowed an outfit: a white tube skirt and black tank top, plus metallic silver flats, stuffing the toes with toilet paper to make them fit. She showered and made up her face, ate some toothpaste, and got dressed. Then, without bothering to tell Trish, she left.

It took her more than two hours to walk to North Hollywood—her chewed-up feet blistered and aching in Trish's sister's shoes—but Mikey's apartment complex wasn't difficult to find. Lise knew she was in the right place: she could hear, from the courtyard, the fast-tempo guitars and machine-gun drumming that was Southern California hardcore. It was the music she wanted to listen to, really, that she *would* listen to now, as Mikey's girlfriend. She stood under a dripping, grumbling air-conditioning unit plugged in over the door and rang the bell of apartment four.

A woman answered. Was this Mikey's mom? She didn't exactly look like a mom—she was beautiful, with thick, dark hair to her waist and a mouth that turned up in the corners, like she was always smiling. Underneath her T-shirt, her breasts were loose, likewise flowing to her waist,

and she wore a miniskirt, like any girl, and bare feet. And
the smell of her: vanilla. The smell of baking. "Can I help
you?"

"Is Mikey here?" Lise choked, suddenly on the verge of
tears. She couldn't stop herself—she was crying. She was
always crying. If only she didn't cry so easily! Why did she
have to be such a crybaby, dragging her unhappiness around
for everyone to see?

"He's inside, honey. What's wrong? Oh, honey, come
here," Mikey's mom said, enfolding Lise in her arms.
"You're all right. That's it. Hush. Hush. You're all right."
Lise sobbed until she shuddered. She felt so sorry for
herself. Her mother had never loved her right, not like this,
never hugging her so tightly. Lise tipped her head over
Mikey's mom's shoulder and let the tears pour out. "Come
on inside now. Everyone's here. I made lasagna and there's
plenty left over. Petra is reading palms—she's telling us our
future. Don't you want to know your future?"

"I guess," Lise sniffed.

"What's your name again?"

"Lise." Lise held her breath to make the crying stop, like
when she had the hiccups.

"Lise. That's a nice name. I've never heard that name
before."

"Didn't Mikey tell you he'd met me?" Lise asked
hopefully.

"Did you two just meet?"

Lise nodded.

"Well, then. I'm Patty." Smile lines softened Patty's blue
eyes as she flashed the easy, quick smile that had put them

there. "Let's go in—it's too hot to be outside. I can't live without air-conditioning."

Lise was grateful for Patty's hand on her back, guiding her forward. There were so many people! She hadn't thought so many people would be there, who knew each other like, really well. Immediately, Lise wanted to go. She felt too outside it all. "Patty," she started to say, and ducked behind her.

But Patty was already calling, "Michael, someone to see you." Mikey sat at a dining table jammed behind the couch. At first he didn't hear his mother, the living room was so noisy and crowded, like a party, kids everywhere, slouched on every surface, filling the floor with their lengths and curled-up widths, a clutter of bodies and their further clutter of accessories: clothes and shoes, magazines, record sleeves, backpacks and bags. It was like no other home Lise had been in, with batik tapestries draped over the windows, band posters lining the walls instead of framed pictures, incense burning, huge stereo speakers like you would only see on display in an expensive hi-fi store. Furniture, mismatched and well-worn, was placed irregularly around the room, as if it were frequently shifted. The way this place was—it was like a teenager's bedroom.

"Michael," Patty called again, louder this time, to combat the blaring music.

He looked up. "What?"

"Someone to see you."

Lise stepped out from behind Patty and waved. Mikey looked surprised and then not surprised—he looked nothing, she thought. For a moment the whole room was quiet, noting the disturbance: the arrival of a new girl, as young and pretty as any of them were or had recently been. There were many girls, more girls than boys—but then it always seemed like the girls outnumbered the boys, that there were never enough boys to go around.

"We're having a meeting," Mikey said. "Sit down or something."

There was nowhere to sit that she could see, without asking someone to move over or give up their place, and Lise was too timid to ask. She really had not expected to find so many people there. Instead, she clung to Patty, following her into the kitchen where three girls were washing and drying dishes. They seemed to know where everything went in the cupboards—they seemed at home, opening and closing drawers. Patty seated herself at the tiny breakfast bar and patted the stool next to her, miraculously free, still warm from the person before. "Do you want something to drink? A Coke? Some OJ? You want some lasagna? I made plenty. I have to feed my hungry kids," she laughed.

Lise shook her head.

"You're a quiet one, I can tell. The quiet ones are the ones you've got to watch. They'll always surprise you."

"I guess," Lise said uncertainly.

"Oh, totally," Patty said, nodding. She even talked like Lise and her friends, like a Valley kid. Lise could tell her anything, she just knew it, and Patty would say the things Lise wanted to hear: that she was pretty and cool and people liked her, that running away wasn't such a terrible thing to do, that Lise was right and her mom was wrong because her mom wasn't like Patty, she didn't *understand*. Patty would say what a thing was and how it worked, like if you liked a boy and you talked once on the phone but he ignored you when you met again, and then you slept with his best friend but you didn't want to, what that meant was . . . what? What was the answer? Patty would know. Maybe she would talk to Mikey for Lise.

"You don't think my eyes are like, small?" Lise asked her. "They're kind of close together."

"No way." Patty shook her head emphatically. "You have beautiful eyes, really soulful and dreamy. I like your makeup. But, you know, you don't have to wear makeup. I don't." Lise thought Patty was the most beautiful woman she had ever seen, even more beautiful than Trish's mom, who had to wear makeup or else she just looked ordinary. Sometimes when Lise saw Mrs. Blue in the morning—or afternoon, when she usually woke up—that's what she thought: ordinary, and tired-looking, like any other mom.

Mikey's meeting was done; FFF adjourned. A dozen handsome boys with crew cuts stood up at once, unified, indivisible, absorbed in their conspiracies, ready to rule. Some left, picking up girlfriends on the way out, while somebody else changed the music: another pounding anthem of suburban teen disaffection. Mikey appeared in the kitchen. "What's up?" he said to Lise.

"Um, I just thought I'd stop by. You told me where you lived, remember? And like, all these other people are here. It's really cool." Mikey nodded. "No, it is," Lise insisted. "It totally is. It's like, the coolest place I've ever been."

"Come into my room," Mikey said.

This was way more than she had hoped for. He wanted to be alone with her! He definitely still liked her. Lise's heart soared. "OK," she said. Her smile bared her braces and made them shine in the overhead strip light, but she didn't care. Mikey liked her! Mikey from FFF *liked* her!

He led her down the briefest of halls to a small room, much smaller than her bedroom at home. A couple squirmed on top of the bed, fooling around, their shirts off, jeans unbuttoned, the girl's exposed belly rounded provocatively—or expectantly, Lise wasn't sure which. Down on the floor, sleeping bags crawled like a tangle of fishing worms. Mikey nudged one with his foot. "Get up," he said.

"What? What time is it?" The sleeping bag's lodger turned his face toward them, eyes half-sealed with sleep, his cheek pleated from the pillowcase: Voyd.

"Here she is," Mikey said, and abruptly left, pulling the door shut after him.

"Hey," Voyd croaked. "Nice to see you." He opened his arms to Lise. "Seriously, I mean it. I'm happy you're here." She knelt down—she didn't know what else to do. Voyd unzipped the sleeping bag and pulled her in. He kissed her, then the night before happened all over again.

Twenty

They were unbeatable. Anyone who called them out, FFF wasted. Even the kids from tougher neighborhoods.

Voyd may not have looked like a man, but he was a man. He fought like a man. He gave orders and they were obeyed. He was smaller and skinnier than most FFFers (small for his fourteen years, period), with muscle wrapped around his arms and legs like cord, and in his small frame was gathered the competitive force of one who has participated in organized sports his whole life. His eyes were hard, but his mouth was petulant; when he suffered, everyone around him suffered. If Voyd had believed in God, he might have said that God spoke through him. If he believed in God, he might have been waiting for his visitation as a chosen one. Voyd believed in FFF. Through FFF he prevailed with an iron fist. The whole of his heart and mind was devoted to FFF, and he was waiting for Ranger, FFF's founder, to personally visit him at Yum Yum Donuts, where Voyd held court.

People said Ranger was in jail. He was in Mexico, where he had three, four, five children with as many women, half-breed bush babies who ran around naked and called him 'Sir'. He was a Hare Krishna now—someone had seen him at LAX with a stack of books he pressed on strangers, wearing an apricot-colored bathrobe, his head shaved but for a topknot. Maybe he worked in a shoe store in Glendale, or he cooked in a health-food restaurant in Santa Monica, surfing in the evenings after work when sharks browsed the shore, looking for dinner. Mikey said he saw Ranger from time to time. Mikey knew where he really was, but he wouldn't tell the others; he said Ranger wanted to get on with his life, that he wasn't interested in being a badass anymore. Mikey and Ranger were still tight, *brothers*, and Voyd wanted to be a brother like that to Mikey. Even more, he wanted to be father to FFF. Father with a capital F.

Voyd couldn't sleep again. It was hot in Pigpen's apart- ment, no air-conditioning, just a couple of tabletop fans looking this way, then that, as if scanning the horizon for an incoming natural disaster or a lost pet. These searing June days felt more like August, when the lit chaparral chased the Malibu Colonists down the Pacific Coast High- way, waving to each other from their convertibles as they fled. Lise was pressed against his skin, stinking like vinegar. Today when they kissed, her lips felt rubbery and slick, not to his taste. He bit her lips. She didn't stop kissing him, so he bit her again: discipline. He bit her again so that she bled and Lise had finally pulled away.

Now he pushed her from him. He made a cradle for his head with his hands and crossed his ankles, the thinking man's position. The dark provided a sanctuary in which he could think and make plans. He made good use of his sleeplessness—Voyd kept the edge on everyone. Each day was rehashed and evaluated, scenes run over in his head, detail picked up that he had previously missed, magnified until it all but exploded, until he was satisfied that he hadn't missed a trick. He had learned his lesson two years ago, when he was twelve, driving home from school with his mother, who had been called in to the headmaster's office yet again after Voyd detonated a pipe bomb on a school playing field. Their car was stopped at a faulty stoplight flashing yellow. The flow of traffic at that intersection was steady east–west; Voyd and his mother were headed north, and no one would let them through to cross. Voyd's mother hesitantly nosed her Mercedes into the intersection, but lost her nerve and reversed to a safer position. As they waited for a gap in traffic, another car—a dented blue Nova with no front fender—pulled up behind them in a cloud of exhaust. Neither Voyd nor his mother thought anything of it, until four boys—four *Black* boys—as topless as Voyd's mother's convertible, their shirts pulled over their faces and banded tightly at the back of their heads, the gathered cloth hanging down like ponytails—blue and black, blue and white, two blue—got out of the car.

Earlier that day, moments after Voyd detonated the pipe bomb, someone—not a teacher—had come out to investigate. They had just a few minutes to talk before the janitor arrived, followed by the Latin and science teachers, and finally the headmaster himself, but in that short time Voyd, who was Boyd then, first heard of FFF.

Mikey introduced himself, shaking Boyd's hand. Boyd already knew who Mikey was. Everyone knew: basketball center, football quarterback, student-council senator, prom king. He was even known at other schools to be the most popular kid in the Valley, practically a celebrity. "You should meet some people. Come to Yum Yum later," Mikey said.

"What kind of people?" Boyd asked belligerently, the way he asked most questions.

"Cool people. The coolest guys you'll ever meet."

The janitor was approaching, a sour look on his face; it was he who would have to clean up the exploded home plate, same as he had cleaned up Boyd's other messes: the full cafeteria trash can that went off like Old Faithful, spraying orange juice, chocolate milk, and pizza crusts, and an explosion of chalk in the music room that left the flute section choking on their instruments. Boyd had never been one for remorse, although he could feign it, of course.

Mikey balanced on the balls of his feet, ready to take off. "Fight for freedom," he said.

"What?" Boyd said.

"FFF. Fight for Freedom. You need us."

Throughout his meeting with the headmaster and his mother, Boyd had repeated it to himself. "Fight for freedom. Fight for freedom." He didn't really hear when the headmaster said he was suspended.

"Boyd," his mother said in her sharp, displeased voice. "What do you have to say for yourself?"

"What?"

"One more incident and you're expelled," the headmaster announced triumphantly. "Do you understand, Mr. Richmond?"

Boyd shrugged. He went through schools like his father, a venture capitalist, went through companies.

"Hey, baby, wanna take me for a ride?" His mother's car was surrounded by youths more legitimately troubled than Boyd, their hopes and opportunities abjectly circumscribed by where they came from, the infusion of crack cocaine and guns, fathers in prison, deteriorating schools, a lack of recreational facilities and strong community leaders—in short, ferment and rot, weakness, danger. "I wanna go for a ride in your nice car." Mrs. Richmond shuddered and shook her head almost imperceptibly, the muscles that bound the right side of her jaw flickering as she clenched her teeth, foot ready on the gas, still hoping for a break in traffic to accelerate through. But no car stopped, or even slowed to rubberneck.

"I like your car. It turns me on." The one doing all the talking, the one nearest his mother—blue-and-white shirt—had his hips pressed against her door. When he stepped back, Boyd could see that he was hard. He had stepped back so Boyd and his mother *would* see that he was, and he laughed, watching their faces. "Quit staring at me, you fucking homo," blue-and-white shirt said, rubbing his erection against the door again.

When Boyd looked away, out his own window, another sweat-studded torso awaited his gaze. "What you staring at, gay-boy?" blue-and-black shirt said. Boyd turned his head again, to look straight ahead out the front windshield, hiding behind his fluffy blond bangs. "Fucking homo hair," blue-and-black shirt said, flicking Boyd's bangs. "Homo-fucking gay-boy."

The other two, both blue shirts (lurkers, quiet until then), suddenly hopped into the backseat. One leaned forward, putting his hands all over Boyd's mother, touching her face, her shoulders, her breasts. She began to scream, until he got a hand over her mouth. She went red in the face—could she breathe? The other blue shirt had a grip around Boyd's neck, daring him to move, pleading with him to twitch an inch and be killed. These were boys who wanted to die gloriously as outlaws, not wash cars for a living.

Finally, hope in the rear-view mirror: another car pulled up behind the Nova, joining the queue to cross the intersection. "Hey!" a voice shouted, and a horn blared. "What's going on?"

Boyd's neck was suddenly cool where the boy's hands had been. A noisy U-turn and the Nova was gone. The scene, from start to finish, had lasted no more than five minutes—in fact, four. Mrs. Richmond said she knew this for sure as she had watched the clock. Neither she nor Boyd could identify their masked assailants to the police, nor did they have a license-plate number. The policeman fiddled with his ballpoint pen's button, clicking it up and down, not writing anymore. "Not much I can do here."

"I know," his mother said, likewise resigned. When she and Boyd finally arrived home that night, she would tell his father what happened in a flat voice—"Yes, that's right, we were carjacked, but they didn't get the car, thank God"— omitting certain details (the *sexual* details, Boyd noted), and they would never speak of it again that Boyd was aware of. But for Boyd, who was soon to become Voyd, the incident was life-changing. From that day on, he hated Black people, and Hispanics, Mexicans, Chinese, Japanese, Filipinos, Koreans—or indeed any person of a non-white color. He hated gays and Jews too, because you couldn't like one and not the other. He hated them all.

Voyd knew the word for the way he felt: ideological. It was a big word, and saying it made him feel proud, that he believed in something. FFF corroborated his beliefs. Over the past couple of months, Voyd had been compiling a kind of Holy Book, his synthesis of totalitarian and revolutionary ideas. He planned to photocopy this book, bind it in white, for white supremacy, and hand it out to all FFFers, with instructions to read and memorize, above all, to believe.

His work done for the night, his thoughts organized, Voyd tried to sleep. But someone stank. Someone in the room had Jew blood—he could smell it, worse than B.O. One drop, that's all it took to poison a well. He would find out who it was, and if they were FFF, he would kick them out. He would never knowingly allow a Jew to belong to FFF. Judaism was a conspiracy against the European white race and he would not stand for it. It was all in his book. A race divided could not prosper. FFF would prosper. FFF prospered now—they were unbeatable. Anyone who called them out, FFF wasted. Even the kids from tougher neighborhoods.

If the Jew in this room looked under the bed for a Nazi, they would find Voyd.

He shifted in his sleeping bag, still wired. He was tired enough, after kicking some serious ass—those metalheads had thought they were so bad! FFF showed them. Voyd flexed his hands, feeling the ache of after-fight, the bones bruised from contact. Power, he thought. His fists had power like a brain has thoughts.

Next to him, Lise shifted and murmured, having a good dream. Maybe they would sneak home in the morning, Voyd thought. They could clean up, get the housekeeper to make them breakfast, chill out in front of the TV while his parents were at work, then escape again before they returned. He would get some money, take them both shopping—the girl only had the clothes she showed up in, and now she was wearing Voyd's Misfits T-shirt, having puked down the front of her own.

Besides, he wanted to impress Lise by showing her where he lived. His parents' house in Encino was huge, but that wasn't all: in Voyd's bedroom, Lise would find the FFF logo spray-painted on the wall over his bed, the letters burning in the torch held aloft by the Statue of Liberty. She would forget about Mikey when she saw *that*. He had his own TV and VCR, an Apple computer, a private telephone line, rows of clothes in his walk-in closet (the good clothes his parents preferred him to wear when the family was together, versus the clothes he kept at Mikey's, his FFF uniform of Dickies chinos, flannel shirts, and black brogues). Downstairs, a game room boasted pinball, Donkey Kong, a jukebox loaded with Motown singles, a pool table, and darts. The kitchen was overstocked, overflowing with food, with fresh fruit on display like a hotel buffet, the many other rooms just as grand, well supplied, and little used. Voyd's parents were business partners in possession of a private jet that was forever in flight across America, while his older brother was at ski school in Lake Tahoe, hoping to go pro. Once upon a time, Voyd had wanted to be a lifeguard, but now FFF was all he cared about—that, and his parents' promise of a car when he turned sixteen: a vintage VW Beetle with the old-style sloping headlights, nothing past 1967, painted bottle green.

He rolled Lise onto her back and her legs flopped apart. He pushed inside, but she didn't wake. No one did. Everyone was passed out, Lise especially, who had insisted on calling him Mikey when she got drunk tonight. The girl was always drunk and passing out, her body willing and *there*—but then Voyd could get sex whenever he wanted. Lately it seemed like all the girls wanted him, just like they wanted Mikey. There were so many girls in the FFF Fan Club.

"Ow," Lise muttered in her sleep.

"Shh." Voyd humped faster.

She opened her eyes. The whites glowed in the yellow clock light. Her brow rumpled, her mouth was an O, expanding and contracting. "Ow. Ow. Ow."

"Shh," he hissed, working hard now, stabbing into her again and again. She yelped reflexively before Voyd clapped a hand over her mouth. She bit at his palm, but could not get the meat in her teeth. The others in the room stirred— someone said, "Shut up," in a sleepy voice. Finally Voyd came, one last great blow like an axe sunk into a tree. Lise whimpered as he withdrew and immediately reached between her legs, holding herself.

"I think I'm bleeding," she said when he took his hand away from her mouth.

"Shut up!" the sleepy voice shouted—not so sleepy now,

but enraged, very close to Voyd's ear. "Shut the fuck up or I'll fucking kill you!"

"*You* shut the fuck up," Voyd shouted back—the voice of the master. "Do you know who you're talking to? Don't fucking talk to me like that."

Lise was afraid, Voyd could tell; she shriveled beneath him, shuddering with tiny, silent sobs, one hand clamped to her fevered mound—how it burned, swollen almost shut, leaking substance, she didn't know what, blood or semen or some *internal* juice that belonged inside, belonged to her organs and not to the air. Whatever it was, it was all over her, mixed with Voyd. There had been other girls than Lise, even tougher girls, older, more experienced, who told him how he made them feel, how torn up, how rough he could be. It only made him more excited and he often took them again, right away. Voyd shoved Lise's hand aside, probing the sticky flesh for himself. She didn't make a sound now. He wouldn't sleep tonight. She couldn't resist him.

Twenty-One

First they crashed at Mikey's, before moving on to the trashed apartment near Phazes where Lise had lost her virginity and where kids slept among the kind of detritus usually found in the gutter — beer bottles and cigarette butts, the newspaper they used for toilet paper, candy-bar wrappers and potato-chip bags and Coke cans. The Pigpen, it was called, after the guy who rented the place. Voyd said they would go to his parents' house one night, but they hadn't made it there yet; they got too drunk, or Voyd would say he didn't feel like it. Lise wished they would only stay with Mikey and Patty. They always returned there at some point during the day, so Voyd could find out what was happening with FFF, and Lise clung to Patty then, a helpful member of her elastic family, assisting with meals and laundry, whatever Patty needed. Patty didn't appear to work a regular job, instead making herself available to the many kids who frequented her home, cleaning wounds (because there were nightly fights, Lise now knew) and consulting on everything from birth control to general-equivalency degrees (instead of a high-school diploma) and the benefits of a year in the Peace Corps. Patty talked frankly about drinking and drugs, and while she made neither available, you could weather a bad trip in her care or drunkenly carouse to the discordant music always blasting from the stereo.

Despite the fact that she had been claimed by Voyd and slept with him at night (or whenever he felt like it), Lise still longed for Mikey. She knew he was in love with someone called Jessica—at least that's what everyone said, although Lise hadn't met her yet. There were so many girls hanging out at Patty's house, it was hard to know who was who. The phone was always ringing for Mikey, different girls calling all the time. "The most wanted kid in the Valley," his mother joked.

Mikey seemed to have forgotten why Lise was there; he thought Voyd was the answer. He'd forgotten that he ever liked Lise himself, and why should he remember? She wasn't pretty enough for Mikey. He only dated the prettiest girls—models, he liked models, and Lise wasn't a *real* model. She had freckles on her nose. Her eyes were too small, set close together, and they were *brown*, not green or blue, or even hazel. Shit-brown piggy eyes, plus she smelled now, having showered only once since she ran away from home. She reeked, she knew it, she could smell herself, and her face purpled with embarrassment. When she blushed, which was often, the color steeped her newly bleached roots (the rest of her hair was streaked black and white and coming out in handfuls—another strike).

It was Voyd's idea to change Lise's hair color. He wanted her to look like the girls who went to the punk shows in Hollywood (like a real runaway, Lise thought, but she didn't say). He told her to always follow him when he left a room, unless he said so, and he kept his arm around her when they walked together, resting on her shoulders, with his forearm at her throat. He was just being protective, but sometimes it was like she couldn't talk to anyone else. She struggled to be natural with him, to just be herself and talk to him like she talked to Trish and Jen or even her mom—not that she was ever really herself in front of her parents.

When thoughts of home or her parents came into her head, Lise pushed them right back out again. She didn't feel particularly homesick, except sometimes when she got drunk, and the longer she stayed away, the more impossible going back seemed. She would be in *so* much trouble. She had phoned Trish to say that Voyd was officially her boyfriend and she was staying with him now, like it was normal (and, slowly, it was beginning to feel normal, this new existence of total freedom from Planet Parent). Trish warned her that her mother was freaking out, hassling Mrs. Blue and Trish both, threatening to sue unless they told her where Lise was. "So where are you anyway?"

"Just around. We're at somebody's apartment."

"Yeah, but where is it?"

"Um, by Phazes."

"Like, can you be more specific than that?"

"I don't want her to find me," Lise said.

"What about your friends? Don't you want us to find you? Don't you want to see us?"

"We can hang out," Lise said nervously. "I totally want to hang out with you guys. I just haven't had time lately. I've been totally busy."

"You didn't call me for four days! Don't you think we're worried? You could have been *dead*, Lise. Like, some rapist could have *killed* you. That's what my mom said."

Lise's eyes filled, touched by Trish's concern. "Ohmigod, I *miss* you guys. I didn't mean to be mean. You and Jen are my best friends, Trish. You know that. We share *everything*. I'm not like, hiding from you or anything right now, I just don't want to go home. I can't *live* there. You know what my mom's like—she's totally psycho."

"So what should I tell her? Because your psycho mom is calling here at least five times a day. She says she can't even go to work, she's so upset. My mom's totally sick of it."

"Tell her—"

What? What could she say that would delete what came before, undo the fact that Lise had run away? Lise was hoping that if she stayed away long enough her parents would be too worried to be mad. By the time she went home—and she did plan to go home eventually—they would be so glad to have her back that they wouldn't punish her. They might want to buy her some presents instead, some clothes or a new stereo to replace the little kid's tape recorder she'd had since she was nine, plus other little things to make her room nice, maybe a canopy bed trimmed in white, effusions of lace at the windows, a gilt-framed mirror, and her own private line to make calls whenever she wanted. Lise could get her ears pierced and be allowed to wear makeup—anything to keep her at home.

Her parents would know, too, that having done it once

before, it would be easy for Lise to just go if she was unhappy. If they made her unhappy.

"Um, just tell her—"

But if her mom was calling Trish's house every day, did that mean that Trish was her spy? As a runaway, Lise had to keep her wits about her now; Voyd was always telling her that she had to be more careful. "Don't talk to cops," he said. "If anyone hassles you, just say, 'I have nothing to say.' And make sure you know who your friends are. Do you know who your friends are? I mean, your *real* friends. Who's got your back. People who won't let you down, no matter what—even if they're getting hassled by the cops." Lise thought Trish sounded like she was trying to get information, like she wanted to pin down Lise's where-abouts so she could send Mrs. Anderson over to take back her daughter.

"Tell her you don't know," Lise finally said. "Tell her you haven't talked to me."

"She won't believe that."

"Then I don't care what you tell her! Tell her I'm dead! I don't care—I hate her! Just leave me alone about it. I'm sick of talking about her." Lise had never shouted at Trish before and there was a shocked silence when she finished.

"Are you on drugs, or what?" Trish huffed. "You sound totally different. You've *changed*. Like, I don't know if I'm talking to the right person, if you're even Lise. You sound totally brainwashed or something. Totally *weird*."

"I have to go. Someone needs to use the phone." It

wasn't a lie. Patty, who had been talking at length to yet another weeping pregnant girl, signaled to Lise: she sliced her throat with the blade of one hand.

"Wait, are you going to Phazes later?" Trish asked.

Lise didn't answer. Voyd had reappeared from Mikey's bedroom, more FFFers in his wake. Gently, so gently, Lise hung up on Trish, replacing the receiver like a sleeping babe into its cradle, as if she wasn't really putting the phone down. As if Trish wouldn't be mad—although Lise thought she heard her scream just as the line went dead.

"Come on," Voyd said to Lise, taking her hand.

She didn't ask, "Where are we going?" She never asked. She looked to see if Mikey was coming, but he wasn't there. He was in his bedroom, probably. Lately it seemed like he stayed behind when they went out to do things, or he said he was meeting Jessica somewhere instead. Voyd called him Mr. Serious and asked him when he was getting married, but Mikey didn't have a sense of humor about Jessica.

In the backseat of someone's red Beetle, Lise snuggled into Voyd's lap. She thought that maybe they were going to get something to eat. Maybe they were going to Yum Yum. Lise was sick of donuts. They went to Yum Yum every day, staying for hours while she picked at crullers, chocolate-iced and jelly-filled and sugar-powdered donuts, or a giant glazed honeybun, mostly eating because she was bored. FFF affairs—their fights and allegiances, the lengthening list of offences against their honor—didn't interest her much. Lise had a sudden craving for Hamburger Hamlet, where she always went with Trish and Jen. She wished she could say to the five boys she was traveling with, "Hey, let's go to Hamburger Hamlet!" and they would all think it was a great idea. She wished she could ask them to turn down the music. She wished someone would offer her a beer from the six-pack sitting on the floor of the backseat— but they were for after. After what, Lise didn't know. No one bothered to tell her.

Twenty minutes later, they were in a parking lot, empty of cars at nine o'clock at night. The boys in the car began to fumble with lengths of pipe, brass knuckles, a rubber police nightstick. Lise shivered as a bad-tempered eighteen-year-old named Napoleon slipped a knife from a sheath in his sock, showing the others its startling, naked blade. When she looked at Voyd to see what he thought, his eyes were shining. "That's the business," he said.

Climbing from the car to let Voyd out, Lise smelled the stagnant, unfamiliar air of Downtown, the worst air in Los Angeles: trapped exhaust mixed with the ammonia tang of sun-baked urine, animal and human. It was quiet. The workers had gone home. No one lived Downtown; they went back to the suburbs if they were lucky, to Compton and Watts if they were not. Graffiti obliterated the walls of the office buildings, tag upon tag upon tag, and Lise knew she was in dangerous territory. Her mother had warned her never to go Downtown at night, not even to the big public library.

"Get back in the car," Voyd ordered. She must have looked scared, because he added, "It'll be over in five minutes." He pushed her into the front passenger seat.

"Stay here. Listen to music or something. Sean left the keys in the ignition. Don't sit in the driver's seat."

Lise didn't protest. The pack of boys—ten of them, from two cars—strode with purpose across the parking lot, headed for a grim, overcast corner shadowed by a high wall. Over the last week, she had witnessed as many fights as days. Was fighting fun? she asked Voyd. He laughed and said yes, fighting was fun, especially when you won, and FFF always won.

The boys were halfway across the parking lot before anyone stepped out to meet them: Mexican boys, dressed like wetbacks in flannel shirts buttoned up to their chins. What had Voyd told her about Mexicans? They were the crazies. Was that right? Or were the Koreans the crazies? The Koreans were the *killers*, fast and wily, always after white girls. The Bloods would tag your front door for a drive-by and—

There was a loud bang, like fireworks, and Lise caught her breath. She peered into the mass of bodies, trying to pick out a casualty or a weapon, a *gun*, but all stood. One of the Mexicans cupped a chunk of brick in his hand like a shot-put, which he heaved in Voyd's direction. The brick fell short and atomized when it hit the ground, spraying dust, then stillness like after a thunderstorm, with the birds still sheltered in the trees, the insects underground, and everyone indoors, watching TV.

Napoleon struck first, having scooped up a handful of brick rubble and massaged his forehead with it. Voyd had someone by his shiny black locks. Cradling the head with one hand, he used the other fist to drive the boy's nose into his screwed-up face, as if he wished to replant the nose on the same plane as his forehead. Blood pulsed from some opening and the boy's body shuddered. Lise looked away.

Twenty-Two

The great airport runway that was the Valley plain at night
was a sticky settlement of smog by day, the smog weaken-
ing the colors of the landscape until the haze burned off,
when everything came into relief, the contrast of sun and
shadow like a tarnished silver service, showing the pattern.
For California, the sauna state, hitting 107 or 108 degrees
on a summer day, air-con was the only way, Edison pumping out 14,000 megawatts of energy to compensate. The
Valley was hotter and smoggier than anywhere in the Los
Angeles Basin, with gluey heat like rosin on the skin. Just
beyond where the suburbs met the chaparral lay a barren,
unfriendly, undeveloped stretch that might once have served
as an airfield for Amelia Earhart in her strawberry-red
Lockheed Vega 5B monoplane. The area was rocky—always
and always rocks in the Valley—and rural, with overgrown
citrus orchards, wild asparagus, succulents the size of
horses, and the occasional solitary, loping jackrabbit. The
San Fernando Valley, mostly dense with housing, its subdi-
visions clumped at the base of the Santa Monica mountains
like fruit fallen off the vine, had a spread of more than two
hundred square miles; here, beyond the suburbs, was the
old land, cheerless and unteachable for now.

In the days before Pacific Electric and William Mulholland's waterway, only a weekly horse-drawn stage had dared rattle along the winding mountain pass between Los Angeles and the scant Valley population. With trains and water came neighbors, and soon enough Van Nuys, Reseda, and Canoga Park sprang up, a city a month built, until Bob Hope was golfing in Toluca Lake. Coyotes still howled at night, sometimes feeding on tasty domestic trash and pets left outside, but otherwise they kept to their dens, run in by traffic noise. Above it all burst Rocketdyne's test flights, nightly fireworks to celebrate the Valley's own Independence Day: they had made it, achieved the American dream, one million Valleyites by 1980.

Five years later, more often than not it was gunshots that everyone heard at night, as scared private citizens sought to protect family and home from those who demanded to take what they wanted, or what they believed was owed to them, or what they saw was cherished most—and this in the civilized world, not two hundred years ago when the frontier was settled, when men quested for Utopia, wary and armed, seeing bears in shadows, coyote in tree stumps, hearing owls as human voices, every rustle, every crack of the underbrush stalking and taunting them, threatening each one's stake of land.

Voyd had his dad's .38-caliber Colt, wrapped like a fish in newspaper inside his backpack. The land FFF crossed to target practice was not drivable, at least for the time being. If they did have trouble with Johnny Law, they might try to explain (their earnest smiles brightly stickered across their faces) that shooting up a rocky ravine wasn't anything so different from what their fathers had done as boys—or even (quoting their school textbooks now) the ancient agrarians of the Valley, dull from lack of protein, living on fruit, olives, and grain, but hungry for a leg of something. Voyd knew their excuses wouldn't hold with a cop: these were modern times, after all, when drive-by shootings tore up the front pages of the L.A. dailies. It was the Eighties, not the Fifties; Reagan was in charge, the dollar was hero, the Soviet Union ready to strike, adding three new warheads a week to its arsenal of ICBMs, Backfire bombers, and missile submarines. Kids were raised in fear; everyone had watched *The Day After* on TV, and some of them prayed to thermonuclear warheads, unseen but definitely there. Voyd knew kids who had picked out what they were going to wear when the bomb dropped, like they were going to the prom. His mother talked about evacuation routines and the possibility of building a shelter in their backyard, stocked with cans of food, drums of water, Saltines, board games, cards, and a radio for tuning in the news reports she had no doubt would come, with a long-range forecast of radioactive rain, heavy fallout, and genetic mutation. Voyd knew better than that. When Russia pushed the button to nuke America (America having nuked them first), there would be half an hour or so to have sex before the mushroom cloud engulfed the country—but he would already have blown out his brains rather than fry to death.

The barrel of his dad's Colt .38 clicked, needing a bullet. Once fed, the gun spat right up, splitting Valley lime like timber. The boys made lace of an old bed sheet they had brought with them. Drunk Wes found a shotgun shell on the ground and tucked it into his shirt's buttonhole like a forget-me-not. Everyone was eager to hold the gun, and over and over it changed hands, an easy transaction: gimme gimme this, gimme gimme that. Dervishes of dust stuffed their mouths. Chaparral nipped at their bare legs. Voyd had the gun again. He had more turns than anyone. It was his dad's gun and the others could get their own if they wanted. This gun was practically his anyway; if his dad noticed it was gone from the bottom drawer of his bedside table, he didn't care, or didn't say he cared.

They were talking about a kid from Montclair Prep, once in FFF, then the Mickey Mouse Club, now prison, who had been caught burgling his own parents' house. At some point during his arrest he'd named at least ten other kids from his school that were in gangs, including two FFFers.

"That clown is dead," Voyd said, taking aim. "See that Mountain Dew can? That's his fucking face." The can exploded, spurting alien-colored streams like Silly String.

"If we don't get him, somebody will," Drunk Wes said.

"Sure we'll get him. We always do," Voyd replied.

"Remember that longhair? The one that testified last year? The one that said we *scalped* him?" Stresser asked, laughing.

"Anyone seen him since Napoleon dumped his ass in that Goodwill box? If I see him," Voyd said, grabbing the Colt off Drunk Wes. Bang!

"So long as the cops don't come knocking at my door, I don't care what happens to rats like that," Damien said.

"How are the cops going to find out? We're *chameleons*," Voyd said. "They don't know what's going on."

"What's going on?" Stresser asked, deadpan.

"Nothing," Voyd answered.

"Nothing," Damien agreed.

"Absolutely jackshit. Stop rubbing my nose in it," Drunk Wes said, and everyone laughed.

"Now then, you see this fucking gun? Mikey doesn't believe in guns. But I know for a fact that other guys are carrying guns. Sawed-off shotguns and shit. Mikey says he's not ready for it. But what if there was a contract on *your* head?" Voyd asked, swinging around to aim at Stresser. "I mean, Stresser, you've got a long list of enemies. Almost as long as mine. Almost as long as Ranger's."

"I bet Ranger carries a gun."

"We should get Ranger to come out here and show us a few things," Damien said.

"Ranger would *love* us," Voyd said. How Voyd wished he could meet Ranger. Lately he'd been bugging Mikey even more—just Ranger's telephone number, so Voyd could talk to him, ask him a few questions, no big deal. Nothing to do with FFF, if Ranger didn't want to talk about FFF. Nothing about the good old days, because as far as Voyd was concerned, the good days were still to come, when he ran FFF totally. That's what Mikey was afraid of: he knew Ranger would love Voyd. He knew they would talk man to man, that they were the *same* man. "I think we got to take FFF to the next level, like he did. Those guys from La Mirada are packing, Suicidal Tendencies are packing. To fight those guys, we got to be packing, too. We're ready. Mikey just can't see it. But I can. I've got the vision." Voyd tapped his head with the Colt's barrel.

"Mikey's always thinking about girls," Drunk Wes said.

"Mikey's a pretty boy," Stresser sneered. "He doesn't have balls anymore."

"We're defenders of this race and we won't be fucked with. FFF is the one you respect," Voyd declared like a true leader, his voice ringing around the canyon. He fired the gun. The bullet jammed, but Voyd didn't panic. He knew that if the gun jammed in a real situation—life or death—he could use his hands. His powerful, almighty, iron fists.

Twenty-Three

"So we're just like, growing in different ways now. I still care about you. What we had was really special." Lise was replaying the scene. They had stood, sweating, just outside the door to Mikey and Patty's place. Voyd blocked the door. Lise reached out to take his hand, but he shook his head. She could hear a bunch of people inside, most of whom Lise knew by then, at least by name and reputation, if not to talk with them. Voyd had made her go outside, away from everyone. It was over in five minutes; it had lasted seven days. Lise had been planning to celebrate their one-week anniversary by dedicating "Time After Time" to him that night at Phazes. "You have to find somewhere else to stay. You can't stay at Pigpen's." Voyd kicked over an anthill, toeing the ants one by one, smearing the sidewalk with their black blood and the flecks of their legs.

Lise stared at the gore stuck to his sneaker. "I can stay here," she choked. "Patty will let me." She put one hand against the wall for support and the many points of stucco crucified her palm.

"You can't stay here either. I was here first."

"You can't stay in both places at once."

"I might want to sleep here some nights, and some nights at Pigpen's. And you can't be where I sleep."

"But Patty really likes me."

"Sure she does. She likes everybody." Voyd grinned at the ants, grinding the last ones like he was putting out a cigarette. "That's what makes her so cool."

"But I mean, like—" Lise was crying now. She was always crying, always, her nose shining red as a Christmas candle, mouth a gaping wet glare. This would be the face Voyd remembered, its features drowned in self-sorrow—and thinking that, Lise cried harder. "She likes me. I know she likes me. I thought you liked me. I thought I really fit in. I thought we were all friends." Voyd didn't say anything. "I mean, can I at least say goodbye to people?"

"Jesus Christ," Voyd muttered, but he let her get past him.

Lise ran straight to Patty and flung herself into her lap, surprising Patty, who was sitting cross-legged on the floor, French-braiding the blue hair of another girl. "He—he—" Lise hiccupped, she was crying so hard.

"I know he did. I know. Oh, I know. That's just too bad. But that's the way love goes."

"But I *like* him," Lise wailed. "Can't you talk to him, Patty?"

"When the light goes out in a relationship, there's no turning it back on." Patty tried to ease herself from Lise's grip, which only made Lise anchor like a bulldog, her arms locked around Patty's neck. Lise didn't care who saw. She didn't care if Mikey saw. She *hoped* Voyd did, to see what he had done. She wanted him to know how much he was hurting her, to feel sorry for her, take her back, never leave her alone, like before. But Voyd was gone; she couldn't see him anywhere. Was he in Mikey's room? Where was Mikey? Where were they? Were they laughing at her, together, in Mikey's room, with girls?

Finally Patty dropped her off at Trish's house. Jen was there, and at first they wouldn't let Lise in—and it was a hundred degrees outside, at least, dangerous heat, the kind that killed old people and babies and dogs left to whine in sealed-up cars, no hope of a breeze. Trish and Jen just stood there, glaring, Jen with a strip of mustache bleach arcing over her top lip, while Lise begged. "I'm sorry. I'm just so, so sorry, you guys. I mean, I don't know what I was *doing*."

"Like we should care. We don't, really," Trish said.

"I'm sorry."

"I think you should go away," said Trish. "I don't think you should be here."

"Please. I said I'm sorry. I don't know where else to go. *Please*, you guys. I mean, I messed up, I know that." She tried to explain that Voyd wouldn't let her do anything without him, that it wasn't her fault, and the phone didn't work at Pigpen's apartment—

Trish interrupted. "I could call the police. You're trespassing."

"Stop it, you guys. You're supposed to be my friends," Lise pleaded.

"Are we? What about those other people you were hanging out with? If you're friends with FFF, then you can't be friends with us."

"I'm not friends with FFF," Lise said, too fast. It was a typical FFF response: deny everything.

"That's not what we heard. We heard you're like, best friends with them," Jen chimed in.

"*You* guys are my best friends," Lise insisted.

"You better not be lying," Trish said.

"I'm not. I swear I'm not. Cross my heart."

"Ohmigod, Lise, your hair," Jen interrupted, pointing at Lise's dye job. "What have you *done*? That looks *so* bad! And your clothes are all like, black. You look like some homeless kid."

"She *is* homeless," Trish reminded Jen. "Remember? She ran away."

"Ohmigod, this stuff is starting to *burn*!" Jen squealed, swiping at her mustache. "Just let her in, Trish. It's totally hot and the air-conditioning is like, escaping."

"She has to confess first," Trish said.

"Confess what?" Lise asked.

"What you've been doing. Where you've been. If you've been having *sex*. You have to tell us how many times you had sex and with how many guys. Like, if you did all of FFF. That's what I heard. That you did them all."

Lise teetered slightly, feeling light-headed in the heat. She hadn't had anything to eat that day and inside the Blues' house, she knew, were Lucky Charms, her very favorite cereal, and Kraft Cheese in a rubbery block, orange juice without the bits, Double Stuff Oreos, mini pizza bagels. "Um, no. That's not true. I mean, with Voyd, yeah, but no one else. Is that really what people said?"

"How many times?" Trish demanded. Her grin was

malicious. Beside her, Jen was fidgeting—she blew on her top lip as if to cool it.

"I don't know. Like, maybe ten?" Lise had lost track; she kept waking up without her underwear, that's all she knew.

"That's it?"

Lise nodded. "Maybe more," she whispered.

"My lip is burning!" Jen cried, running off into the house, and that's when Trish finally let Lise in. To break the ice—Lise was so nervous her hands were shaking—the three girls raided Mrs. Blue's liquor cabinet; she was out, but she wouldn't have cared. Anyway, Lise had a broken head and they were helping her, Trish explained to her mother sometime later.

"A what?" A broken heart, broken heart, broken *heart*.

"You need a shower. You totally stink. And you've got hairy legs," Trish told Lise.

"I know what we should do! Let's go to Phazes. It's only midnight. There's two hours left until it closes," Jen said.

"Lise can't go looking like *that*," Trish said.

"I'm not ready," Lise agreed. For the hundredth time that day, she replayed the breakup scene in her head: untouchable Voyd, even though he stood right in front of her, not looking at her, and she engrossed in his features, more handsome than she had ever thought before. She saw the ketchup stain blotting the white front of his T-shirt, the orange blossoms shriveling in a pot by Patty's front door. One hysterical ant had crawled up her bare shin like an itch and Lise had watched Voyd's sneaker lift, then hesitate, as if about to squash the escapee with a swift kick. Already it was a flickering image—Voyd's face became less clear to her the more she needed to see it.

"You need Vidal Sassoon ASAP. I'll get my mom to make you an appointment," Trish said.

"She needs to *wash* her hair," Jen giggled.

"I like it," Lise muttered, insistently raking its length with grubby fingers tipped in black nail polish.

"You like looking like a *skunk*?" Trish said, wrinkling her nose.

"A *homeless* skunk," Jen added. "And you smell like one, too."

"Your breath is totally bad, Lise. When did you like, last brush your teeth?"

Lise wanted to say, what did it matter? Patty didn't care. Who said it had to be twice a day, morning and night? Not Patty. She wasn't that old-fashioned kind of mom. So long as kids kept their orthodontist appointments and had their braces tightened every month—you could still see the orthodontist if you didn't live at home, Patty said (parents didn't like missed appointments, paying all that money). Lise threw herself face down on a pile of lacy pillows on Trish's big bed and pulled the covers over her head. "I like the way I look," she mumbled into a pillow. This wasn't exactly true. When she was with Voyd, she had thought she looked cool, but now that she was back with Trish and Jen, she wanted to look like them—with her hair and nails nice, her clothes bright and clean, no skulls around her neck.

"You can't be serious," Trish snorted.

"Lise, you look *gross*," said Jen. "Come on, we have to

make you presentable. It's our little project. Like, we're having makeover night."

Lise sat up in bed. Mirrors hung on every wall in Trish's room so that wherever she looked she was sure to see her own beautiful reflection. But Lise, seeing herself, all healthy color drawn, replaced with shadows and blotches, her skin broken out from being unwashed and too many donuts, lips cracked, the white pancake makeup that all the punk girls wore concentrated in those fissures and nubs—Lise began to cry again. "I like, can't forget the nice things he said. And it's totally bugging me that I can't forget, because I know I have to forget to get over him."

Jen unscrewed the lid to a sticky bottle of crème de menthe and poured each girl a glass of the bright green stuff, then added milk (she insisted it tasted like a milkshake when served this way). "A toast," she said.

The three girls recited together: "We promise to meet on October 9, 2002 in the lobby of the Beverly Hills Hotel at 7:30."

Lise gulped her glass. Jen handed her another shot. Jen was smiling, Trish was smiling. They hadn't changed in the week Lise was gone, not like Lise had changed, living among strangers as if they were her own family. But here, *here*, in this house, was her family. They were drunk, drunker still—who would be the drunkest? Lise always was. She had another shot. It tasted like a milkshake. Jen was right. Lise *loved* Jen. She loved Trish. They were her *best friends* and she just wanted to have fun with them and pretend the bad stuff didn't exist. Because it didn't. It could be as simple as that.

Then Trish was shrieking. "Ohmigod, is that your hair on my pillow? Your hair is like, falling out, Lise! Like, a whole bunch of it—you have a bald spot on the side of your head! It looks like some animal died on my pillow. A big dead skunk! I am totally grossed out. Where am I going to *sleep*?"

"Totally!" Jen agreed.

Lise wept. She wanted to go home.

Twenty-Four

There was something there that was unsettling. They'd lived in the house about two years, but Voyd had spent most of the last year living out. It wasn't just the house that drove him away, but deep down he knew the house really was part of it. Their other houses didn't feel like this one. They'd moved at least every other year since he could remember, the process beginning with a big sale at work followed by the first faint stirrings of departure: talk of neighborhoods and who lived where. Then the real-estate agent would appear, and the interior decorator, to ask Voyd what color he wanted his room this time, did he still love sailing, or skateboarding, or NFL, or maybe there was a new theme they could explore? Out of nowhere, the packers and movers turned up one day to dismantle everything that was going, and Voyd went home from school a new route.

Sometimes his parents were away when they moved. That had happened at least three times, and Voyd was left on his own to cope with finding his way around, where the light switches were, and the thermostat, to get the air-conditioning turned on. As the houses got bigger, he occasionally got lost, and one night he slept on the kitchen floor, having arrived home after dark, after baseball practice, too tired to bother looking for his room. Two houses ago, his brother decided he'd had enough and went away to boarding school, becoming an Easterner (living anywhere east of California, even in Tahoe, made him so) and rarely coming home, but even in this house he had a bedroom furnished—loaded, was his father's word—to his specification: skis crisscrossing the ceiling, forming a colorful lattice, and replica Olympic medals dangling from the curtain poles, whose swags were stitched from Olympic flags.

Little remained of the life known in each house, just a few framed snapshots taken with new cameras, the boys always standing in the blazing sunshine. There was less life lived in successive houses, as his parents worked harder on bigger deals and Voyd spent more time with friends. Even Thanksgiving and Christmas were spent away from home, at a hotel in Hawaii or skiing in Colorado, staying in resorts where the holiday meal was shared with many people, people they only saw once a year, year after year.

His mother hadn't always worked. She was at home when he was little, raising Voyd and his brother, part of their kindergarten carpool, but then she went to business school because she never had the chance to go to college. At business school, something became real for her—she *felt* real, that she measured up to men, or movie stars, or whoever. Upon graduation, his mother joined what became, at the moment of her joining, the family corporation—his father's term for the buying of shoestring operations and small businesses, aided by a sizable inheritance; his father's angel investor was his dead mother, who found oil in her backyard just months before she passed away. Venture capitalism was half luck, half logic, Voyd's dad always said. If Voyd's grandmother had died any sooner, before her septic tank packed in and needed replacing, they would have sold the farm and never known what lay beneath the hard land just steps from the back porch. It was oil leaking into the septic tank, pumped off four times a year and driven away in a tanker full of slurry, Voyd's dad laughed, for *thirty* years. They never could figure out why that tank filled up so fast before then. But there was plenty left, enough to make the family rich.

What it was about the house they were in now—it wasn't that it was like a hotel, because Voyd had lived in houses furnished like hotels before, as his parents became more and more corporate, always staying at the Four Seasons because the rooms were alike no matter where they traveled, and then they wanted their home like that as well. The interior decorator was even able to get the sheets the Four Seasons used on beds all around the world, and Voyd's mother, who liked everything just so—the way the towels were folded in the closet, what flowers were used in what rooms, what scent of cleaning products and laundry detergent and shampoo and soap smelled right to her particular nose— gave him a thrilling bonus.

They'd lived in the house almost two years and there was no bigger house to move to without leaving the Valley, so his parents were buying property in Maui and Aspen now, flying the decorator around in the company jet. *Those* houses felt fine to Voyd. It was cool to say they owned a house in Hawaii, or that his friend Peanut's dad had the same stereo that Voyd's parents had in their ski chalet. It was cool to say *ski chalet*.

There was just something strange going on. The house was great when Voyd invited his friends over to graffiti his bedroom and watch TV or make long-distance calls. His kitchen had the best food, his game room was huge, and, of course, no parents—but he always wanted to leave with his friends. He didn't like to be alone there. The housekeeper locked herself in her room at night—maybe she was afraid, too.

Voyd wasn't *afraid* of the house. That wasn't it. He didn't believe in ghosts. They didn't make sense to him, like religion didn't make sense to him. He couldn't just *believe* without proof; he had to see things for himself. He had to have a reaction to an actual event for it to count as real. One house they lived in his brother swore had a ghost, a little girl who flew out the window one morning when he was tying his shoes. That, and sometimes he heard what sounded like a distant radio, but really old-fashioned music, wartime dancehall stuff, tinny like it was coming from the attic, down through the air-conditioning vents—but there was no attic. It was playing in a room that didn't exist in the house.

Voyd didn't believe in ghosts, but maybe it was more like he felt another *dimension*. Like when he was in the pool by himself, he sometimes thought the pool might swallow him. He felt, even, like he couldn't get out; the water held him and his arms and legs went dead. He couldn't paddle, he couldn't kick, but he didn't sink, he didn't drown, and he wouldn't, not until the pool was ready to take him. He hung there, suspended, in limbo, the pool water having thickened to a suffocating, colloid-like gel. The drain cover on the bottom of the pool—that was something to stay away from, what might be a door, or a mouth, with some kind of suction power, for sure. And if it got him somehow, if a hand or a tongue or some kind of nozzle reached out and grabbed his foot, he would disappear.

But these were crazy thoughts, Voyd told himself. It was like thinking a man-eating shark lived in the deep end of the pool, or that if you closed your eyes while floating on your back, ever so calm and drifting off, you would wake up in the middle of the Pacific Ocean.

Yet that feeling of another dimension, that some rooms had different spaces in them that weren't for the living— but weren't for the dead, either—that feeling was there in the house. When he was home, he felt like he didn't matter. Whatever it was, it was much bigger than him.

His parents wouldn't say if someone had died there, or been killed, or committed suicide. They said they didn't know, and did it really matter anyway? They didn't believe houses held on to *feelings*. Voyd wasn't sure if his parents had even been inside this house before they bought it. It was one of those houses everyone wanted, they didn't care what it was really like. The kind of house that was a celebration of success and wealth, a house in which to count a bounty in the number of bedrooms with en-suite bath-rooms and how many garages and how long a table the dining room held. A house that everyone knew wasn't a rental. A house without clutter, with intercoms so people could find each other without having to walk around and shout.

Mikey's house wasn't even a house, but still everyone wanted to be there. Mikey didn't have a double bed or a TV in his room, and the living-room couch was a futon, and there were mice and bugs lurking, and nothing matched, nothing was the nicest thing from a store (except Mikey's clothes, which were always the best, always designer label). So many people wanted to stay at Mikey's house that Patty had to kick them out—and even Voyd couldn't always stay when he wanted to. Then he went to Pigpen's. Not home.

When Voyd's parents were home, they didn't seem to mind the feeling that something was pushing against the painted surfaces of the house. It wasn't like *The Amityville Horror* or *Poltergeist*; it was something else. Something was in that house, and lately Voyd felt that it wanted to be found. Something would come after them if it weren't found soon. It was coming already.

Twenty-Five

Mikey's new girlfriend was a total knockout and it was serious, Lise heard. That's what everyone said. She was a real model, not just a one-off in a mall fashion show, but someone whose pictures appeared in *Seventeen* and *Mademoiselle*. Lise saw her talking to Mikey at Phazes, and she knew Voyd, too: Lise saw them talking and it made her eyes water. Voyd ignored Lise when she went up and stood by him—Mikey's new girlfriend was gone by then, not that Lise was afraid of her. One of the little kids always following Voyd around, a short kid built like a Coke can who called himself Cop, started hitting on Lise instead and she walked away. He was only like, twelve.

Lise didn't think Mikey's new girlfriend was that beautiful. Not as beautiful as Trish. The camera loved her, that's all, and there was a difference between those kinds of beautiful. Her nose was too big, Lise thought. In fact, the only really pretty thing about her was her hair, which was kinky like all the magazines were showing. When she passed Mikey's new girlfriend on the dance floor with her friends, Lise hissed that she'd better not go to the bathroom alone or Lise would kick her ass, ruin her face with her fingernails.

Trish and Jen watched Lise closely for further signs of degeneration. Whether she had been affected to her core by the week spent with Voyd, they weren't sure, nor did they want her to escape again and return to his influence. That's what they called it: his *influence*. It was why, they said, Lise had run away in the first place, because she met FFF and they were bad, a totally bad *influence*. Lise tried to show them she was a good girl, really, like always. She said FFF was OK, they weren't that bad, some of them were really, really nice. Like, only a couple of them were *really* in jail, and they were totally older, not even FFF anymore.

Lise showered twice daily, borrowed Trish and Jen's trendy clothes, let Jen French-manicure her nails, and ate the same fruit they ate for breakfast, salad for lunch and dinner (the girls were supposed to be on diets again). The few freckles of rot that blemished her skin when she first returned to them, the chemical hair, body odor, and ratty T-shirt, proved nothing malignant. Dumped, Lise mostly moped around Trish's house. When she was left alone for a minute, which she rarely was, she dialed Mikey and Patty's house, but always hung up when someone answered. She dialed home the same, just to run her fingers over the familiar pattern the numbers made, hanging up before it even rang.

Trish said she could stay indefinitely, and Mrs. Blue didn't care; she was in Las Vegas anyway, with the new man in her life, a casino developer. Trish let the answering machine deal with Lise's mom's calls, and how often she called, Trish didn't say. At least every day. It bothered Lise, but she was too afraid to call back and say, "I'm here.

I'm fine," or even, "Come get me." Her parents didn't know what to make of Lise and she wanted to be with people who did, who *understood* why she did things. Besides, Lise couldn't face a whole summer grounded, her tape recorder confiscated, her secrets festooned around the house like travel mementos, there to remind her of what she had done, where she had been.

She heard one message from her mother and that was enough. "I'm warning you, but you won't listen. I've got the police looking for her and they'll arrest you if you don't help. Listen to me: if you want to do the right thing here, then do it now before the police get you. If you don't do the right thing, there's no excuse for you. God help me if you've got her there. God help me find my girl. I just want to find my girl." Lise's mother sounded deranged and Lise had laughed with Trish and Jen—had laughed cautiously, but still laughed, the three girls standing around the answering machine, Jen urging Trish to turn up the volume. Her mom was nuts, Lise agreed.

"No wonder you don't want to go back there," Trish said.

Besides, Jen was sleeping over, too, the friends inseparable now that it was summer and there was no school. The reunited trio vowed to protect Lise, their runaway, to straighten her out, beginning with her hair, the color of which had been reversed to a nondescript, dried-out brown, not at Vidal Sassoon, as Trish had promised, but at some anonymous strip-mall salon, the kind of place Lise's mom would go to—if she didn't cut her own hair, that is. But she did, standing outside on a sheet of newspaper in good weather, or over the sink, snipping at the split ends that she could see, ignoring those she couldn't.

Lise wasn't allowed near anywhere FFF hung out, but outings to keep up her spirits were organized by Trish and Jen—to the Galleria and Golfland and Hamburger Hamlet and Baskin-Robbins, and to Michelle, Tracey, Natalie, and Kirsty's houses, all friends, who were never home, of course. Lise shopped and nibbled fries or cones without much appetite (the girls were always breaking their diets), but she robbed more gleefully than before. It was tricky, now that it was summer vacation, to determine whether a family was home or not, but they got lucky—plus they were faster, in and out in five minutes, max. Lise carried away makeup and perfume, an opal-drop necklace from Natalie's mom's jewelry box, tapes of music that Trish and Jen approved, trendy clothes she kind of liked, two pairs of almost-new Reeboks in yellow and pink, a carton of cigarettes she was determined to smoke, a sticky bottle of peach schnapps and another of sweet vermouth. She thought about the bulging I. Magnin box under her bed at home, its lid strapped down with one of her dad's old belts buckled on the last hole, and wondered if her parents had discovered it yet. They probably ransacked her room the minute she left, trying to learn about her, to figure out who their daughter really was. Would she ever be able to go home and not be in trouble?

One day Lise proposed a destination to Trish and Jen: Mikey's new girlfriend's house in Encino. "I mean, it's supposed to be super nice and everything."

"*Whose* house?" Trish asked suspiciously.

"This girl I know. You don't know her, but she's got like, totally good stuff."

"Is she one of those weirdos you were hanging out with?"

Lise shook her head.

"We don't know anything about this girl. Like, if her mom works or if she has brothers and sisters. Her dad could be *unemployed*. He could be at home." Trish wrinkled her nose. "We'd like, see him in his *underwear*, watching TV. *So* gross."

"In his underwear drinking a *beer*," Jen added. "In the *afternoon*."

"She lives in Encino. Her dad's totally rich. He's a lawyer or something. She's a professional model," Lise told them, and it killed her to admit these facts. "Her brother drives a red VW Cabriolet. Her mom's dead." The fact of this loss didn't make Lise feel sympathetic towards Mikey's new girlfriend; it was just punishment for being so perfect, a model, lucky that Mikey loved her, rich enough to buy whatever she wanted, to live in *Encino*. Better yet, she didn't have a mother she had to run away from. As far as Lise was concerned, the case against this girl was solid, whereas other targets had been justified by pettier slights: Kirsty flashed her breasts at Trish's Romeo one night, while Jen hated Natalie for kissing Robo in front of her at Phazes.

"Weird. Her mom's *dead*," Jen said, shuddering. "That's so creepy."

"Why should we do her house?" Trish wanted to know.

Lise hesitated. "Forget it. It was a stupid idea. I don't

even know her. I'm not sure where she lives. Maybe it was Glendale. Who cares?"

Trish gazed at Lise. "Jen, we have to watch her," she said, as if Lise wasn't there. "She might turn on us again."

"I know. You can totally see it in her. His *influence*," Jen hissed.

"What?" Lise asked, halfway to tears. "I'm fine. I'm totally fine. I'm staying right here with you guys, I promise." Where else could she go? Once she and Voyd got back together (or she and Mikey, which was like, impossible, but maybe not, because like, Mikey could still *like* her and then she would live with him and Patty), she could stay with him again. Maybe they would even get their own place. Voyd was always saying his parents were so rich. She'd been to apartments that belonged to kids whose parents paid the rent for them. Those kids said it was like boarding school, but a hundred times better, and Lise said, "Yeah," like she knew what they meant.

When she broke into Mikey's new girlfriend's house, it was a solo mission. She walked all the way to Encino, her hair wrapped in a blue bandanna for disguise (and wearing sunglasses, always), one of Trish's pillowcases stuffed down her shirt so she looked fat. Lise walked, despite a Valley high of 107, past lawns that should be dead except that sprinklers whizzed in them at night, and she soaked every bit of fabric that touched her skin as if the cloth, too, cried out for rain. Tickles of sweat ran down her sides and legs. She couldn't even *think*, it was so hot, just kept walking. By the time she reached Mikey's new girlfriend's house, she was exhausted and could only half-heartedly perform what had become the usual security check: garage windows, looking for cars, then the front house windows for movement or people; around the side to the back, checking all windows, and find the key under the door mat, or in a flowerpot, or slotted into the plastic underbelly of one of those fake rocks—people were *so* predictable, like Trish said. If there was a burglar alarm, get out fast, back to the street where no one would suspect a pretty teenage girl, fashionably dressed, who looked like she lived in the neighborhood. Mikey's new girlfriend's house was exactly the kind that would have an alarm, with the key in a birdbath, but the back door swung open to a silent, utterly still kitchen, no sirens. Lise was in.

The air-conditioning gave immediate relief. Lise drank from the kitchen faucet, using her hands as a cup, but stopped herself before she'd had enough, thinking she had heard voices over the thundering tap. She listened to the house: nothing. There was no one around. When she finally began to move, she found endless rooms littered with white tennis sneakers and racquets, golf clubs and balls and shoes, sports pages, *Time* and *Sports Illustrated* and *Newsweek*, golf tees scattered like loose change on the couch cushions, ghostly dry-cleaning bags that billowed and drifted, stirred by Lise. In a house that reeked of the male sex and its necessities and habits, Mikey's new girlfriend's room was easy to find, peaches and cream at the top of the front stairs, all fluff and satin, heavily draped around the windows and bed. It was Lise's dream room. The adjacent bathroom had brass taps and a lacy shower curtain and fuzzy peach towels, a fresh one for every day of the week, stacked up on a white wicker shelf. Products and perfumes filled the countertop, with yet more tucked inside the mirrored vanity cabinet. A walk-in closet, fanatically arranged, brokered the passage between bed and bath, and Lise tore through its contents, verifying what she already knew: this girl had everything. She had more than Trish.

Lise stood in the middle of the bedroom and breathed. She just stood there, breathing. She *could* breathe, and it seemed a long time since she had breathed so well. Her head cleared and suddenly it all seemed so easy. As her feet rooted in that little plot of peach-colored carpet, her legs felt warm, her whole skin reflected the room's color. The things that soured her simply disappeared—she was sweet. How good and sweet she was!

Lise did something then that wasn't careful: she got into bed. She kicked off her Reeboks, turned back the peach bedspread (it was lined in white satin—Lise shivered when she saw that), and lay down. She wanted to feel what it was to go to sleep and know that Mikey loved you. The sheets were smooth, ironed sheets, but Lise didn't know that (her mother never ironed *anything*, especially not Lise's father's shirts; he wore a sports shirt to work, and Mrs. Anderson wore polyester, which didn't need ironing). The pillows were stuffed with down instead of the foam she got at home. From the bed, she could look out the window, hung as extravagantly outside as in with green willow branches and some kind of vine, white flashes of flower shaped like the secret parts of a woman's body. She saw a trampoline and a pool and the red-tiled roof of the pool house, on the edge of which sat a fat calico cat, its hooked tail switching back and forth like it was fishing.

Lise took a pillow in her arms and pressed it tightly against her chest. "Mikey," she murmured. "I love you, Mikey." The words, the act of holding the pillow to her like a human form, filled her with desire. Lise knew what sex felt like now, just as she knew what it felt like to wake up in this room and have beauty and luck with her. She kissed the pillow, tagging it with her lipstick, and pressed another pillow between her legs, seeking the seam, a ridge of eyelet, a twist of down to rub her tickle bone—the bone with a nerve-riddled soft spot, the tip of her pubis, sensitive to bicycle seats and dips in the road—until she sighed like the passengers on *The Love Boat*.

There was a noise at the door, a sharp intake of breath, two be-ringed hands clacking against each other like castanets. "Dios mio!"

Lise sat up. Her wide, alarmed eyes matched those of the maid, who was babbling in Spanish—a warning or a curse, it sounded like, spit bombs launching through the air, parachuting on silken threads. Lise threw back the covers and swung out of bed, shoved her feet into her Reeboks, and took off. Reaching both maid and door, she violently pushed through, using her right shoulder the way a football player cradling a golden ball would do. The maid cried out as she pitched backwards into the hall, cracking her head against a baseboard, a jolt that followed through the rest of her, her body landing unnaturally at a right angle to her neck. She lay as if dead. She *looked* dead. A stain, growing fast, appeared in the dark carpet—was that blood? Lise wouldn't touch her to find out: no fingerprints! No mess on her clothes! They weren't even her clothes, but Trish's shorts and Jen's top. She couldn't get them messy with blood!

Before anyone else could come along and Lise would have to explain, she fled. She ran for what seemed like miles until she tripped over her flapping shoelaces, skidding on her hands and knees on the macadam, trembling all over with what she had done. No one died from just hitting her head! The woman was hurt, that's all, and she would recover, just like on TV. She might have amnesia. She might not remember a thing. She might not remember Lise's face. No fingerprints, no fingerprints (that was Trish's voice, scolding her and Jen)—but Lise had been in Mikey's new girlfriend's bed. She had left the print of her whole body on the sheets. She had tagged Mikey's new girlfriend's pillow with a kiss—Cover Girl Lipslicks "Hint of Pink," sticky stuff, long-lasting. If the maid was dead, Lise would be traced. She could never go home now. She wrung Trish's empty pillowcase, pulled from her shirt—no loot for it today—making a length of rope with it.

Twenty-Six

"Yin Shin," someone told Voyd. The Korean Killers. Voyd nodded. One of them was trying to talk to Mikey's new girlfriend, Jessica, who danced with a group of her friends in front of the mirrors at Phazes, lights strobing over them, stabs of light slashing their clothes, dislocating their limbs. The girls splintered in the mirrors, the lights making more of them, making them seem everywhere, a girl for every guy. The mirrors reflected the faces of the dozen Asian boys who had gathered to watch. Mikey was out in the parking lot; someone had been sent to get him while Voyd kept an eye on things inside.

The dancing girls, all of them FFF girlfriends, were encouraging Yin Shin to look at them, talk to them, to think they were theirs for the taking. They were inciting battle between Yin Shin and FFF. Beautiful girls were the worst. They had to prove that every guy in the room wanted them. Voyd raged, pacing the edge of the dance floor like a cage. He was supposed to wait for Mikey to do anything about it. "You got to be more careful. Don't talk so much shit. There's all these guns and shit around, you never know," Mikey had told him yesterday. Voyd knew what Mikey was really saying: that Voyd was too hot. Kids

250

were kissing *his* ass now and Mikey was jealous. Voyd didn't need Mikey telling him what to do all the time. He could handle Yin Shin himself. It was bullshit that they were karate experts, he didn't believe it.

There were FFFers who said they wouldn't get involved in what they called the real gang stuff. They said that wasn't what FFF was about. They said FFF was about being the cool guys in town, the best-looking guys, the best dressed, the guys who got all the girls. Pussies like that really pissed Voyd off. They didn't deserve to call themselves FFF, but Mikey wouldn't kick them out. If Voyd was in charge, he'd lose anyone who lost the scent for a fight.

By now, the Korean Killers were outright dancing with FFF's girls, tugging playfully at their hands, mesmerizing with long-lashed, bead-black, speed-bright eyes. What was he waiting for? Backup, Voyd told himself. He only had a couple of little kids with him, new recruits who weren't fighters yet. He needed Mikey and his boys, the old-timers, experienced fighters, who were hanging out in the parking lot drinking vodka from Sprite bottles.

Here they were. "What the fuck is going on?" Mikey demanded, and for a minute Voyd felt nervous about calling Mikey in like this. *Starting* something. Voyd pointed. Mikey looked, his handsome face hardening, before he marched out and seized Jessica's arm, dragging her from the dance floor. One of her sandals came loose, still strapped on but the sole shoved to the side of her foot, and she shouted at Mikey that it hurt, he was *hurting* her—ohmigod, she'd stepped on something that *burned*. Then FFFers surrounded them, ranks closing in to protect their elite, and

251

Jessica finally shut up, realizing this was serious. Pressed alongside her, making sure she didn't escape, Voyd held his breath: Jewish stink. How could Mikey stand it?

One of the Asian boys came over and pushed at them. "What's your problem?" he asked.

Mikey was too slow responding for Voyd, who lunged with a punch, shouting, "You!" It was *you*, a great purge, all the day's anger and frustration, the little things that got to him added up, vomited from his guts—and Voyd *had* guts, more guts than Mikey. This fight was his. "You, you, you!" Each word was a jab, connecting with flesh and bone at last.

The fight went to the floor. FFFers came out of nowhere, over the railings and through the emergency exits like soldiers from a wood, camouflaged until that moment by their trendy clothes and good looks. It was a movie scene of a fight, bodies dropping all over the place, arms and legs flying like a crowded swimming pool on the Fourth of July. Next thing anyone knew, the club bouncers had charged, dragging everyone out front to Wolf for judgment. Wolf, who had been busy with his isometric exercises, jogged in place while he considered the boys. "All of you are eighty-sixed out of here," he decided.

Twenty-Seven

"Ohmigod, it's *so* crowded," Jen said. "Like, even the parking lot is packed."

Trish's Romeo had dropped them off at Phazes, promising he would return in an hour with more Romeos. Trish sulked; she didn't want to walk into Phazes without her Romeo now that everyone *knew* he was her Romeo. People would talk. They would think there was trouble, that Romeo wasn't faithful, that he was *available*. "They're probably all from Huntington Beach," Trish said. "Look what they're wearing. They're trash. Phazes shouldn't just like, let anyone in."

Lise recognized FFFers she knew standing around, some of them holding clubs of what looked like white picket fence, glowing arrows clumped with dirt and straggly grass where they had been pulled out of the ground. "It's a fight," she said, but it hadn't started yet. More kids were spilling out from Phazes, the crowd getting rowdy, worked up. FFF would choose their moment; they would make it worthwhile.

The girls were drunk. Always. Lise, wasted, was forgetting her problems: the dead maid, Mikey, Voyd, her mom at home waiting for Lise to return so she could really be in trouble. Her problems were like the miniature bottles she had secretly swiped from Mrs. Blue's liquor cabinet that morning, easily swallowed once she got started (sitting on the toilet, the only place Trish and Jen left her alone), the empties stashed under the ash pile in the fireplace. Tonight, with Trish and Jen, she shared bottles fully-grown and elegant, nips of this and that they mixed in champagne flutes. A straight shot of whiskey, two teaspoons of strawberry schnapps, Irish cream and Coke, bourbon and apple juice. "We promise to meet on October 9, 2002 in the lobby of the Beverly Hills Hotel—We promise to meet—We promise—" they repeated, each toast a new taste. Now Lise felt the alcohol beginning to roil somewhere beyond the root of her tongue, drawing in the sediment of her lunch—a turkey sandwich, no cheese or mayo—to an almighty storm, and she set her jaw stubbornly. She wouldn't be sick. She wouldn't pass out. Not tonight. Tonight she had a mission.

There he was, talking to friends, laughing, throwing back his head, except he wasn't relaxed. Those shoulders—she knew those shoulders and what they did when he was stressed. Mikey was a defense lineman, a football hero, his shoulders as broad as if he already wore his pads, but his neck wasn't thick from working out every day. No way. He was naturally built like that. He didn't have to lift weights until his eyes went dead.

It wasn't like Mikey to be afraid, and Lise wanted to talk to him, find out what was wrong. They were *friends*, she thought. She'd been at his house every day for a week and she knew his mom *really well*. They were friends, but they could be more, and if not Mikey, then Voyd, who had to be somewhere nearby, if there was a fight—but Trish grabbed her arm, making her stumble. So totally drunk, just like, totally. "Um," Lise said.

"Where are you going?"

"I just want to know what's going on."

"It's a fight. You already said so."

"Mikey looks upset," Lise said.

"They're just dumb boys fighting," Jen said. "Let's go inside. I want to dance."

There was shouting, then a general push. Something was happening now. Lise saw Voyd stalk into a clearing in the middle, and Mikey followed.

"What do you want?" Voyd asked. "Do you want to fight?"

The answer sounded like, "I'm going to tear you to pieces." An Asian boy, lean and taut as a greyhound, stepped forward. He spat on the ground and raised his fists. Voyd struck out at his opponent's cheek—he never missed. The boy sprang backwards, swearing, and reached into the waistband of his jeans.

"I think he has a knife," Lise heard someone say.

"I'll kill you," the Asian boy threatened. He was looking at Mikey, not Voyd. The Asian boy advanced, knife in hand.

"No knives. No knives," Mikey insisted, backing away.

Lise's nose was numb from drinking. Her tongue crackled, needing spit. Then everyone was running for cover, people were shouting, reaching for the doors to Phazes, trying to get back inside. Trish and Jen—she didn't know where they were, but Lise wasn't scared. Not with Mikey and Voyd there.

"I'll kill you all!" the Asian boy screamed. Lise opened her eyes and she was still standing in the parking lot, voices like explosions around her—someone was trying to wake her up, get her moving, but Lise had to watch. Her lips touched her fingertips, as if in prayer. The blade was within inches of Mikey's chest. Next to Mikey, Voyd wielded a club and he swung as if for a grand slam. The Asian boy was too quick, knocking the club from Voyd's grasp with a swift sideways kick, while the knife never strayed from its target. "Motherfuckers!" The Asian boy pounced, but Mikey ducked, just escaped being cut. He turned to run. Before he could take two steps, the knife was in his back. "I'll kill you!" the boy screamed as he stabbed Mikey to death. Anyone could see he was stabbing him to death. Mikey twisted his back against the blade, resisting it, *fighting*, killing himself. He wanted to get away, but the knife held him. One minute he was standing, the next he was dying—he dropped to his knees, a surprised look freezing on his face.

The Asian boy took off down Van Nuys Boulevard in the direction of the freeway, and Voyd was running, too—Lise saw him get into a car that sped away, leaving Mikey to die alone. Wolf was here now, with his bouncers, and Trish and Jen, tugging at Lise's hands.

Lise didn't know who drove them back to Trish's house. Just some guy Jen had met, who wanted to come in but Trish wouldn't let him, so he left two savage streaks of reeking black rubber on the driveway. Lise couldn't panic about what Mrs. Blue would say when she got home, and she couldn't get upset that they didn't know where Trish's Romeo was. She wanted to tell them to shut up—but she couldn't, because she was crying too much.

Trish accused her of overreacting. "I mean, it's not like you were going out with him." She picked up the phone to check that it was working. She was waiting for Romeo to call. "I could have been *hurt*. It could have been *me* who got stabbed. That guy was just waving his knife around, and everyone was like, pushing each other, and people falling down, and people getting stepped on. It was like, people, please! And I could have been hurt and he doesn't care." Trish was crying now.

"I know," Jen said, hugging her.

"I'm going to bed," Trish wailed, and Jen followed, holding her hand.

They left Lise alone in the kitchen. She took Trish's last cigarette—her lucky cigarette—from the pack and tried to smoke it, but the picture of Mikey's death kept getting in the way, as if it came from the smoky, stinging haze. She really needed to talk to someone. She picked up the phone. The line was busy, but she kept trying until it rang. "Patty!" Lise cried.

"Patty can't talk right now," whoever said. A girl. Lise hung up.

Twenty-Eight

Gangland had infected the romantic suburbs; it was news, with police and politicians predicting that FFF's numbers would swell and kids would be incited to further, retaliatory violence. "I hope we don't have to get a Patton tank, but there is a war going on and maybe we should mobilize every resource," a city councilman intoned. The LAPD promised that from now on, every patrol car in the Valley would be alert to kids who should be in school, despite that it was summer vacation. "What kind of parent lets their teenager stay out until two, three o'clock in the morning?" the district attorney wondered. "We can only do so much. It's the parents who need to be on top of the situation here. Kids need discipline. They don't know what responsibility is. They're the future of America, and what they need most is discipline. They're coming from families where every-thing's given to them, no questions asked. I am sorry for the victim's family, I truly am, but this could have been prevented with some good old-fashioned discipline."

The night Mikey was killed, Voyd went home. He and Deano had been driving around for five hours, trying to keep the cops off their tail, and Voyd got sick of it, sick of it all like he got sick of the constant sun or anything that wouldn't go away when he wanted. For the first time in a long time, he was afraid of what might happen. He had been at Mikey's side when he was killed, his right-hand man, his little brother. Mikey *died*, and Voyd was crying now, his chest alive with noise like the wilderness at night.

A few FFFers remained at Phazes' parking lot, watching over Mikey's blood, by then crisscrossed with tire tracks, polluted with torn-off sheets of cop notepad paper and cigarette butts. Later, someone scratched FFF in his blood on the macadam, so everyone would know what Mikey was.

Some kids helpfully supplied their names and addresses to the cops, as if they had suddenly sobered up after a long drinking binge and walked into AA, honest for once about who they were and what they had been doing. Some of them were FFF, breaking code. Voyd would hear about them later, after he went home.

He could have gone to Patty's. Most kids did. When the apartment filled up, they sat outside the door, filling the courtyard, and then the sidewalk, hundreds of kids, eventually joined by reporters and photographers and camera crews. Voyd thought that if cops were sure to be anywhere, it was Patty's. "Let's go to Yum Yum, like we always did," Deano said. Or Pigpen's, but that place was such a hole and Voyd was sick of slumming. What he really wanted was to go to sleep for a long time in his own bed, the stillness of the well-built house like he was buried in a snowdrift, a pure white vault, safe as God in heaven. If the cops came for him, his dad would pay for the best lawyer in town — let *him* deal with this. Voyd just wanted to go home and like, watch TV.

He struggled with the lock—the door was double-bolted; his parents weren't expecting anyone, especially not their son. Were his parents even there? The house was dark, the kitchen lights flickering at first, as if the house didn't want to wake up. Out of habit, Voyd opened the refrigerator door and saw the trays of cold cuts, plates of salad, cans of New Coke and Diet Coke and Sprite and ginger ale lined up three deep. Turning on more lights, he wandered down the hall, checking the living room, dining room, library, and game room for signs of life. He finally sat down in his father's den, the TV remote control in hand, not turning it on. Outside the window, he could see Mikey's death fixed as a new star, and Voyd had a feeling it would never leave him alone.

"Well, hello," his mother said.

He didn't know where she came from, or when she had arrived, but there she was in her robe, sitting next to him on the couch. Maybe she'd been there when he went in and he hadn't noticed, too much inside his own head.

"Hey, Mom." Voyd tried to sound vacant. It was his usual voice for parents—but tonight, or this morning (it was almost seven o'clock, he saw on the VCR clock), the voice cracked. Voyd turned his face from her, his eyes filling up again. He just couldn't make them stop.

His mother didn't understand. "I heard something. I thought someone was trying to break in. I thought you were in Malibu, Boyd."

Is that what he had told her? Voyd half-remembered something about staying at his friend Casey's house on the beach. His parents had given him money to buy a surfboard and wetsuit, but Voyd had rented a suite at Le Mondrian instead, to party with a stripper named Bunny. That was three nights ago. Bunny had made a 'B' of hickeys on his chest—he could have lifted his shirt and showed it to his mother, told her, "This is what I got for nine hundred bucks." That, and the greatest blowjob of his life, Bunny dislocating her jaw to do it a way that only professionals could. It seemed a long time ago now. It seemed like another life. Another person checked into that hotel, someone he thought he knew but now wanted to avoid.

"Did something happen?" his mother wanted to know.

Voyd studied the remote control in his hand, looking for the TV power button. It should be red and round, like an M&M. The buttons blurred together with his tears. Grabbing at detail, he remembered the shirt Mikey was wearing when he died, green-and-black plaid, and the way the Asian boy's hair had been styled, slicked back like a Fifties greaser or a Wall Street broker. For what seemed the hundredth time, he watched the knife pounce on its meat. Mikey looked surprised, but he didn't scream, not once; the only sound he made was that of choking on his own blood. His eyes—always charged, his gaze intense as if a fiery furnace burned deep within him, his eyes the fissures through which its heat escaped—were suddenly transparent, the simple, clear blue of pool water. It was the moment Voyd knew that he was dead.

"Boyd, are you on something?" his mother asked sharply. "Look at me."

Voyd looked. The hallway light behind his mother was a

bright and distant spot. He wanted to go toward it, to be delivered somewhere else.

"You're on something," she decided. The clouded look on his face, skin gone gray, mouth slack, the way he slumped in one corner of the couch, seemingly puzzled by the remote control—that's what it added up to: drugs, not loss, not sadness, but drugs. "I'm telling your father when he wakes up. He's not going to be happy about this."

Voyd stumbled on stairs he couldn't see clearly, shoulders just beginning to shake as he shut his bedroom door behind him, the pillow ready to take his sobs. He was so fucking scared, he realized that now. Shitting-himself scared. So scared he pulled the covers over his head. So scared he wet his pants—there, he did it, felt better, too tired to get up and go to the bathroom properly, to stand at the john and go like a man, like Daddy . . .

He woke to find his parents at his bedside. "We know," they said, and what a relief it was. From now on he would tell them everything, he promised. He even signed one of those rehab contracts saying he would. Voyd cried for his parents. Mikey was his best friend, his mentor, his hero, his boss, his savior, his loss. In the days to come Voyd would remind everyone of that. When they talked about Mikey being gone, Voyd would always say that he was the hardest hit, after Patty. He had been standing right next to Mikey when he got stabbed—he was *that* close. It could have been him dead. No one disagreed with Voyd, except his lawyers, who would teach him a better way to tell his story when the police came looking for him. And they did. Everyone knew they would. Voyd was ready. He cried for the police, too. He knew by then that he wanted to stay at home, not jail, not heaven, not hell. He just wanted to be home for a while.

The house, full of parents and lawyers at all hours, still felt possessed, but Voyd could get used to it—and besides, there wasn't such a great gap of experience to separate them, Voyd and the house. The house had seen terrible things, he was sure of that, and so had Voyd. Night after night he dreamt the house was burning down, with all the people he needed most trapped inside, their bodies pulsing with flames in the windows, but in the morning, the house stood. Both he and the house still stood.

Twenty-Nine

Scratch had the scoop on everyone, but his motor mouth made him seem unreliable. He had to be making things up as he went along, to make his information—the *detail* of it—so good. "Scratch as in like, starting from scratch. Like zero. That's me, baby. I'm a zero. I'm a member of the Zero Generation." Grimy, scabby Scratch, missing teeth, with a shabby, flapping trench coat wrapped around his emaciated frame, had a hand in every pot cooking on the street.

The young hotdog vendor, working that summer on Hollywood Boulevard, listened endlessly. Scratch talked until Ed's head ached, his nose long since grown accustomed to Scratch's stench. There was no escape: Ed was saddled with a clumsy aluminum stand, even if it was on wheels. When Scratch bought a hotdog—and he always bought *one* hotdog from Ed, making a point of giving him business—he made that hotdog last. First he nibbled the bun from both ends until he met the meat. Then he licked out the onions and relish, mustard and ketchup, applying more in generous, artistic squiggles, state-shaped dollops, delicate dabs like punctuation. Finally, one baby bite at a time, spaced out by ten or fifteen minutes during which he talked nonstop, he began to work his way through the dog, replenishing regularly with condiments. Scratch could make a meal of condiments, he bragged.

Besides being homeless, Scratch was possibly deranged, inhabited by a legitimate mental illness—or maybe he had just taken too much speed, like every other skinny, forsaken punk in Hollywood. To get by, Scratch panhandled, grinning crazily, which didn't help his luck. Ed didn't like to call anyone a weirdo (as some people, most often the cops, seemed to enjoy calling Ed—*and* criminal *and* gay-bait, fuckhead, punkass, etc.), but Scratch had introduced himself to Ed in a strange way, saying—as he said to everyone, Ed now knew, including the pedestrians he was begging for change—"Excuse me, do you speak American?"

"I guess," Ed replied.

"OK, that's great. Looks great, baby. Work it, work it! Hey, baby, did you know I played high-school basketball with Akeem Olajuwon? And I was quarterback for the Jets. And I played golf with Jack Nicklaus—nineteen holes and I won!" Scratch shuffled his feet, clad in ill-fitting Nikes minus their laces, the canvas split to show crumbling yellow toenails, track marks studding his toes. Ed had to turn away. He clanged the pot lids to look busy, wiped up a drip of ketchup, fished in his pan for broken pieces of hotdog, bloated as a dead cow's belly, and chucked them in the wastebasket. "Hey man, I could've *eaten* those," Scratch whined.

That was the first day of Ed's summer job. Three weeks later, Scratch was still with him, hanging around the hotdog stand for most of Ed's shift. Perhaps Ed had made the mistake of buying him cigarettes one day early on, when Scratch skipped his daily dog, claiming he was full, not broke, because he could always suck some dick for ten bucks—a pretty teenager like him could always suck dick for a living on Hollywood Boulevard. Ed wasn't sure that Scratch was a teenager, maybe twenty or twenty-one, but it was hard to tell. Scratch carried his body like an old man, moving slowly, arthritically, sometimes curling around an unknown pain in his middle—but his face was young and lean, his skin congested with acne.

"I'm the King of Hollywood Boulevard," Scratch announced. "One day I'll find my queen. There's this girl I love. She goes to the Glam Slam on Wednesdays, the Bar D-Lux on Thursdays, the Zero or the Fetish or Opera Loco on Fridays, and Club Soda on Saturdays. She's the girl who always requests 'Bela Lugosi's Dead.' She's an angel. I'm in love, but she ain't saying yet. I'd do anything for her. I'd treat her good. The thing is, she thinks I don't have a dick." Scratch made like he was going to pull down his pants.

"Don't," Ed said, looking across the street where a preacher was trying to round up a couple of homeless teens, promising them shelter and food.

"I love that little bitch," Scratch declared. "Who do you love, Ed?"

"No one," he answered, automatically skimming the fat spume from his tin pan of hotdogs—reflex, after just a few weeks of work. He could have done this job with his eyes shut. The boiling water spit, nicking his wrist, and when he got home later Kelly would want to rub his burn with butter. Lately she rubbed butter into everything, her lips, her eyelids and cuticles, Ed's scrapes and burns. Kelly did her mother's nails before she went out at night with her new boyfriend, Dexter, finishing the color with a final gloss of butter, and Mrs. Costello joked about her popularity with dinner rolls. She *joked*. She was feeling well enough to joke, taking her medication, controlling the hours she worked, not crying so much. Going to an aerobics class at the Y, which seemed to help. Dexter took good care of her, too, and when he slept over, he was still there in the morning. He had already bought Ed's mother a pair of earrings for her birthday, which was two months away; he wanted to take her to his high-school class reunion and show her off wearing them—it was twenty years since he graduated! He was almost forty, for Christ's sake, could Ed believe it? He still felt like a kid himself, Dexter said, and Ed's mom said the same, and then they looked at each other and laughed.

There were girls Ed saw that he liked. He liked the look of them. What they wore and where he saw them told him they were the same kind of person he was. He stared at them when they weren't looking, and sometimes a boyfriend appeared and Ed would curse his luck (one girl even wore a wedding ring, but smiled at him tenderly when she caught him staring, as she would an old dog blown over by the wind or a child with thick glasses). He willed them all to look back, but the moment it seemed like one might, he turned his head. The ones that came to his hotdog stand made his hand shake as he gave them change, trying not to touch their open palms and give it away that he liked them.

They never returned for another hotdog; there were no second chances. He never got to say, "You look familiar. Have we met? I remember: no mustard, extra ketchup."

Scratch had told him that all life's grandeur was a girl in summer. Ed liked that line and repeated it in his head. He would like to have a girl this summer, a girl whose picture he could put by his bed, and then in a box, and when he was middle-aged he would drag out the picture, like his mother used to do when she was drunk, and say, "I should have married *this* one. My first love. If I had married this one, none of the bad things would ever have happened."

"You got the time, Eddie?" Scratch asked.

"Nine o'clock. Nine-oh-seven exactly," Ed said, reading the Timex his mother had given him when he got the job.

"Guess you're off in an hour, then. I got to find my girl. She needs me. She's insecure. I got to find her."

"Good luck, dude."

"You going to the Meat Puppets show?"

"Yeah." Ed didn't have to hide anymore. FFF was done. He heard a bunch of FFFers had been shipped east to summer camps and boarding schools. The only kids calling themselves FFF anymore were ten-year-olds who didn't know any better. The walls around the Valley that bore FFF's graffiti had been tagged over, and no one talked about them—except Mikey, the one that got killed at the beginning of summer, who everyone said was just like James Dean: live fast, die young, and leave a beautiful corpse. The flattop was out as a hairstyle, the male ponytail in—suddenly girls loved long hair on men, even FFF girlfriends.

No one bothered Ed, and if one day they did, there was a knife at his hotdog stand, a small vegetable knife, the blade flimsy, serrated, its cheery red plastic handle with a visible, insecure seam, not quite healed in the heat of the machine that cranked them out by the millions.

After Scratch had shuffled off down the street, tugging on the greasy strings that streamed from his patchy, ripped-up head, Ed kept working, pitching dogs to the tourists and fortune-tellers, waitresses and store clerks on break and the incredibly dressed hookers. The Hollywood crowd would be exciting to someone who didn't see it every day the way Ed did, a squalling, festering scene, a procession of living corpses and hustlers. Now and then a police car or ambulance would scream by. Scratch prayed for the ambulances, he told Ed; you never knew who might be in there. A lot of his friends had died.

At ten o'clock, Bones, Cashdollar, Pellet Head, and Jeff Air appeared. Together, they rolled Ed's hotdog stand to the garage off Hollywood Boulevard where it slept, then waited while Ed turned in his red-striped baseball cap and apron to be laundered and pressed by his boss's wife for the next day—and every day after that, minus his days off, until school started again, his final year at North Holly-wood High. Cap off, Ed wasted no time getting his Mohawk upright, seven inches and growing. His boss said, as he did every night, "When you going to get a haircut?"

Ed just laughed. "Never," he said.

The yellow was gone from their bruises. Split lips had healed and bones emerged from the swelling that swaddled them. Ed was waiting for his broken teeth to blacken and fall out—the dentist had promised him they would. It was why he had this crappy job: to buy new teeth.

"Did you hear that preacher? How can he feel my pain? He's standing in the middle of the street, talking about radical revelation and the power of Jesus. He's not even looking at me, but he says he feels my pain. *All* of our pain," Cashdollar said.

"Don't listen to him. It's for the street kids," Jeff Air said.

"I can feel your pain!" Ed heard the preacher shouting. "Be prepared for the Lord!"

"Jesus never said shit like that," said Bones, fiddling with a chain and lock around his neck. He couldn't stop playing with it. Bones had a girlfriend now, for the last month, and they had exchanged necklaces. She was meeting them at the Meat Puppets show with four friends—four *girls*. Ed knew he smelled like hotdogs and wished he didn't.

They all had jobs. Bones and Pellet Head were parking cars, saving for guitars, and Cashdollar was stacking shelves in a grocery store for a bass. The Latchkey Kids were still a possibility. They were still kids with mothers who worked full-time, with fathers who lived away from them in condos or hermit holes or with new families. The Latchkey Kids still had something to say: we don't fit, except for a hole in the shape of a key, down which they had tumbled, Alice in Wonderland-style, and found the crazy hardcore scene. Pellet Head's uncle knew a guy who said he could get them rehearsal space for free, and Cashdollar had a contact at SST, someone he'd met at a show selling T-shirts and LPs.

Jeff Air was working in a copy shop and he would do the flyers for their shows on his breaks. Once Ed bought his teeth, he'd buy some drums. The Latchkey Kids would be launched, and if they were lucky, if they were *good*, they could quit their shitty jobs and make music for a living.

Inside the club was a mob of thrashers, ready for mutiny or the Meat Puppets, whichever came first. The atmosphere was tropical, full of sweat and smoke and people wanting to get into fights. Four girls with sticky-looking Krazy-Kolored hair already had their tops off—guys were always baring their chests at shows, dripping bloody gashes from spikes and chains that caught them when they slammed, and now girls wanted to do it, too, their breasts showing the first red scars. Onstage, the opening band paced, alternately pounding their instruments and screaming at the crowd. They hadn't started playing yet, baiting their audience instead with taunts of "Faggots!" and "Hippies!" and "Hillbillies!" Then someone grabbed the singer's balls and gave them a twist and the place exploded.

This band was good at making people lose their shit, Ed thought. Beer bottles smashed the wall behind the drums, dousing the drummer in foam-and-glass confetti, and the drummer retaliated with his sticks, skipping them like stones over the heads of the crowd. A bunch of drunken punks hurled gob, English-style, while the youngest kids, eleven and twelve years old, attacked at waist-level. An amp shorted and began to smoke—nothing extraordinary; things were always going wrong with the gear at shows. The guitarist investigating the amp called out, "We need a soldering iron. Someone here got a soldering iron?" Next thing anyone knew, the singer's arm had been sliced open from elbow to wrist with a broken bottle—blood, serious blood, and plenty more where it came from, making the crowd roar. The long neck of a bass guitar swung wide like a crane, striking its target: a skinhead's shining pate, marked out in scar-rivers and scar-borders, lines that had been crossed before.

Ed crept around the edge of the crowd while Jeff Air, Cashdollar, and Pellet Head charged for the stage, Bones still outside, waiting for his girlfriend. Ed always knew where his friends were now. When a badass showed up, inviting kids into the pit to slam and prove they were men, Ed disappeared to the toilets to groom his vertical black hair for as long as it took things to settle down. More often than not, his friends joined him there, and they pretended that they didn't watch the door.

He had just started on his hair, picking out his reflection from the graffiti on the mirror, when a girl came in. She was a little girl trying to look older with heavy makeup and provocative clothes: tiny skirt, cutaway T-shirt, boots with heels just making her reach Ed's shoulder. She looked familiar. With her head shaved to the scalp, he couldn't be sure—but he thought she was the girl from the night FFF kicked the shit out of him in Puppet's garage.

That night, she had pushed through the fighting boys, her Misfits T-shirt huge on her. "Stop fighting or I'll tell Mikey," she said. "Mikey said no more fighting."

"Go ahead and tell him," said the kid who was beating up Ed—the little kid from the Cathay de Grande, the FFFer who started it all with the Rats.

"I'm telling Mikey."

"Mikey doesn't give a shit," the kid said.

"He does so. He doesn't like fights. Mikey said no more fighting." The girl was drunk, wobbling like a spun-out top. She grabbed the kid's arm to stop him—or to steady herself. The kid pushed her down. "Leave me alone," she said, starting to cry.

"I'm getting sick of you," the kid said. "You better watch out."

"Where's Mikey?" the girl mumbled, crawling off. "Where's Mikey? Has anyone seen Mikey?"

The kid just laughed and resumed kicking Ed in his kidneys—kicking him until he bled when he peed for a week.

Now Ed touched her arm. "Hey."

The eyes that turned on him were glossy and sorrowful, with black cobwebs stenciled in their corners, matching her black lipsticked mouth and black fingernails. She wore spikes on bracelets and a dog collar wrapped around her neck. Miniature skeletons dangled from both earlobes, and her face was made up to look dead in white pancake. Death was the latest thing in Hollywood—death and Doomrock and Creep Chic clothes with bat wings.

"I know you," Ed said. The girl shook her head. "I'm serious. I've seen you before." He hesitated; he had been humiliated that night, his beating public and brutal. "In Puppet's garage. There was a fight."

"I don't know what you're talking about."

"The night Original Sin played."

"Who?"

Original Sin had been together for about five minutes, and then disbanded, re-forming with a new name, its players rearranged. It was always happening to bands. Ed tried again. "The night of the fight."

"What fight? I've seen millions of fights," the girl said.

"It was you. I swear it was you," Ed insisted. "FFF."

The girl's face flushed, giving her away, he thought. He knew she was Mikey's girl. She had tried to save Ed that night—she had gone to get Mikey to stop the fight. He remembered clearly that she had wanted to break up the fight. "FFF's dead," she said.

"I'm sorry about your boyfriend."

The girl's eyes dripped, pure liquid now. She took a breath. "Thank you."

"What's your name?"

"Rat."

Ed nodded. "Nice to meet you, Rat. I got a rat. His name is Darby Crash." It sounded like a pickup line, and he flushed.

But Rat seemed to want to talk to him. "Cool name. I love Darby Crash. 'Blue circles and hard drugs are every-thing—one day you'll pray to me.' He said that. It's like, on his gravestone. You know, it's better to be a rat than a person."

"You think so?"

"Yeah. People take care of rats. They're nice to them—nicer than they are to other people."

"Not everyone," Ed laughed. "I could name some people that are scared of rats, including my mom."

"It's good for people to be scared of you, too. Like, rats are mysterious. *I'm* mysterious."

"Are you?"

Rat nodded. "I'm getting a rat soon. My, um, mom has rats. She has two of them and they like, run around our house. Yeah, my mom's cool. Everyone says so. Like, if you have a problem, you can stay at our house. I mean our apartment. We have this cool apartment that's like a bedroom, with lots of posters. Do you have a cigarette? I'm totally tweeking. Come on, give me a cig—I'm jonesing so bad."

"I don't smoke," Ed said.

The girl looked disappointed, but only for a second. "You like my hair? I stole this girl's leather and now I have to hide from her. I had to cut off my hair. And I got lice before that. You pick them out and pop them with your fingernails. Or you burn them with a cigarette. Or you stick a pin in them. Pop! Juice everywhere, man." Rat loved the gory details and spat them out.

"I recognized you," Ed said. "From before."

She wasn't happy, hearing that. "No one knows me. They think they do, but they don't. I was born a wicked child."

Life without Mikey wasn't good to Rat; she was all messed up, fucked on drugs, her lips blistered, her gums edged in blood. "I wouldn't forget you," he said. "You helped me."

"Fuck you, I did not." She pushed at him, but her needle arms were useless so she pinched him instead, choosing the soft flesh above the elbow, just like Kelly would have done. He grabbed her hand and tried to hold it, to calm her down—she was trembling all over—but she jerked free and fled the room.

Later, Ed watched as she climbed onstage, shirt off, her breastless, skeletal chest glowing. When she dove, the crowd parted so that her falling body crashed to the floor. Ed pushed through, trying to reach her, but she had already disappeared.

"You look like you've seen a ghost," said Pellet Head.

Ed wanted to find the girl. She was beautiful, and possessed, definitely a runaway. She smelled like a skillet that had never been washed, the creases in her neck rich with black oil. Her bruises were flowers. She was the kind of lonely girl to write songs about, the kind that got swallowed by a room or the night taking her like a mouth. He wanted to know the facts of her life and drink her answers the way some people drink wine: like there was never enough. He would write a song about her tonight—the words were already coming to him, his first song. Tomorrow he would ask Scratch where to look.

Thirty

Rat pushed on the door, to which a flyer had been attached bearing the following message: It is unlawful to tell the future in Los Angeles, to furnish any information not otherwise obtainable by the ordinary processes of knowledge by means of an occult psychic power, faculty, or force, clairvoyance, clairaudience, cartomancy, psychology, psychometry, phrenology, spirits, seership, prophecy, augury, astrology, palmistry, necromancy, mind-reading, telepathy, or by any other craft, art, science, talisman, charm, potion, magnetism, magnetized substance, gypsy cunning or foresight, crystal gazing, or oriental mystery.

Rat didn't care what was unlawful or not. She broke the law all the time now. She was a thief, a drug-user, a jaywalker, loiterer, trespasser, vagrant, panhandler, vandal, and possibly—she had never found out for sure if that maid died or not—a murderer. She told the kids she hung out with that she definitely killed someone, to keep them from fucking with her.

Now here she was, ready to talk to Mikey in heaven. He had a question he wanted to ask her. He had never asked her his second question, and she had been waiting all this time. It wasn't too late. Whatever he wanted to ask, Rat knew the answer was yes. From heaven, he could see her devotion: the homemade FFF tattoo on the inside of her wrist—the most tender spot; the locket she wore around her neck with chips of his dried blood in it, scraped from Phazes parking lot; the flowers she regularly laid in the space where he died, always gone by the next day. It made her so mad to have her flowers taken away that she wrote on the door to the club, 'Wolf has AIDS.' The meanest thing she could think of.

There was so much she remembered about Mikey! All the little things she went over and over in her head every day. And there were new things she learned, gleaned from the newspaper cuttings and kids she met on the street, some of them, like her, from the Valley, others from much farther away: New York, Ohio, Tennessee. Even those kids knew about Mikey. He was more popular than ever—she hadn't known someone could be that popular without being a movie star.

The crone whose business it was telling the future motioned to Rat from the near-dark. The room stank of sour milk and wet carpet, and it was no larger than the walk-in closet of a rich girl. Rat heard noises from upstairs and remembered what she had been told about thunder as a child: God was rearranging his furniture. God was really upstairs in some room off Hollywood Boulevard. It made Rat giggle.

"Do you want me to read your future or not?" the crone snapped.

"Shut up," Rat said, but she sat down and handed over two dollars, warm and damp from her sock. What Rat wanted more than anything was for this crone to crack open and she would find Mikey standing there instead, ready to take her in his arms. At the very least, she would see him in a crystal ball, tiny but complete, waving to her, waving her in with him. If there was a door somewhere, the crone would tell her where to find it.

After this, she planned to head for the hills to the old Errol Flynn estate, where she heard the peace punks lived. You hopped the fence and you were in—at least that's what Scratch told her. He wanted her to go there with him and they would live together forever. He said they did satanic rituals in the guardhouse, but you could sleep indoors with the dead movie stars, maybe in a real bed. Those movie stars inspired dreams, Scratch said. Freckles would give her a ride; he wanted to be her boyfriend, too. He wanted her bad, even more than Scratch did, but she wasn't so sure about him. He wasn't really freckled: his skin was a constellation of scars where his dad had thrown battery acid at him, or something like that. Everyone had a story. If you didn't have a story, you made shit up. Some people lied about what their parents did to them.

They had talent shows up there, at the Errol Flynn estate, and real agents came looking for models and actresses. That's what Scratch told her. Rat had modeling experience. She didn't always look like this. She could be clean-looking, if that's what they wanted.

She was getting sick of Hollywood. Holly*weird*. She wanted to go to New York and be a model—when she didn't know what she was doing in Hollywood, it made her think she should go there for a while. But like, she had a lot of friends here, more friends than ever, and it didn't matter if her old friends were mean to her or pretended they didn't see her. She didn't go to Phazes anymore, except to lay flowers. Phazes was so over, ever since Mikey got killed there.

Every day out of her mind on something, and now she didn't even remember why she ran away, just knew it was something to do with Mikey. Everything for Rat had to do with Mikey. TLF—true love forever, another tattoo for her knuckles.

Going home just wasn't an option.